About the Author

Gary D. Rudé has a background in education, with a concentration in English, journalism, and photography. He taught in public schools for several years and then left the academic scene for a corporate business career. He is an avid sportsman and fisherman and has traveled extensively in the US, Canada, Europe, Australia, and the UK. He was born in Northern Minnesota but currently resides in Las Cruces, New Mexico, with his wife, Elaine, and their two champion Bichon Frise dogs.

Keezheekoni
Burning Fire

A Hank Walhberg Series

Gary D. Rudé

Keezheekoni
Burning Fire

Olympia Publishers
London

www.olympiapublishers.com
OLYMPIA PAPERBACK EDITION

Copyright © Gary D. Rudé 2024

The right of Gary D. Rudé to be identified as author of
this work has been asserted in accordance with sections 77 and 78 of
the Copyright, Designs and Patents Act 1988.

All Rights Reserved

No reproduction, copy or transmission of this publication
may be made without written permission.
No paragraph of this publication may be reproduced,
copied or transmitted save with the written permission of the publisher,
or in accordance with the provisions
of the Copyright Act 1956 (as amended).

Any person who commits any unauthorized act in relation to
this publication may be liable to criminal
prosecution and civil claims for damage.

A CIP catalogue record for this title is
available from the British Library.

ISBN: 978-1-80439-693-3

This is a work of fiction.
Names, characters, places and incidents originate from the writer's
imagination. Any resemblance to actual persons, living or dead, is
purely coincidental.

First Published in 2024

Olympia Publishers
Tallis House
2 Tallis Street
London
EC4Y 0AB

Printed in Great Britain

Dedication

I dedicate this book to my wife, Elaine, who put up with my hours of writing seclusion while she patiently proofread my material and made appreciated suggestions, and to my father, Henry, who introduced me to the world of fishing at a young age. Finally, I share this dedication with all my fishing friends, who shared my passion for the great northern pike over the years.

CHAPTER 1

The lake was unusually calm that crisp October evening in 2000. The aurora borealis danced across the northwest sky in a mirage of bright green and deep purple rays. It reminded him of the sparkling, dark velvet curtains that hung across the stage at the old Minneapolis Orpheum Theater on Hennepin Avenue. They were called northern lights in Minnesota and produced a cosmic display that easily surpassed the fireworks at Sydney Harbor on New Year's Eve.

Hank Wahlberg had made this journey more than two dozen times during the past twenty years, but tonight he was troubled as the campfire dwindled to a roasted-red glow. It wasn't a coincidence that he had taken an extended Canadian fishing trip at this particular time. When he crossed the border at Pigeon River and entered Ontario, a nasty feeling came over him. His instincts told him something was amiss back home, but this well-deserved vacation meant weeks of no phone calls, emails, or interruptions. He rarely took his cell phone with him on outings like these. There was no cellular service once you were a few miles out of Thunder Bay, so not having a phone was no big deal. However, Hank's wife Lydia begged to differ each time he ventured, phoneless, into the back country.

He left his company, VisualFish, Inc. in the hands of CFO, lawyer, and friend Winston (*Winnie*) Farrell. But this time, as he departed the Twin Cities, Hank was experiencing an uneasiness that felt like a developing ulcer in his already acid prone stomach lining.

Things changed for Winnie after he lost his wife, Camila, in a terrible accident. They had only been married a short time, but he seemed never fully recovered from this tragic loss.

Winnie's moods had become erratic and unpredictable. He had missed an important board meeting and two staff sessions, giving no apologies or excuses for his absence. His actions were really out of character for a man who prided himself in managing details and adhered to a Vince Lombardi approach to punctuality. Maybe he was having a few bad days. Troublesome memories can wreak havoc at the most inopportune times. But more importantly, he knew Winnie had developed an affinity for small, line hits of cocaine. Hank had walked into the men's room early one morning after his wife's accident and found him snorting up. Winnie had pathetically responded, "I just needed something to get through the day. Camila weighed heavily on my mind, and I didn't realize how lost I was without her. But I promise it won't happen again." Winnie said he would consider checking into a drug rehabilitation center, but it was an empty promise that Hank knew he would find hard to keep.

Paul Nordstrom, Plant Manager, was also a witness to his drug use. He took the time to write Hank a letter describing how he had accidentally caught Winnie in a compromising set of circumstances.

Promise or no promise, friendship be damned. He would schedule a meeting with Winnie on the day he returned to the office. He'd confront him with the facts, demand an explanation, and take necessary corrective action. This time Winnie was testing their friendship. He asked his wife Lydia, the Company's Chief Legal Officer, to keep a careful eye on him and the business while he was away. Lydia was an accomplished attorney and used her intuitive abilities to uncover potential problems before they jumped up and bit you on the ass. He valued Winnie's skills and intelligence to manage the financial end of the business, but the trust he placed in his dear, old friend, was starting to unravel.

Many years ago, Winnie purchased a stunning villa near Santa Maria in the State of Oaxaca, Mexico. As an astute and cunning lawyer, he completed the purchase using a dummy corporation to keep his anonymity. This isolated retreat gave him the seclusion Winnie sought whenever he needed to escape. It was also where he first met his late wife, Camilla.

To add more fuel to the fire, Hank was unaware that the FBI had begun compiling a dossier on Mr. Farrell. He had established a low-keyed relationship with the *Farmaco* drug cartel that operated up and down the Pacific Coast of Mexico. The cartel provided him with his drug of choice, and in return, he offered legal advice to the organization. The FBI's interest in Winnie peaked when they discovered a large quantity of cocaine masterfully hidden in a decorative gift box. It had arrived at the FedEx Facility at the Minneapolis Airport with special delivery routing to VisualFish: attention, Winston P. Farrell. But once a well-trained drug dog sniffed it, the parcel was confiscated and held for an FBI pickup.

When the overnight parcel did not arrive at his office, Winnie knew he was in trouble. But as his luck would have it, Hank had already left for Canada, so Winnie immediately enacted his breakout plan:

First, he liquidated their joint stock portfolios.

Second, he withdrew every cent from the corporate bank accounts.

Third, he discreetly sold several company-owned real estate properties in the metro area, sliding all the profits into his Mexican bank account.

As CFO of VisualFish, he had cleverly established complete control and access to all company assets, requiring only his signature to make withdrawals or changes. It put Winnie in complete control of a small fortune. He finished the conspiracy in a few short days and was on his way to Mexico before the slow-to-act Feds could stop him.

Hank shrugged off most of his concerns, and none the wiser to Winnie's astonishing actions, settled into his down-filled sleeping bag, and the Canadian solitude lulled him into a deep sleep.

He awoke at the crack of dawn to an ominous sound in the still morning air. Slowly pulling himself free of the warm nest he had created during the night, he could feel his fear rising as the sound grew louder and more distinct. Due to recent Canadian changes at the border, nonresidents were no longer allowed to carry any firearms into Canada unless they possessed a valid hunting license that coincided with an open game season. Camp guns were often used as a defense to scare off unwanted visitors. Unfortunately, animals don't recognize these claims. Now, without a camp gun, all he had for the defense was a slightly dull, fillet knife. Combined with a considerable amount of adrenaline that was striking sharp pains in his lower back. Then, as suddenly as the sound materialized, it ceased and dissipated into the dark, jack pine forest surrounding the campsite. Hank slowly unzipped the front bug screen of the pup tent and untied the dry canvas drawstrings that held the two protective weather flaps. He popped his head outside the tent and surveyed the visible 180 degrees that were allowed from his kneeling position. Nothing stirred. Nothing moved. Silence, once again, was the only sensation he could comprehend. He withdrew to the confines of the tent and began the arduous job of dressing in cramped quarters.

Hank could finally lace up his newly purchased Keen hiking

boots and break free of the canvas prison. Examining the immediate area around the tent site, he looked for tracks or any sign of the intruder. Having found nothing, he decided to start a small fire and get some blistering coffee into his aging veins. Hank had acquired a taste for roasted coffee beans, consisting of a fifty-fifty blend of pure Kona and high-grown Colombian Supremo. This formula produced a low-acid, scant-caffeine but full-bodied drink. He could consume it at midnight and still get a good night's sleep. His mind drifted into peaceful solitude as he took his first long, addictive sip.

The sun slowly rose in the east, peaking around a few massive white pine trees, reluctant to give way to its rays. Lake Keezheekoni was again calm and reflective in the early moments of the day.

To hell with all the potential problems south of the border, Hank decided to fire up the trusty Evinrude and travel down the rock-embedded shoreline to one of his most productive pike holes. The cool morning air slapped him like a scorned woman. However, some freshwater shark action would mask his paranoia and provide a bit of optimism for what surely would be a crackerjack day.

In the Chippewa language, *Keezheekoni* translates to English as *burning fire*. The shores and woodlands around the lake held stories and tales from explorers and indigenous people which dated back hundreds of years. However, Hank Wahlberg could only relate to personal experiences he encountered on many adventurous trips to the region.

But today, a nagging question kept coming up: *Hank, what the hell are you doing here, by yourself, in this remote setting?* The answer was simple; Keezheekoni cleared his mind and opened it up to powerful possibilities. Some of his most extraordinary ideas came to fruition when he was on this water.

CHAPTER 2

Hank was a young boy in the late '50s when he became intrigued and excited about fishing for the great northern pike. (*Esox lucius*) His father, Gunnar Wahlberg, used Sunday afternoon fishing excursions to escape the dangerous work he performed as a lumberjack in Minnesota's Northwoods.

Approximately four hundred primary wood-processing mills in Minnesota had sprung up in the past few years, so Gunnar was always able to find work. As a young lad, he started in this industry, working teams of horses that pulled enormous wagons, removing felled trees from the expansive forest of Norway pines. When abundant pine trees dwindled over the years and government regulations imposed more industry roadblocks, Gunnar's efforts changed to harvesting fast-growing and sustainable tamarack trees slated for pulp production. Although mechanized harvesting equipment threatened to change the industry, loggers like Gunnar Wahlberg were still working the forests, eking out a meager but gratifying living.

Hank's father was a very frugal man. He would never throw away or waste an item with current or potential value. Living through the days of the Great Depression (the 1930s) had instilled in him a need to conserve all available things. Gunnar would bring home rejected slabs of wood that the mills could not use. He used some of the wood to help heat his home in the cold winter months, but he used the best pieces to construct furniture or make decorative art.

He saved enough money to buy a used 2 ½ horsepower outboard motor but could not afford a fishing boat. So, he took some of his wood collection, including several sheets of marine plywood, and built a flat-bottom, twelve-foot fishing boat. He had no boat trailer or money to purchase one, so he took more lumber and built a car-top rack to haul this homemade vessel. He devised a pulley and rope system in his garage that supported and hung the boat from the rafters. It allowed him to drive his rack-equipped 1949 Ford into the garage and lower the boat onto the vehicle. He never went fishing alone because it took at least two people to unload the weighty craft from its position on the top of the car.

Fishing with his father on Sundays led Hank into his first business venture at age nine. Filling out a legal limit of northern pike or walleyes was never a problem. The lakes in north-central Minnesota produced large quantities of fish. He and his father would clean enough fish for a family meal and sell the extras to the neighbors. Then, pulling his Red Radio Flyer wagon loaded with fresh catch, Hank would show up at certain designated homes and ask if they would like some tasty morsels. He'd retrieve a quantity of fish, stringing them onto a piece of soft, yellow twine for easy handling. He never asked for money, but the grateful fish-eaters always slipped cash into his nervous, outstretched hand. The going rate was fifty cents a fish, which beat the hell out of babysitting or mowing lawns.

Fishing with Gunnar also produced events that left indelible marks on his impressionable mind. One fantastic Spring day, after launching the homemade boat on a small mud-bottomed lake just outside Trail, Minnesota, all hell broke loose! Hank and his dad decided to use poorly painted red and white Daredevil lures while trolling around the circular, weed-filled lake.

Equipped with level-wind antique Mitchell reels, a thirty-pound green rayon fishing line, and two six-foot, rusted steel rods, the trolling adventure began. The first pass produced nothing but freshly emerging green lettuce weeds. The next pass, much closer to the heavily wooded shoreline, saw Gunnar suddenly kill the engine and pull-set the lure into what he thought was a substantial fish. Because the wind had picked up, he yelled at Hank, "This could be a big pike! Throw out the anchor, so we don't drift into the nasty shoreline."

He listened intently and then watched as his father pulled and jerked the object affixed to the end of the line. Finally, after over ten minutes of futile maneuvering, Gunnar said, "I'm tired of this shit, and I am going to reef into the snag to see what happens."

The Daredevil came free. It appeared hooked on a piece of water-logged brush. When the loaded lure reached the boat's port side, Gunnar's face turned ghostly white, dropping the rod to the boat's floor.

Concerned, Hank asked him, "What's the trouble?"

But he was unable to speak, and his hands were shaking violently. Hank peered over the side of the boat and saw a chunk of bloated flesh with curly, silver locks of hair attached to the lure. It looked like a settler's scalp taken by an Indian in a recent Randolph Scott western. Finally, Gunnar regained his composure, started up the Evinrude, and headed for the muddy public landing. They loaded the boat in silence and drove immediately into the small village of Trail. Gunnar telephoned the sheriff and went back to the lake to await his arrival. A farmer searching for a lost Holstein heifer had lost his way in a November snowstorm. He had fallen through thin ice and drowned in the freezing, murky water. His body was lodged and held securely in a pile of rotting tree limbs. At least now, some closure could occur for the mourning family, who had been living with false hope through the entire miserable winter.

As years passed, the fishing routine continued with his father. However, Gunnar began venturing further from his home base, exploring inviting waters that might produce better results. One such area to be explored was the east side of Upper Red Lake, north of the City of Bemidji. Lower Red Lake and the western two-thirds of Upper Red were controlled by the Red Lake Band of Chippewa Indians. Their annual income came from walleye harvesting from this section of the lakes, and the sandy waters were highly regulated and protected by the tribe. Unfortunately, waters like Lower and Upper Red Lake became somewhat neglected as the Indian tribes developed and secured gaming rights to casinos and other business ventures. They didn't enforce the existing laws, and unregulated fishing almost destroyed that source of preservation.

In the late 1950s, Gunnar and his fishing partner Ben Theer had begun fishing the Upper Red Lake out of the village of Waskish, just off Minnesota State Highway 72. One day, Gunnar asked Hank if he would like to go fishing on the big water.

He took a deep breath and yelled, "Heck, yes! When do we leave?"

Several local fishermen had taken the enormous northern pike out of the shallows earlier in the spring. The Indians appreciated the removal of these toothy carnivores as they devoured their cash crop of walleyes and often became entangled and destroyed their commercial fishing nets.

The wind blew gently out of the west when they launched the homemade dingy into the sandy waters. The two men and the boy carefully lowered themselves onto the hard, wooden seats, and Gunnar said, "Put on the life jackets as the wind seems to be gaining strength. We'll troll into the area where pike have been active and see what we can do."

They were using medium-sized sucker minnows as bait, attaching them to a simple, 6/0 Kahle, single hook that dangled from a forty-pound test steel leader. The party caught nothing for the first two hours and didn't even experience a heart-stopping nibble for all their efforts. Then ominous clouds began growing in the west, and the wind shifted violently, blowing out of the east. The old saying, wind from the east, fish bite the least, came to mind.

The little boat was being deluged with two and three-foot white-capped swells and began taking water over the gunwales. Then finally, Gunnar turned the vessel, veering directly into the gusting wind. The boat seemed to remain stationary in the dark water eerily, but the endless onslaught of riled liquid kept coming over its bow.

Gunnar yelled, "Ben, you have to jump overboard. Grab hold of the anchor rope and begin pulling us toward the shoreline. The puny Evinrude can't do it on its own! Stay on the sandy, shallow shoals, and don't lose your footing. Hank, an empty, two-pound Butternut coffee can is under the front seat. Get it and start bailing water as fast as possible!"

Slowly the vessel began making headway. The rope stretched over Ben's shoulders, battered by the relentless wind and ice-cold water. Besides hearing a periodic, muffled curse word, little Hank kept bailing the incoming waves. Between tears of shivering fear and outright bawling, he knew he had to keep the boat from sinking.

Hank looked at his father and with much trepidation, asked, "Are we going to die out here?"

Gunnar rapidly replied, "Hell no! Just keep doing what you're doing, and we'll make it safely to the home shore."

When Ben staggered up the sandy bank and collapsed on an island of green grass, they all exhaled a well-deserved sigh of relief. Ben removed a pint bottle of Four Roses Whiskey hidden in one of the zippered pockets of his faded, green coverall. He uncorked it and took a giant swig. He then handed the firewater to Gunnar, who repeated the exercise. Then both men broke out in a piercing cry of relief. That day, Hank learned northern pike hunting could be rewarding, unpredictable, and dangerous. This simple prophetic lesson would have a profound effect on all of his future fishing trips.

CHAPTER 3

Hank was an ambitious, over-achieving student. He graduated from a small Minnesota high school with Valedictorian honors in 1964. Because there were less than a hundred students in the entire high school, graduating with honors wasn't as difficult as it might sound. He traveled extensively with his family in his youth through many of America's great state and national parks. These memorable excursions instilled in him a curious desire to seek out discoveries and often dangerous adventures. As a result, he had evolved into a die-hard risk taker.

Right after graduation, he embarked on an arduous journey up the Alaskan Highway through Canada and ultimately onto the border of the forty-ninth state. He had read an article about "hook and line" fishing opportunities along the great Alaskan coast. No experience is needed! The United States granted statehood to Alaska on January 3rd, 1959. It was still remote, unpopulated, and full of closely monitored growing pains. Officials were now enforcing newly written regulations for visitors who made their way to Alaska. Hank was unaware of them as he was preparing his loosely knit plans. A 53 Ford F100 pickup truck, repainted in a British racing green, was his vehicle of choice to tackle the 1,422 miles from Dawson Creek, British Columbia, to the port of entry at Delta Junction, Alaska. The so-called Al-Can Highway had hazardous areas deemed almost impassable. Ungraded roadway, with potholes the size of Rhode Island, meant crossing these stretches was not for the faint of heart. Extra gas cans filled with liquid gold and non-spoilable, canned food supplies were part of his short preparation list. He had saved some money working odd jobs after school and on weekends, which amounted to about three hundred dollars, a goodly amount of money in those days. At the onslaught of the trip, his only thought was: *What a great way to spend the summer months and make some fast money.*

The magnificent scenery was overwhelming for a small-town boy from the lower forty-eight. The Tanana River Valley had luscious, green foliage and color-washed wildflowers as far as he could see. In addition, the entire area had three spectacular mountain ranges: The White Mountains to the North, the Granite Mountains to the Southeast, and the Alaska Range to the Southwest. But little did he know, his fishing dreams were coming to a dramatic end as he drove on the mud-soaked road leading to the border crossing at Delta Junction. It was the site of the historic milepost sign '*1422*', which signified the end of the highway. Having had no problems entering and traveling into British Columbia and the Yukon, Hank thought the border crossing into Alaska would be a literal cakewalk.

After showing a Minnesota driver's license to the friendly border agent, many questions came streaming out of the official's now disesteemed mouth.

The agent asked, "Why are you coming to Alaska? What provisions do you have to sustain yourself while you are here? How much cash do you have on your person? Do you have someone to stay with while you are seeking employment? How long do you intend to stay in Alaska?"

The answers Hank slowly uttered to the agent did not impress nor meet the regulations and qualifications for entrance into this untamed land.

Hank asked the agent, "After hearing what you have just told me, what can I do?"

He sternly replied, "Turn your pickup truck around, purchase food and gas at the first provision station in the Yukon, and go home! Sorry, you're not crossing into Alaska today!"

It took Hank a little over three weeks to get back to Minnesota. Then, broke, discouraged, and somewhat ashamed of his failed trip to the wilderness, he impulsively decided to enlist in the United States Army. Fort Leonard Wood, Missouri, and Company Delta 3-2 became his new home for fourteen weeks of laborious and intense basic training. After completing boot camp, several DIs (Drill Instructors) reassured him that five or six more weeks of AIT (advanced infantry training) would lead him directly to the rice fields of Vietnam. *A sad and scary revelation.* Hank, however, was pulled away from mundane duties such as KP (kitchen police) and nightly guard duty to partake in classes on highly controlled intelligence programs developed by the US Army and the DOD (Department of Defense). He suspected his military career was heading in a unique direction.

CHAPTER 4

After graduation from Ft. Leonard Wood, Missouri (AKA *fort lost in the woods misery*), he was sent to an obscure, little-known post near Augusta, Georgia, named Ft. Gordon.

He had never visited the Deep South and was uncomfortable with a community that posted signs like *"colereds to the back of the bus,* whites-only drinking fountains, and segregated bathrooms. In addition, laws formulated and based on *separate but equal* were found in several southern states.

Hank recalled the first time he had ever seen a person of color. It was 1958, on a hot summer day in Northern Minnesota. A neighborhood baseball game had just ended, and he stopped by the local Dairy Queen for a malt. As he was waiting for his order, a lady, who had been hitchhiking, got out of the cab of a grain-hauling Peterbilt that had stopped for a red light. She quickly entered the store and went directly to the counter. She wore a loose-fitting, heavily stained black dress and an ill-fitting leather jacket that could have come straight from a Marlon Brando movie. But one item she was wearing caught everyone's attention; a black beekeeper's veil that covered her head and rested uneasily on her shoulders. She paid for a large, soft-serve ice cream cone and immediately exited the premises. Once outside, she raised her veil, and for the first time in his isolated twelve years of living, Hank saw a Negro. But unfortunately, he was not his hometown's only naïve and curious member. Word spread like wildfire. It seemed as though every resident with a car or bicycle made a slow, staring pass as she exited the hamlet, periodically sticking out her arm with a raised thumb. Although he couldn't quite comprehend what happened, it was an undisputed introduction to racism and discrimination.

The second time he experienced overt discrimination was when Hank and his bunk buddy, Marnie Monson from Oregon, decided to take a military bus into Augusta. It was late afternoon, and the bus stopped in front of a red brick building that resembled his old high school in Minnesota. It was a theater of sorts, and the lights on the marquee were flashing, announcing a concert that would start in about an hour.

Hank looked at his friend and said, "What do you think? Should we buy a ticket and enjoy some music?"

Marnie replied, "Let's do it. If we go into town, we'll probably find some dive, get drunk and thoroughly regret it tomorrow."

They purchased one-dollar tickets and entered the theater. It was empty, and because there was no assigned seating, they moved to the front of the auditorium and took seats in the center, third row. The theater began filling up with a lively crowd, and the first performers came out promptly at seven. The MC introduced the first act. The Temptations sang their hits songs, *My Girl*, and ended with *Just My Imagination*. Both he and Marnie had heard these songs on the radio, but to listen to them performed in person was a real treat. The second act that followed was another early soul group called the Four Tops, and they performed three numbers, including *I Can't Help Myself*. The final act, before intermission, was an ensemble called the Drifters. They belted out *There Goes My Baby* and *Save The Last Dance, For Me*. The lights came on, and he and Marnie were still seated and discussing the excellent music for the price of one dollar when Hank felt a tap on his shoulder.

He turned around and saw an intimidating police officer who asked, "Whatcha all doin' here?"

Marnie showed his ticket and said, "We paid admission for tonight's show."

The officer frowned, and deep wrinkles appeared around both eyes as he responded, "You boys must not be local? Don't you know this is Black night, and you certainly don't look like any black folks I know! So, I suggest you get your asses up from your chairs and leave the premises peacefully. I mean now! Come back next weekend when they feature Country Western singers, and I think y'all will fit in much better."

They left the building dejected and racially confused—another indelibly etched wake-up call.

Fort Gordon had a defined area within its boundaries that housed German POWS during WWII. The barracks were incredibly uninspiring and fit the definition of an internment camp to a tee. They had faded, red exterior tiles, unofficially given the apropos name of *tile city*. Heat to the barracks came from a simple wood-burning barrel stove in each structure's center. There was no insulation in the walls or ceilings and no hot water for shaving or showers. Having been raised in rural Minnesota, where an indoor bathroom was considered extravagant, Hank had no real problem adapting to these conditions. However, the three-month winter stint in the Peach State was depressing and bone-chilling cold.

Time passed rapidly at Fort Gordon as training was more acute and focused primarily on military intelligence. Four other high-clearance grunts were assigned to the city, each coming from a small town with fewer than four thousand population. Later the Army revealed it had purposely selected potential candidates who grew up in small towns as it made security clearance vetting easy.

Departure orders came in mid-January, and Hank reported to the office of the Assistant Chief of Staff for Intelligence at the Pentagon. Being a lowly PFC, the world's most extensive military complex fostered feelings of inferiority. The building was large, with over 6.5 million square feet of office space. Bicycles were often used for transport within its massive halls. Pentagon police placed electronic speed traps in the hallways to keep bicyclists from speeding. Offenders could be fined and lose biking privileges. Then they had to figure out how to effectively get from point A to point B in the maze and miles of corridors without pedaling.

Most captains and majors were nothing but errand boys in the Pentagon's chain of command. The numerous stars in many offices weren't constellations but epaulets on the shoulders of innumerable generals. Hank did not fit well into this environment.

A year passed, and his training and clearance levels became top secret. At night, he wondered what the future held for him while billeted in the Fort Myer compound. He took two weeks' leave to return to Minnesota, and visit friends and family over Christmas of 1966. Upon his return to the Pentagon in January, Hank was called into the personnel office, commanded by a newly appointed Brigadier General. He was asked to take a seat for what he thought would be disciplinary action for something he had done wrong.

The General looked up from his desk and asked, "Walhberg, are you happy with your current assignment here in the Pentagon?"

To which Hank responded, "No, Sir! I joined this man's

Army to see a bigger portion of the world. My assignment here is important, but I would rather be elsewhere."

The General removed his military-issue reading glasses and quite frankly asked, "Where would that somewhere be?"

Walhberg replied, "This is the Army, Sir. You tell me where and I will gladly go!"

Without hesitation, the General said, "I have immediate openings in Paris, France; Bangkok, Thailand; and Rome, Italy. Take your pick."

As quickly as he heard about the opportunities, Hank chose Rome, Italy, for no reason other than wanting to be in a warmer climate but not too close to Vietnam.

They told him he would no longer wear a military uniform. Instead, they classified him in what the Army called civilian status. He was given a substantial procurement voucher and told to report to a men's clothing store some forty-six miles away in Baltimore, Maryland. A military driver was waiting at the south entrance parking lot and would immediately take him to the designated store. White shirts, sports coats, three-button suits, civilian shoes, and all the undergarments were sized, packaged, and delivered to the front counter of the quaint haberdashery. A somewhat envious Army Corporal escorted him back to Fort Myer in less than two hours.

He was to stand by and await written orders, the issuance of a diplomatic passport, and a Pan Am Airline ticket transporting him to Rome, the Eternal City.

The flight from JFK to Ciampino International Airport in Rome was an exciting and memorable trip. First, because the flight was at half capacity, Hank was offered seating in the first-class section of the big 707. Second, the service from the friendly attendants was superb, and the four-course dinner served on real flatware china was one of the finest meals he had ever eaten.

Finally, upon landing at the Rome airport, Hank was among the first passengers to start the deplaning process. Paparazzi and other local press members had gathered around the base of the portable staircase. Flashbulbs flashed as he began his dissent, and cheering and applause erupted from the rowdy crowd. Hank was unbelievably impressed with the reception until he turned and looked up behind him.

Claudia Cardinale, the famous Italian actress, was returning from America after starring in *The Pink Panther*. The gala event was for her! Now totally disillusioned, he finished his debut on Italian soil, and two grim US Embassy staff members whisked him away in a drab government vehicle. Hank often said, "I never had a bad day in the Army," which was a true understatement. Being stationed in Rome, Italy, was an absolute dream. He readily found a fabulous apartment, within walking distance to the Embassy, just off of Via Volturno, in the city's heart.

He began taking Italian language courses and became quite fluent in proper Italian. He committed to exploring every nook and cranny of this metropolis during his free time away from work. However, after four years of conducting many excursions into Rome proper, he realized it would take a lifetime to complete the exploratory task he had set.

His work at the Embassy was quite rewarding, working with all military branches, especially with Ambassador Frederick Reinhardt's embassy staff. He compiled a stellar record in the intelligence field. If fate had not intervened, Hank would have moved into a Foreign Service Officer position within the State Department. His father had suddenly succumbed to high blood pressure, resulting in a fatal stroke. He could not return to Minnesota for the funeral but concluded that living the good life had its limitations. Hank missed his family and close friends. With a certain amount of apprehension, he returned to the States.

CHAPTER 5

It was the winter of 1969. The Vietnam War was at a feverish pace, with no end in sight. Richard Nixon was elected the 37th President of the United States. Hippies seemed to be ruling college campuses with massive help from illicit-trip drugs like LSD.

Hank found himself in a slight quandary. He had taken enough college courses while stationed in Italy to complete a bachelor's degree in business administration. A move back to the classroom was a decision he'd make after spending the upcoming summer just loafing around and doing some serious partying.

Before university classes began in September, he applied for unemployment benefits to support some of his frivolous expenditures. Unfortunately, after making the application, the government, in their infinite wisdom, decided they could use someone with top-secret clearance to work on a unique missile field construction project in North Dakota. Hence, his plans for a wild summer evaporated when he was issued a firm "no" for applied benefits. Instead, Hank took the job as Branch Field Manager with a small construction company in Grand Forks. The company bid on a three-year government contract and won the bid. He knew nothing about construction or missiles, but he would quickly learn what was necessary to handle the appointment. After his first week on the job, it was apparent Hank's security clearance was the primary reason he had the position.

Nevertheless, he took the job seriously and used his leadership skills and street smarts to become a proficient field manager. He worked with the Army Corps of Engineers and Air Force personnel at the Grand Forks Air Base. During one of the ordinarily mundane Friday meetings at the base, he overheard a conversation between an Air Force Colonel and an engineer.

The Colonel said, "Did you know if North Dakota seceded from the Union, they'd be the third largest nuclear power in the world?"

That statement overwhelmed Hank as he became aware of North Dakota's strategic importance in the Cold War with the Soviet Union. In addition to the possibility of nuclear war, Vietnam was also on his mind as he watched B-57 bombers taking off from various runways. Fully loaded with so much armament and fuel, their wings seemed to touch the ground as they rotated and made a successful takeoff. He thought about their foreign missions and marveled at how innocent they looked, staged like wild Canadian geese on the black tarmac.

That year, the ever-changing climate in North Dakota produced dry fantastic weather, and the multi-year contract was completed in only nine months. Hank was now unemployed, and his future was up in the air. A rather tricky internal debate welled up inside him: *Should he seek other employment opportunities, or consider returning to the classroom and completing the few credits he needed for a four-year degree?*

The Fall quarter at Bemidji State University was about to commence. He went to the campus and then directly to the registrar's office to see a list of needed courses. He also wanted to know if he could use accumulated G.I. Bill benefits to help fund the plan. The answer was yes to both points, and he began taking classes that very week.

Adjusting to campus life was not a problem, but finding off-campus housing proved extremely difficult. Then, by chance, he was perusing the personal ad section of the local newspaper (*The Bemidji Pioneer Press*) when he noticed a request for someone to perform caretaker duties at a small fishing resort located several miles north of the city. He phoned the listed number and set up an interview for the following day. After a short but positive meeting with the owner, he took the offer. Although the salary was minuscule, the massive main lodge as his rent-free residence more than made up for the paltry wages. Twelve fully furnished rustic log cabins were on the property, but renting them was impossible during the cold months because they had no insulation. He was responsible for cleaning and repairing the cabins, maintaining the fleet of rental boats, making repairs to the other resort accouterments, and above all, security for the entire compound. It was a good job that afforded him an abundance of leisure time.

Getting back into the classroom was easier than Hank anticipated. He enjoyed all the classes he was taking and was consistently on the quarterly dean's list that recognized students with high GPAs. His age, maturity, and dedication probably kept him from the enticing parties and drugs, enabling him to stay focused on his goals and achieve his bachelor's degree.

He was also trying to find a way to earn extra money while attending school. Being surrounded by pristine wilderness and hundreds of glacially constructed lakes, he devised a plan to set up a fishing guide service at the resort. During the six months of tolerable Minnesota weather, when the lakes were ice-free, he would offer his services to the resort visitors, guaranteeing them a rewarding fishing excursion. For only ten dollars per person per day, he provided the necessary fishing gear, transportation, and a prepared shore lunch for an entertaining day on the water. Hank advised his clients that he generally practiced a "catch and release" policy when fishing but for an additional dollar per fish, he would boneless fillet and package any daily catch. If someone caught a trophy class fish and wanted to have it mounted, the same charge would apply, and he would skin and treat the fish, making it ready for a taxidermist to create a masterpiece.

But before Hank could proceed with this venture, he needed to find a vehicle to haul an aluminum fishing boat, outboard motor, and all the essential supplies while accommodating up to two fishermen. With a meager budget of one hundred dollars, he found a 1957 Studebaker Champion advertised in a local newspaper. Hank phoned the seller and arranged a meeting for the following day. The Studebaker turned out to be the perfect vehicle, but before he closed the deal, he spotted four massive truck rims and tires on a pallet in the seller's backyard. They were painted drab olive green and had probably been removed from a military vehicle.

Hank asked, "Are those truck tires and rims for sale?"

The owner replied, "Yes. I bought them at an auction sale several years ago, thinking I'd use the tires for flower planters, but I never got around to it. You can have the lot for another twenty-five dollars."

A firm handshake solidified the deal, and Hank arranged to get the entire acquisition out to the resort the following day.

He planned to convert the Studebaker into a flatbed pickup truck. He removed the front and rear fenders from the car and cut away half the roof and trunk, exposing the vehicle's frame, which would become the base of the truck bed. A neighbor who lived a short distance from the resort offered to help with any welding that might be required. Using a Lincoln arc welder, the

Studebaker rims were affixed and welded to the freakish truck wheels and then carefully positioned and bolted to the vehicle. When it was removed from the jack stands and lowered to a free-standing position, the *pikemobile*, as Hank had named it, possessed almost two feet of ground clearance that could have easily competed with early versions of *Grave Digger* and *Bigfoot*. The newly painted, boat-carrying unit was bolted to the rear frame of the car, and the creation was ready to do some serious business.

Taking the pikemobile out on its maiden voyage was a real challenge. A six-cylinder engine powered the Champion, with 101-horsepower, coupled to a three-speed manual transmission. It soon became evident that the vehicle was highly underpowered. With the added boat rack, additional parts for body strength, and the massive truck tires and rims, the car's weight had increased beyond a level considered safe. If the contraption was driven more than twenty miles per hour, violent shaking would occur because of the poorly balanced wheel design. However, this did not deter or suppress Hank's enthusiasm for the project, and the plan continued to evolve with no regrets.

Hank had made friends with two elderly Red Lake Chippewa Band members. They told stories of lakes in the region with large populations of northern pike, but because they were so isolated, they were almost impossible to reach. He had the Indians pinpoint the locations of two of the most promising lakes on an old forestry map. Using a compass and Yukon snowshoes, he made a winter trek to each of the lakes and devised a workable plan to secure an entrance to the bodies of water. Over the Winter months, Hank cleared and finished two trails into the wilderness. He constructed primitive log bridges over several streams that zigzagged the forested topography. Using three bound logs, Hank designed a two-log ramp affair that fit the enormous width between the wheels of the pikemobile. He did this to keep curious explorers and unscrupulous, hungry fishermen from entering his private kingdom. The average vehicle of the day did not have the extreme axel width to fit on the ramps, and at that point, anyone attempting the crossing would be forced into an abrupt halt.

As the opening fishing weekend approached in mid-May, Hank had already made several trips to each lake. He cleared out a boat landing area and fabricated a small wooden dock at each site, providing nervous clients a safe way to get in and out of a moored boat. It was an arduous trip in the best weather conditions, plagued with many hidden dangers. On the second day of opening weekend, Hank agreed to guide two pig farmers from central Iowa into lake number one. They had been trying to catch a "mount-worthy" northern pike for years. Both gentlemen were suffering from deteriorating health issues, and agreed that this trip would likely be their last hurrah. Fully loaded with one sixteen-foot Lund aluminum fishing boat, a scuffed-up, ten-horsepower Johnson outboard motor, and all their gear, the journey began. A light fog had settled on the area, and a sprinkling of cold drops of nearly-frozen rain came with it.

As they approached the first bridge, Hank stopped several feet from the log ramps. He instructed, "Both of you guys get out of the vehicle and cross to the other side. Position yourselves at the far end of each ramp, and guide me over the structure, ensuring the tires stay directly in the middle." Each cautiously crossed the bridge and took positions as they were told. They, in unison, yelled, "We are ready when you are." The vehicle slowly climbed onto the awaiting ramps, now caked with a coating of thin ice. Edging the vehicle forward, the rear wheels scaled the ramp but began sliding to the left and then violently back to the right. Without fanfare, both ramps shifted together, dropping and supporting the helpless vehicle on its frame, with all four wheels now airborne above the ominous waterway. Recovering from the sudden jolt, Hank called to the farmers, "Are you okay? Stay back from the ramps! The timbers could crack, and I don't want anyone injured." He slowly crawled out of the vehicle and carefully made his way to solid ground. He knew he could do nothing to rescue the pikemobile from its current stead.

However, he had a plan. A logging operation had recently moved into the area and was currently working timber less than a mile from their location. He would travel cross country to reach their location and bring back help. He assured both fishermen that he would be gone less than two hours. They looked discouraged and scared. To keep their spirits up and their minds occupied, he suggested, "Gather some dry kindling and start a fire. Carefully get an aluminum pot and some coffee from the car's rear. You can dip some water from the stream and make a hot cup. I'll be back before you know it!" Having deflected their agitation, Hank quickly disappeared into the thick pine forest.

True to his word, he returned with help. The loggers had a John Deere 540 Skidder on site and agreed, for a price, to help extract the vehicle. The skidder is a valuable piece of equipment in the logging industry. It is used to move and efficiently position felled timber. Equipped with tire chains and all-wheel drive, it becomes a force to be reckoned with in the woods. Postioning the skidder at the rear of the pikemobile, massive logging chains were attached to the car's frame. Within seconds, it was all over. The vehicle was on high ground, and ramps were still bound and unscathed, although squeezed out of position. With assistance from the logger and the two fishermen, Hank was able to reposition the ramps into their original lodgment. He asked the Iowans if they wanted to continue the trip. They replied with a unanimous, "Yes." With the ice now removed from the ramps, they could make a successful crossing, and they ventured onto the lake and were rewarded with a very successful day of fishing. The two farmers spread the story of Hank's fantastic fishing enterprise by word of mouth.

Hank did gain an enthusiastic following of northern pike anglers over the summer months. Some stayed at the resort, but most were avid fishermen who wanted a chance to land a trophy pike. The money he earned was sufficient to maintain his current lifestyle. His business had grown to a point where he guided customers almost daily. As he thought about his adventures on these two lakes, two additional rewards became evident: one, he was delighted, and two, Hank could hone his fishing skills because he actively fished along with his compensating clients.

CHAPTER 6

September 1970 marked the end of Hank's first summer at the resort and the beginning of a new quarter of study at the University. Because some of his needed classes to complete his degree were only offered in the winter quarter, he took a very light load and began looking for part-time employment within the city. He stopped at the 3rd Street municipal liquor store and ordered a bottle of Leinenkugel beer.

He began bullshitting with a fellow barstooler and asked, "Have you heard of any job openings in the downtown area?"

Dressed in a blue Hart Schaffner Marx sport coat, with perfectly creased, tan Hager bell-bottom trousers and newly polished western boots, he replied, "I am the manager of the Thriftway Clothing Store, right next door, and I have been searching for an assistant manager."

Hank could barely believe what he heard but had the wherewithal to spit out, "I'm your man! When can I start?"

This chance meeting led to a steady job and a new friendship with manager Victor Hungarford.

Victor, who preferred to be called Vic, had owned and managed the business for over ten years. His only assistant was his wife, Theordos, whom he lovingly called Toto, after the dog in The Wizard of Oz.

Toto had flaming red hair piled in a bun atop her head, increasing her height from a mere five feet to something approaching the elevation of a center on a men's basketball team.

Her facial features were distinctive and idiosyncratic.

She used a makeup base resembling the plaster of Paris, coupled with a faded orange rouge that was supposed to emphasize her high cheekbones but produced a clown-like appearance. Toto's smile was endearing but overwhelmed by her two lips, often hastily painted in an awful shade of ruby red. Finally, her brilliant green eyes gave her the total appearance of an unwanted Christmas tree ornament. She contracted polio as a child and consequently walked with a well-worn crutch. Toto used it as a weapon to ward off bullies who often tormented her because of her disability.

In time, Hank was able to tolerate her appearance. By doing this, he discovered an intelligent and highly motivated lady.

She taught Hank many valuable tricks of the clothing trade, including a specially developed code on each saleable item in the store. When deciphered, it revealed the wholesale cost of any commodities in the store and became a sales tool when a customer demanded a special deal or discount. She also possessed an unreal ability to magically gift wrap items for special occasions and holidays, turning ordinary wrapping paper into a work of art. Hank became Toto's training challenge. She exclaimed, "I've never met anyone more devoid of artistic abilities, but we'll work on it!"

Vic, on the other hand, was all business. He was always dressed impeccably and had a fetish for western bolo ties and Tony Lama cowboy boots. Vic had been a lightweight boxer when he was a young man. He made appearances in several Golden Glove competitions during the Great Depression with surprising victories. But time and booze had taken their toll on his body, and he had shrunk in stature and weighed only a hundred and fifteen pounds, soaking wet. However, his positive attitude and the repetitive twinkle in his eyes more than made up for his physical shortcomings. The success he experienced in the clothing business was something to write home about with pride. He developed a niche in the marketplace, and if you were searching for high-quality outdoor clothing or footwear, you would go nowhere else but to Vic's Thriftway store.

He was also an avid fisherman but preferred the muskie or muskellunge (*Esox masquinongy*) over the northern pike. Vic favored this species because of their laid-back aggressiveness and picky eating habits, making it a monumental challenge to hook and land one. There was an old saying amongst dedicated muskie muckers: It takes ten thousand casts to catch one. He always felt that this crazy amount of effort was all bunk. Vic devised a technique to increase his chances of catching the prey every time he ventured out on the water, albeit somewhat illegal. He would purchase live, yellow baby ducklings, hook them through their bills, and cast them out over a likely muskie haunt. The success rate was never officially measured, but it did not come close to ten thousand casts.

Vic also knew how to poach deer whenever his meat freezer ran low. This practice stemmed back to his survival days during the 1930s. One Sunday afternoon in late October, Vic invited Hank to do some end-of-season walleye fishing on Lake Bemidji. Vic drove out to the resort to pick him up. Because he only drove Cadillac automobiles, he was quickly recognized. His latest purchase was a 1964 solid gold-colored Coupe de Ville that towed his model FDR Alumacraft boat and trailer. Fortunately, this walleye junket ended with a total limit of tasty morsels. After filleting them on a well-worn picnic table near the public access, they headed north on County Road 9 to take Hank back to the resort. About two miles from home, they were driving into the brilliant setting sun when a giant whitetail buck suddenly appeared in the middle of the road. Vic hit the brakes but regrettably made violent bumper contact with the creature, knocking it into the nearby ditch. The Caddy came to a complete stop on the narrow shoulder of the roadway.

Without hesitation, Vic shouted, "Get out of the car and watch for any on-coming traffic. If you spot any headlights, yell a warning."

Vic dove into the ditch and straddled the helpless animal. He removed his bowie knife from its worn leather sheath, grabbed the massive antlers with his left hand, and lifted the head of the deer, preparing to slit its throat. As he raised the knife in his right hand, the unconscious deer began trembling and sprang to its feet. Vic dropped the weapon and instinctively gripped the antlered rack with both hands. The animal made one hulking leap toward a six-rung barbed wire fence on the far side of the ditch. It cleared the obstruction with Vic still on its back. The creature ran directly toward the nearby tree line when Vic finally released his grip and fell off the panicked steed. Hank began a fit of uncontrollable laughter as Vic re-emerged on the far side of the ditch. Gathering his composure, Vic blurted, "Don't you ever tell anyone about what happened here tonight, or you'll be very sorry you did. Now, let's get the hell out of here!"

After the Whitetail incident, they remained good friends for many years, but they never raised the buck story again.

CHAPTER 7

It was early December, and wet, *heart-attack* snow fell as several Alberta clippers descended on Minnesota. The clippers brought frigid, below-zero temperatures and high winds resulting in severe blizzard conditions. It was as though time had come to a standstill. No humans were moving around, and most animals were sleeping beneath the blanket of white. Nevertheless, he had completed the outdoor projects (thank God), and Hank had begun preparing for those needed classes in the upcoming winter quarter. He had plenty of LP gas in the one-thousand-gallon tank that rested in a deep mound of the white stuff outside his kitchen window. He had also harvested around two cords of dry firewood that he had split and neatly stacked in the entry mudroom at the rear of the lodge. It was peace of mind for Hank. If there was a gas shortage or the antique Rheem furnace, located in the damp bowels of the storm cellar, failed, he could survive by burning wood in the stone great room fireplace. At one time, it had been the only source of heat for the lodge. In addition to supplying warmth, the fireplace also projected a homey and cozy atmosphere in the lodge. Hank would settle into a comfy lazy boy and easily get lost in a good book, often accompanied by three fingers of Bonnie Prince Charlie's favorite treat: Drambuie.

The rising heat waves also radiated into the upstairs bedrooms. Hank installed a high-intensity bedside reading lamp in the master bedroom. He could now plop onto a queen-sized mattress and comfortably read until he'd drop off to sleep. One evening, having flipped off the reading light, he was awakened by the feeling of tiny, hairy feet slowly moving along the hairline of his neck. His reflexes took control in total darkness, and he swatted his hand at the unnerving sensation. He felt for the lamp switch and turned it on. The room flooded with light, and as his eyes adjusted to the illumination, he spotted an immense gypsy moth that had lit on the faded-window shade. With added heat to the upper level of the lodge, the moth probably was awakened from hibernation. *No harm, no foul*, he thought to himself as he turned over and extinguished the light.

Coasting in and out of needed sleep, he finally probed his mind for a favorite dream and fell into a trance. After several hours, he again was booted out of serenity with the same sensation he had felt earlier. The moth had not moved from its perch, so Hank knew something else in the room. He retrieved a flashlight from a nightstand drawer and torched the walls, floor, and ceiling for clues.

Finding no evidence of other creatures in the room, he slowly knelt and aimed the beam under the bed. To his shock and disbelief, he found the intruders. Fourteen Northern Long-Eared bats hung upside down from the metal bed springs. Hank rose to his feet and quietly exited the bedroom, slamming the door shut while bounding down the rickety stairs. He spent the remainder of the night, covered with a patchwork quilt, trying to find a comfortable position in his recliner.

Hank's older brother, Arvid, paid an unexpected visit the next day. He had not seen Arvid for several years, and a memory-filled reunion took place over the next few hours, each catching up on events and adventures that had shaped their lives. Returning to the present time, Hank told Arvid of the bat encounter and asked for advice. He listened as Arvid proposed a plan to remove the unwanted visitors. They would each place a metal-screened wastebasket over their heads, affording them defense but not impeding their vision.

Arvid explained, "Bats will attack or roost on the highest object in the room, and we will be protected while wearing the basket headgear. Next, if you have them, we need a fish net and a tennis racket to capture the little bastards."

Hank remembered the items he had placed in a nearby storage building. He put on his down-filled navy-blue parka and a pair of original Manitobah mukluks, ventured into the bitter cold, and retrieved the items. Now completely outfitted with protective gear and so-called weapons, they made their way to the top of the stairs and gently opened the door to the bedroom. They entered the room and quietly closed the door. They pinned themselves to the nearest wall in total silence. Arvid took the tennis racket and got on his hands and knees beside the bed.

He murmured, "I'll swing the tennis racket under the bed, so be prepared for all hell to break loose! Hold the fishnet upright and get ready to catch some flying vermin."

He repeated the racket procedure several times until all fourteen members of the bat family had been netted and collected for removal without sustaining any nasty bites.

Hank never slept in the master bedroom again.

In Minnesota, Winter had a way of playing tricks on you. One day the temperature would drop to an unbearable minus forty-five degrees, and within twenty-four hours, the mercury would read a balmy forty-five above zero. The weather pendulum raised hell with animals, birds, insects, and humans. Birds couldn't decide if they should migrate. Animals poked their heads out of their insulated beds and contemplated the state of hibernation. Insects emerged from the frozen ground and tested their collapsed wings, and humans couldn't figure out how to dress the kids for school.

Confronting a problem like this, Hank decided to take some

of the guide money he had socked away from last year's successful season and go south for a vacation. The University had just ended the winter quarter, and many students were preparing to hit beaches in California and Florida for their annual bash. Mexico appealed to Hank.

He had developed a camaraderie with a young attorney named Winston (Winnie) Farrell, who had recently purchased a small property in the Mexican State of Oaxaca. Last summer, he had guided Winnie, as Hank called him, on several successful pike outings. With this mutual interest in fishing, their friendship grew. Finally, he told Winnie of his "spring break" plan to go to Mexico. Winnie, without hesitation, suggested they could go to Oaxaca and spend the two weeks in his renovated villa. He made arrangements, and the pair flew into Mexico City, rented an off-road vehicle, and made the harrowing drive to the Pacific Coast. Santa Maria was an undiscovered gem. Although Winnie's villa was not oceanfront property, it was a well-designed private retreat less than an hour away from uncrowded white sandy beaches. They could find no obnoxious, drug or alcohol-infused students. Oaxaca was paradise! Hank spent two full weeks lounging around the Olympic-sized pool and made occasional trips to the beach. Winnie introduced him to some gorgeous, sun-worshiping senoritas. They loved the sun-drenched sand and often came scantily clad, leaving little to the imagination. Mexican cuties with naturally dark skin were a welcomed change from pale Scandinavian blondes who had not seen the sunshine since late August. Waking up next to a gorgeous senorita had a deep cleansing and rejuvenating effect on his anatomy and mind. Hank would stand in front of the full-length bathroom mirror in the guest quarters and pinched himself while hollering, "This must be paradise. I could get used to living like this!"

But Hank knew all good things must end, so it did for his first visit to Mexico.

CHAPTER 8

Hank finished his four-year degree in business administration in the spring of '73. He contemplated another summer of guiding, managing the resort, and laboring in Vic's clothing store but realized his future was outside Northwoods. So, using the local paper and university bulletin boards, Hank put some feelers out for someone interested in taking his position at the resort. Within a week, he found a grad student who wanted the job. The resort owners instantly approved, and Hank was off the hook. However, the student wanted to avoid running, purchasing, or administering the guide service Hank had painstakingly built. In addition, he was studying for his MBA, which gave him very little free time; besides, he hated fishing.

Hank tried vainly to sell the guide service and finally accepted that there was no market for it. However, he did advertise to sell or swap the pikemobile and received a phone call from a Blackduck farmer with a 1964 Chevy Corvair, which he wanted to trade. Taking an entire morning, Hank drove the pikemobile twenty-five miles on backroads to the farm. The minute the farmer saw the car, he wanted it. He said, "This contraption will transport me around my swampy two hundred acres and never again see road or highway service."

Although Ralph Nader had successfully destroyed the Corvair's reputation, calling the car "unsafe at any speed and a one-car accident." Hank was delighted to own a low-mileage vehicle that could effectively transfer him out of northern

Minnesota. Hank also traded two outboard motors for a small, enclosed trailer. Finally, he carefully sorted out his belongings by creating two distinct piles. One was junk or giveaway items, and the remaining pile he kept, loading it into his trailer.

Vic and Toto were unhappy to see Hank go, but they knew this would happen someday. Anticipating his departure, they had successfully recruited a salesman from a next-door competitor. Hank hugged them both and promised not to be a stranger. Then, he drove away with tears spilling down his cheeks.

Next, he telephoned his brother Arvid to inform him of his plans. Arvid offered to let him temporarily stay at their lake home near Brainerd. Hank thanked him but declined the offer. Instead, he told him he had made previous arrangements to stay with Winnie at his condo in downtown Minneapolis while he embarked on this new chapter in his life.

Moving to Minneapolis presented a monumental change. He was unaccustomed to strange city sounds, unbelievable traffic, and people who seemed to rush to get somewhere but still needed to arrive. Hank planted himself in the guest bedroom of Winnie's piece of the sky. For the first time in his life, he felt remorse, loneliness, and borderline depression settle oppressively on his shoulders. After two weeks of isolation, Hank instinctively knew he had to break free from this prison or face unwanted consequences. Winnie had the *Minneapolis Star Tribune* delivered daily to his office, and he brought a copy home every evening. He encouraged Hank to read it and possibly find inspiration to move on mentally and physically. So, he did what Winnie suggested and ran across an article on the newly named College of Business Administration on the campus of the University of Minnesota. The article spelled out a series of changes in their business curriculum and mentioned opportunities to apply for scholarships and other funding to enter their MBA and Ph.D. study programs.

Hank wasted no time making tracks to the registrar's office on 19th Avenue to determine if he would qualify for such a formidable undertaking. The acting dean and department heads would interview him to see if he had a future with the University. At the same time, he received word that the unused portion of his G.I. Bill benefits was approved. In addition, his undergraduate transcripts were in order. He gathered the necessary forms, filled them out, and included testimonials and references. Finally, with a stroke of the dean's pen, Hank was in the university's graduate program. He earned a generous scholarship and a grant from a local corporation that offered an internship and possible executive employment when he completed his degree. Hank was dumbfounded. His future was bright, and he could now clearly formulate realistic goals.

Strategic management and entrepreneurship became his favorite topics of discussion as he wended his way toward a post-graduate degree. Hank could visualize a world where the computer would be more integral in everyone's life. As a result, he became enthralled with any course that embraced computer science.

While taking one of these seminars, he met a grad student who fit the description of a nerd in the most definitive form. His name was Arnie Morgan, and he was a genius at developing software with a knack for writing code.

Hank had been working on an invention involving special software. Users could install this software into most existing screened fish-finders or locators. The revamped instrument would allow the specific identity of every known freshwater or saltwater fish. Arnie was intrigued by Hank's idea and volunteered to work on it in his spare time. He had a complete computer lab in his basement apartment in Dinkeytown.

When Arnie completed his MBA, he was offered a position with a large manufacturing firm in St. Paul. They curtailed work on Hank's software until Arnie became secure in his new job. Arnie desperately needed a regular paycheck to begin paying back some of the student debt he had accumulated while attending the University. At that moment, Hank could not have fathomed Arnie's prominent role in his future business endeavors.

Hank's daily routine now included taking classes, teaching undergraduate sessions, and studying for his degree. In addition to all of that, he began his internship with FishNautics, Inc. The Company was headquartered in Forest Lake, Minnesota, and had recently opened a two-hundred-thousand-square-foot retail outlet in Ham Lake, just west of Interstate 35W. Furthermore, the Company planned to open eight new locations in various Midwest cities in the next three years. This ambitious stratagem would haunt day traders with nightmares of speculation about where this Company was heading.

The internship FishNautics offered Hank included a generous stipend to demonstrate their vested interest in him. As a result, Hank started on the low end of the corporate totem pole. He performed tasks like sweeping and mopping the store aisles, stocking shelves with merchandise, unloading semi-loads of ordered products, and many other mundane tasks. Presumably, this training scenario was approved and blessed by the corporate gods. Unfortunately, his assigned mentor, Maynard Fulstrom, was a crusty, well-seasoned manager with little patience for new blood. Trainees often lasted only a few short hours when he would unleash his unyielding charm. Hank, however, persevered and flourished while Maynard compiled thorough weekly progress reviews on him, sending results to the corporate office for review.

Maynard always wore an English tweed sport coat with elbow patches and dark brown corduroy trousers. This attire worked well in the cool winter months as additional heft kept him warm. But he also wore the ensemble during the hot, humid summer months. He was even seen at home, mowing grass and puttering in his garden, wearing the same outfit.

Work was Maynard's primary motivation for getting up every morning. As a result, he avoided any meaningful social activities and developed few friends. However, Hank appreciated his dedication and the tremendous business expertise he had acquired. Hank became a literal sponge, absorbing everything Maynard shared with him.

Hank mastered all managerial and relevant floor positions at the retail level. The store training took over a year, and then shifted to the corporate headquarters. First, he spent several months in the personnel department, studying corporate policy and the operations handbook. Next, he participated in employee reviews and was required to participate in the hiring process of new employees. He then graduated into the finance department, sitting elbow to elbow with the CFO. Accounting had never been his forte, but he soon understood how dependent the Company was on cash flow and receivables. This financial exposure would tremendously affect him when he cut the ribbon on his first start-up venture.

Next, he advanced to sales, training, and marketing. He always considered himself a damned-good salesman but quickly realized he had much to learn. This arena was rapidly changing, revamping, and progressing at warp speed. It was mindboggling to see how much technology could play in company growth. On one particular day, he attended a sales training class in the newly constructed company amphitheater. The instructor from a local consulting firm introduced a state-of-the-art sales tracking and marketing program to FishNautics. At center stage, he positioned a hospital gurney with a mannequin in a prone position, obviously deceased. He dressed him as an old-time, classic salesman; white shirt with a button-down collar, obnoxious silk tie secured with tarnished gold clasp, a battered and frayed navy-blue blazer, and scuffed-up penny loafers, desperately in need of re-healing.

He loudly asked the attendees, "Besides this salesman's general attire, do you notice anything unusual about his appearance?"

They all stared at the enormous bulge, several inches high, that protruded from under his right jacket lapel. The instructor explained the mound was a collection of business cards and hand-written notes that constituted his career accomplishments and possibilities. Unfortunately, not recorded and compiled for continued company use, this data died with him.

Stories like this brought many problematic business issues and concerns to the surface and forced executives to reassess where they placed customers and employees in their business hierarchy. Terms like; intellectual property, non-compete clauses, and non-disclosure agreements were now regularly discussed in most corporate offices. In retrospect, Hank was undoubtedly aware of business dependency on technology. He embraced the process and appreciated what a springboard it could be for the future. But during his internship, Hank uncovered many policy flaws, technological shortcomings, inadequate company procedures, and leadership weaknesses that he would be obligated to address and correct. For now, he kept his mouth shut.

CHAPTER 9

Hank received his MBA degree with his name boldly embossed in the center of the certificate. It was 1975. The British Conservative Party had just nominated its first women leader, Margaret Thatcher. The Vietnam War ended with a communist takeover. Patty Hearst is on the FBI's Most Wanted list, and unemployment reached a staggering 9.2 percent.

Hank became the new Vice-President of product development at FishNautics. This promotion represented two years of intense study and hundreds of hours of internship service. Management created the position for him, and he needed clarification about how much latitude he would have in the overall design of this department. His concerns were put to rest when the CEO, Mark Branigan, came to his rescue. Mark told him to begin interviewing and hiring an entire staff. Next, he was to prioritize a list of companies and products that he would like to see marketed and sold within all the retail stores. Then Hank was to set up a field-testing program to evaluate all selected products. They gave him a free hand to partake in all in-house and field testing.

Finally, in the corporate chain of command, Hank was to report directly to Mr. Branigan, with no exceptions. With this game plan, Hank moved confidently and blissfully into the new position, now outfitted with a pair of "big-boy pants."

Within a few short months, Hank had organized a team so solidified and efficient that it became the envy of the home office and put some of the weaker management CCAs (corporate climbing assholes) on alert. Hank had arrived with gusto. He was spending more and more time outside the office while meeting manufacturers deemed to be on the cutting edge of outdoor innovations. Although his passion for the northern pike was evident, he still maintained an interest in all fish species; saltwater and freshwater. Hank worked with companies like Lund Boats, Ranger Boats, Eagle Claw, Eppinger, and many smaller companies to experience their products firsthand in real-life settings. With over ten thousand lakes (probably closer to fourteen thousand) in Minnesota, he could pick and choose lakes by size and known species of fish that inhabited the waters. Hank also fished in tournaments around the country, partnering with well-seasoned pros. He experienced a real wake-up call with these activities and quickly realized how little he knew about the complete sport of fishing. But he was a fast learner, and from his education from all these sources, Hank evolved into an accomplished expert.

His hunger and thirst for a world-record northern pike had not subsided or grown less intense as the years passed. Hank now had the money and the opportunity to confront this goal. At that time, the heaviest recorded northern pike was caught in Sweden and weighed an astounding forty-seven pounds, four ounces. However, rumors and tales of much bigger pike have been reported but have yet to be substantiated. Most pike fishermen believe a new record would come from undisturbed waters with no genuine interest in them or easy access to pursue this toothy beast. To grow to world-class size, the pike requires an ample supply of live prey to satisfy its enormous appetite. It is a curiously adaptable fish. It is found in the Baltic Sea and thrives in brackish waters along the Norwegian and Swedish coasts, where they gorge themselves on salmon, herring, and sardines. Generally, pike over fifteen pounds are female and have a life expectancy of over twenty years. Hank never lost his uncanny respect for this species and continued to practice catch-and-release tactics to sustain and ensure their longevity.

Hank had met, purely by accident, two Canadian loggers while fishing in a largemouth bass tournament on Lake Okeechobee in southeast Florida. The loggers, Jean and Jullian Monet were on a mid-Winter retreat from their operation in North Central Ontario. Logging in the severe winter months was no longer in the cards for this elderly pair of French-Canadian brothers. Jean spoke very little English, but Jullian had perfected American slang and was quite outspoken. Their conversation with Hank eventually led to fishing.

They were curious about fishing contests, and Jullian asked, "Can you make a living competing in these tournaments?"

Hank responded, "As in all professional sports; baseball, football, hockey, etcetera, only a select few can make the grade, succeed and enjoy an impressive salary, often shirt-tailed with lofty bonuses. The wannabes are on the outside looking in, with no sponsors and money. So, the answer is yes and no, but only about one percent ever make it big."

Hank explained he represented a sporting-goods company and was not participating in the contest but evaluating certain products used by professional anglers. They shared some stories of fishing in Canada for their favorite meal: walleye or, as the Canadians call them, pickerel. Hank asked if they had any knowledge or interest in northern pike. Jullian informed him that the pike was considered rough fish and not a delicacy for the table. They are commonly called jacks in Ontario and were considered a nuisance for most native and non-native commercial fishing enterprises, destroying nets or devouring their cash crop. He asked if they had ever come across any remote lakes in their logging area that might hold trophy pike. Jullian disappeared for a few minutes, returning with a detailed surveyor's map. He pointed out a place northeast of the remote railroad village of Armstrong. He had ventured into several isolated lakes, searching for pickerel, and was amazed at the number of giant jacks he caught. Hank excitedly copied down as much information as he could concerning the location of these lakes. Finally, he asked the loggers where they would be situated come springtime. On the map, they showed him where their base camp would be and extended an invitation for a visit. Hank was beside himself, looking forward to the ice breakup in the spring and the Canadian fishing opener. He would combine a fishing trip with promising lures and tackle products that he would test in pristine Ontario waters.

CHAPTER 10

It was during May 1980 when Hank and a representative from HotLures, Inc. began preparing for a ten-day journey into Canada. They flew into Thunder Bay and rented an off-road vehicle.

Galen Greene, the rep from HotLures, arranged for all of their tackle and camping necessities to be delivered to the Valhalla Inn, just minutes from the international airport. He also successfully obtained the use of a Canadian-made Princecraft aluminum pike boat. After checking into the Inn, Hank and Galen decided to go for dinner at Uncle Frank's Supper Club. From all reports, this restaurant had the finest steaks in the city and had a generous supply of hand-rolled Cuban cigars for sale. Unlike America, Canada was freely trading with Cuba. Although Hank never picked up the cigarette habit, he had acquired a taste for good cigars. He called them as "all-day suckers" because of their tight roll and slow, cool burn. First, they both ordered a twenty-ounce T-bone steak with all the trimmings. Next, they sucked down a big slice of authentic tiramisu for dessert. Finally, they each had a double shot of Drambuie in a chilled glass with one ice cube topping off an end to a delightful evening. They were in for a lucky outing if the fishing was half as good as this meal.

The late meal had curbed their morning appetites, so they drove to Tim Horton's on Valley Street and settled for some donuts and black coffee. Next, they needed a non-resident fishing license and a set of daily camping permits. The Canadian tire store on Fort William Road offered these services. Only a few hundred yards away was the LCBO (Liquor Control Board of Ontario), where they stocked up on two cases of Labatt Blue Beer and a liter of twenty-year-old Canadian Club Black Label. Before heading to the bush, their final stop was the Safeway grocery store on Arthur Street, where they stocked up on food and sundry items like paper towels and toilet paper.

The weather turned sour as they began heading northeast up Highway 17, passed the Terry Fox Memorial, and proceeded north on Provincial Highway 527. In 1976, Ontario added many improvements to old 527, including pothole repair and asphalting. Before that date, the one-hundred-and-fifty-mile road was little more than a sandy, poorly maintained trail, susceptible to incredible flooding and washouts in many areas. Most of the improvements to the highway were to accommodate the increased traffic from logging trucks that were hauling timber from remote regions to the pulp mills in Thunder Bay. A battle ensued between the truckers, who destroyed the road base while the road maintenance crews attempted to repair it. The results of this unending melee were evident as soon as they hit the highway.

The pair arrived in the village of Armstrong ten hours after they started their trek. They were wet, muddy, and miserable. Several times they were forced to drive off-road, seeking higher ground, due to standing water on the roadway. Relentless, soaking showers had not diminished their enthusiasm, but they wanted to avoid pitching a tent in the rain. Luckily, they found the Chateau North Motel on King Street, with a neon vacancy sign flashing an invitation to come in. The rooms were cheap and dry. Hank believed the mattresses came stuffed with river rock, but after a hot shower and a couple of shots of Canadian Club, he didn't care and fell into a restful sleep. Galen knocked on Hank's door at the crack of dawn and suggested they find a restaurant for breakfast before they headed out to find the loggers, Jean and Jullian.

Armstrong had a population of under one hundred eighty, with about eighty identified as indigenous. Abuse of illegal drugs and alcohol was evident everywhere in the community. Walking from the restaurant down King Street, they encountered a knock-down street fight between locals who jostled over the final few drops of liquid remaining in a bottle of Thunderbird wine. An officer from the nearby Provincial Police Station stepped out of his office and quickly broke up the brawl with a verbal threat of jail. The LCBO store opened at eleven a.m., but thirsty folks were already in the solemn queue, patiently waiting. The rain had ended, but a human cloud of despair permeated the surroundings. Hank could not wait to get the hell out of Dodge. They fueled their vehicle with expensive, sulfur-smelling, shale-extracted gasoline at the Can-Op Mini-Mart, then began heading northeast on the Airport Road, passing the Armstrong landfill on the left and the Armstrong Airport on the right. After a few minutes, they could see a flagman waving a red warning pennant at a small railroad crossing. They stopped, and the flagman approached, saying, "The road is closed to all traffic beyond this point. A massive spring run-off destroyed the main bridge over the Ginoozhe River. It'll be several months before they can make the needed repairs."

Discouraged, they managed to turn their rig around and headed back to Armstrong, and not a word was spoken. Hank's mind was utterly blank until he remembered seeing a small bait shop on the outskirts of the village. He would stop and ask the owner for advice: where could they find a lake with populations of good-sized jacks?

Victor Lowbranch and his wife Eleanor, owners of the business, provided some excellent suggestions, all west or south of Armstrong. Hank felt the information was credible, and they went down Highway 527 to the river crossing between Kopka Lake on the west and Pishidgi Lake on the east. They drove into a clearing above the river, partially occupied by a group of bear hunters out on their annual spring hunt. After some small talk, the hunters showed them where they could set up camp and pointed out a perfect inlet to launch their boat quickly. It was late afternoon when they finally set camp. They decided to prepare a meal and remember about fishing the next day. The bear slayers had a successful evening, bagging a near-record-setting, six-hundred pound boar. Celebratory partying went on well into the night.

Early the following day, Hank and Galen quietly made their way to the awaiting boat, anchored at the river's edge. They pushed off and drifted on the river toward Pishidgi while preparing their rods and deciding on an irresistible lure. Moving slowly along the riverbanks, they began casting their choices into likely spots where pike could be waiting for a defenseless meal.

They each caught, weighed, and released two pike over twenty pounds within minutes. The non-stop action continued throughout the day. They were both exhausted by late afternoon and decided to pack it in for the day. The largest fish taken topped the scale at twenty-six pounds; not near a record breaker, but still a fabulous prize.

Returning to the camp, they decided to make a quick trip to Kopka Lake and catch some dinner-sized walleyes for their evening meal. Using an enticing spinner bait and ultra-light fishing rods, they collected a limit of twelve fish before the sun disappeared behind the inflamed, red-cedar horizon. Then, they boneless-filleted, packaged the walleye pieces into zip-lock bags, and put them on ice. However, they kept out four nice slabs for their early dinner.

The jubilant bear hunters departed the camp. After a terrific meal, they were left alone with a roaring campfire, flavorful cigars, two tin cups of Canadian Club, and a boatload of first-class memories. While dozing in their ample chaise loungers and listening to a George Jones cassette, they became aroused by a commanding voice from the darkness, who hollered, "I am a Canadian Game Warden. Keep your hands where I can see them!"

He approached their campfire, dressed in a camouflage uniform and outfitted with night-vision goggles. He flashed his badge and demanded to see their fishing licenses and camping permits. They produced the documents, and he seemed satisfied.

He then asked, "Have you been fishing today?"

Hank answered in the affirmative, then wanted to see the catch. He opened the insulated cooler and showed the warden packages of walleye, each with a recognizable portion of fish skin still attached to each fillet. The warden began a systematic count of the packaged goods and declared that the total was less than the legal possession limit, which Hank already knew.

Galen asked, "What if our walleye count had exceeded the limit?"

Thinking momentarily, the warden responded, "If you guys would have been over the limit, I'd confiscate your truck, boat, and trailer, along with all your camping equipment, and I'd lock you up in the Armstrong jail."

The river rewarded them for the next seven days with several good-sized pike. The tackle and other test equipment met all the established criteria. Moreover, they were about to be put into

FishNautic's active inventory. Good news!

Later in the week, they uncovered an interesting tidbit while making an emergency beer run into Armstrong. They found out the warden they encountered at the campsite had recently completed his training, and Armstrong was his first official assignment. With his unacceptable, inflated, gung-ho attitude, the local citizens, being pissed off, rebelled and demanded an immediate replacement. They wanted someone who wasn't trying to impress the ranking constabulary with his growing arrest record and his use of intimidation tactics on law-abiding visitors who were bringing needed dollars to the community.

When he returned home, Hank received a phone call from his friend, Victor Lowbranch, who said, "The kid lasted through July, when a seasoned officer from the Toronto District took his place."

Hank thought, *There is some justice in this old world.*

CHAPTER 11

The return trip to Thunder Bay and the air flight to Minneapolis with Galen went off without a hitch. Ten days in the bush had cleared Hank's mind, but he was not ready for the stack of paperwork, unanswered emails, and voice messages, all designated urgent. Thoroughly frustrated, he started dreaming about his next trip to some faraway land as he sat in the corporate lounge and sucked on a robust cup of coffee.

Rose Climber was one of his first new hires after he accepted the Vice-Presidency. Rose graduated from UCLA with an MBA in international business. They offered her several management positions, which all involved relocating outside the country. In addition, her father was suffering from the early stages of Alzheimer's disease, and she had lost her mother to breast cancer two years ago. Being overqualified for the open secretarial position, Hank vetted her through a background investigation, personal references, and several phone calls to professors at UCLA. When they all checked out in flying colors, Hank sat down with her and said, "If I offer you this position, will you be able to commit to an employment term of at least two years?"

She tearfully responded, "Yes, if you will be somewhat flexible with my scheduled work hours, allowing me to respond to my father's needs as the disease progresses?"

He agreed, and it was probably one of the best business decisions he had ever made.

Then, like magic, Hank's next outing materialized from a

long-distance phone call. Rose, now his office manager, filed paperwork when a call came in on his private line. She hesitated and let it ring several times before she answered it. A lady with a distinct English accent began talking before Rose could say hello. The English lady continued a one-sided conversation about how her London-based company needed an entrée into the U.S. market through a significant player like FishNautics. When she finally stopped speaking and gasped for needed air, Rose interjected a few words, explaining who she was and that Hank was out of the office.

She apologized profusely and asked, "When will Hank be available to take my call?"

She checked his posted schedule and said, "I expect him in the office tomorrow at nine a.m. So, if that works for you, I will block out one hour from nine-thirty to ten-thirty a.m., making it four-thirty in London." She happily agreed to the offer and hung up without leaving her name or the company she represented. Rose assumed Hank probably had previous conversations with her because she had phoned on his direct, private line. Still, she carefully detailed, in writing, the entire episode and left a copy on his desk.

Hank arrived early at the office the next day. He had stopped at a little-known coffee house on Lexington Avenue and had the new Canadian thermal mug he purchased in Thunder Bay filled with rare Jamaican Blue coffee. Expensive but darn well worth it!

Settling into his plush Herman Miller executive chair, he noticed Rose's detailed account of the phone call from England. It was almost ten o'clock when Elaine Edwards finally made the phone call. She was the CEO of a highly esteemed manufacturing company based in London. They introduced a line-up of rods and reels that utilized carbon fiber yarn in their manufacturing process. This process was patented in 1963 by British scientists W. Watt, L.N. Phillips, and W. Johnson of the U.K. Ministry of Defense. It created a much stronger carbon fiber product and was initially licensed to Rolls Royce and used in the manufacturing of jet engines. It produced a lightweight, extremely durable material that replaced standard metals. She rightfully claimed that this material and process would revolutionize fishing products known at the time. Elaine explained to Hank that he would receive exclusive distribution rights for all fishing items that Delmar produced. They had secured ample yarn supplies, so keeping up with production volume as sales increased was not an obstacle. Hank presented this proposal to the Board of Directors, who unanimously approved it.

Two days later, Elaine was ecstatic as she listened to Hank's positive response. They immediately made plans for a London departure. Hank would accompany CEO Mark Branigan and one of their corporate attorneys. The group toured Delmar's facility in South London. Once satisfied with the agreement's details, they signed it with only one stipulation: *All products had to be tested and approved.* Hank would conduct the testing in English waters, and as soon as the products passed the rigorous examination, he would sign off on the open stipulation.

Very pleased with the events that had taken place, Mark and his attorney departed London for Minnesota, and Hank planned to go north into the Lake District to begin ardent trials.

CHAPTER 12

Later that evening, Elaine Edwards joined Hank for dinner. She volunteered to go with him to the Lake District, offering her new Range Rover as their means of transportation. Elaine could only be physically described as perfection personified. She was an inch short of six feet with long, silky, brown hair that laid perfectly over her shoulders. Her inviting smile and hypnotic green eyes only added to her seductive demeanor. She wore a tight-fitting, black Emporio Armani creation that caressed every curve of her body and undoubtedly would suck the oxygen out of any room she entered. As she made her way to their table, lingering stares from patrons at Wilton's on Jermyn Street followed her every footstep. Seeing the waitstaff hovering around her like vultures searching for a meal was also embarrassing.

First, they enjoyed a great Chateau Palmer Margaux bottle and generous angels on horseback serving as appetizers. Then, they moved on to the main course by selecting a good cut of Beef Wellington for two, paired with brussels sprouts and baby carrots. Next, Elaine ordered sticky toffee pudding, and Hank had a delicious piece of Banoffee Pie for dessert. Finally, two healthy servings of Grand Marnier capped the feast.

The restaurant was near Piccadilly Circus, in London's West End. Elaine suggested they stroll down Regent Street and then pass by The London Pavilion and the Lyric Theatre before returning to their hotel. Hank walked Elaine to her hotel room, and like a gentleman, returned to his quarters, invigorated but sadly alone.

The following day, Hank woke to the dreadful noise of a bedside phone, and no matter how hard he tried to ignore it, the ringing persisted until he picked up the receiver. Elaine's voice drew his immediate attention, and she asked, "Would you join me for a proper English breakfast in the hotel restaurant in about an hour?"

He responded in the affirmative and quickly rolled out of bed and into a hot, soothing shower. He entered the restaurant and saw Elaine's transformation from Armani to Patagonia. She donned rugged outdoor apparel, right down to her Lowa hiking boots.

She had a stack of maps and paperwork on the table and immediately spelled out the plan she had devised for the next two weeks.

Hank had never experienced traffic conditions like those found in London, and driving on the wrong side of the road was an absolute nightmare. However, Elaine controlled the big Range Rover and exited the city without a hitch. Entering the M1 Motorway, they headed north to Sheffield, meandered on A roads to Manchester, and caught the M6, which took them to the Lake District. Thinking like a typical Minnesotan, he assumed traffic would become light and manageable as they departed Greater London. Instead, he was astounded at the traffic on the major motorways throughout the day. A two-hundred-and-eighty-five-mile trip back home would take about five hours to complete, give or take. The journey to the Lakes took slightly more than eleven grueling hours due to several traffic accidents and other unknown backups without explanation. Finally, they arrived at the town of Windermere, entirely spent. They had made reservations at the Cragwood Country House Hotel, about a mile from the town center and spitting distance to Lake Windermere. Exhausted, they struggled to their rooms and ordered a light meal from the room service menu, and called it a day.

Refreshed after a good night's rest, they met for a quick breakfast, went directly to the boat rental office, and secured a twenty-foot Mastercraft boat equipped with a 330 HP inboard. Hank thought it was too much of a cruiser for their needs, but Elaine explained, "Windermere is a large body of water with constantly changing weather patterns. I think you will soon appreciate a big boat with hefty horsepower." Elaine was right. The rain came down in buckets. Although it was mid-summer, the daytime temperatures were relatively cool; upper fifties for a daytime high and down in the low forties at night. He thought: *Thank goodness I brought my heavy-duty Columbia rain gear.*

Elaine came decked out in a new Eddie Bauer Charly Parka and pro-lined guide pants. With all the equipment slated for testing, they needed as much time on the water as they could muster.

The days passed quickly, and the more Hank used the equipment, the more impressed he became. The carbon fiber construction used in all the products proved lightweight, durable, and easy to use in all weather. Hank experienced absolutely no failures in any of the evaluations. Finally, Elaine, testing a medium-weight rod and reel, hooked into an impressive pike in one of the shallow bays. A battle ensued for over twenty minutes. Windermere produced pike over thirty pounds, and she had a monster on the line. The fish darted between open, sandy shoals and thick cabbage weeds as it vainly tried to spew the razor-sharp lure. It reeled off several vicious runs, but in the end, it emerged completely exhausted at portside with no fight remaining. The fish weighed an impressive thirty-two pounds, four ounces and was a shade over fifty-seven inches long. Then, after shooting several photos, Elaine released the pike into the water to fight another day.

Elaine was drained, physically and emotionally, after the contest. She suggested they quit for the day and head to the Crafty Baa, located on Victoria Street, to celebrate. This establishment was the most haunted pub in the Lake District, with a fantastic selection of craft beers. What an interesting combination; Crafty Milk Stout and ghoulies. Having downed several rounds of the good stuff, they made their way from the bar to a table. They started with an appetizer of Scotch eggs. Next, they both ordered traditional fish and chips in honor of the trophy pike Elaine had caught. However, Elaine had haddock, and Hank ordered cod. Then they washed it down with two more icy cold stouts. Instead of taking a taxi, they decided to walk back to the hotel to take off some of the calories and possibly sober up a bit. Holding hands to balance each other was how the walk started, but handholding soon led to several lengthy embraces, and as their lips met, their bodies seemed to meld into one single entity.

They awoke in unison the following day in Hank's overstuffed bed with demure smiles on their faces and slightly reddened complexions. He had never really developed a long-lasting relationship with any woman, and he knew, as she did, that this would not happen now. Elaine used the bathroom and quickly dressed. They agreed to meet for breakfast, and she hurriedly retreated to her room. After breakfast, Elaine reserved a small conference room at the hotel. She presented the test results, neatly compiled for each proposed product. Hank carefully reviewed each document and signed off on each one. Then she handed him the binding contract containing the test stipulation, and Hank signed it. Finally, they went to their rooms, packed their gear, loaded everything into the Range Rover, and departed for London.

Hank celebrated with a first-class upgrade on his return flight to the Twin Cities. As a result, he could catch up on some paperwork and got several hours of much-needed sleep in his spacious, comfy cubicle.

Rose Climber met him at the airport baggage area. She congratulated him on the Delmar agreement, but she had some bad news concerning her father. He had taken a turn for the worse, developing a severe case of pneumonia. Due to his diminishing mental state and other complications, the doctors did not expect him to survive much longer. As a result, Rose would need time off from work, not knowing how long it would be.

Hank told her he had no immediate plans to be out of the office for several months, so she should take all the time she needed with full pay and benefits. Relieved and happy, she dropped him off at the office and departed for the hospital.

He was pleasantly surprised to see how the team had managed without him during his trip to the U.K. Sales were up in all categories, and they had already slotted space in the warehouses and created display fixture areas, at store level, for all Delmar products.

The display fixtures, designed by Elaine's marketing department in London, arrived within a few days to be set up in all locations. Elaine also sent in marketing and training staff to ensure a smooth and successful introduction. Hank was happier than a pig in shit.

Hank addressed the Board of Directors the following Monday and presented the agreement signed with Delmar Industries. He explained how the product was being introduced into the stores and asked Eldon Vatsaas, Vice-President of Marketing, to review the advertising and projected sales campaign. Next, the Vice-Presidents of finance, warehousing, shipping, training, and sales added their carefully crafted support plans to ensure Delmar products succeeded now and in the future. Hank saw how enthusiasm for this project had infected the entire organization. He would sleep soundly tonight.

Two weeks to the day, Hank received a phone call from Rose.

Her father had passed away that morning, and funeral arrangements now had to be made. He offered his condolences and wanted to know where the funeral would occur. She gave him all the details and informed him that she would return to work within a week.

He reiterated, "Don't worry about work! Take as much time as you need."

She responded, "I have been preparing for this eventuality. I have grieved, cried, and loved my dad to the very end. I am ready to get back to work!"

Hank agreed and told her he would see her at the funeral.

Within a few days after the burial, Rose returned to the office and was welcomed with open arms by the entire team. She experienced a few moments when the reality of loss caught her off-guard, but she was performing above and beyond the call of duty, for the most part. Hank realized he was truly blessed when Rose entered his office door.

CHAPTER 13

Hank was in a fiery staff meeting when it was interrupted by a phone call. He told everyone to take a break as he picked up the receiver. It was his brother Arvid, and Hank immediately sensed something was wrong. Not so. Arvid was interested in making a fishing trip into Ontario and wondered if Hank would be available. It was the first week of September, and work on the Fall and Christmas seasons was almost complete, so Hank joyfully accepted the invitation. Arvid would meet him at his home near Brainerd, and they would depart from there. Arvid had a Ford F150, 4x4, with a long truck bed that allowed him to place the fourteen-foot fishing boat directly into the back of the truck, forgoing the need for a trailer. Trailers were always a pain in the ass when venturing off-road. The tires always seemed flat, wheel bearings dried up and needed repacking or replacement, and fenders were always falling off from violent road vibrations. Making the trip without a trailer would be a welcomed advantage.

    The drive to the border and Thunder Bay was long but uneventful. They checked into the Valhalla Inn and spent the evening reminiscing about past fishing adventures while chugging at least a case of Labatt Blue in the woodsy Skal Lounge.

    Arvid wanted to tackle the Ginoozhe River Road, which corkscrewed northeast of Armstrong because he had heard the bridge over the river had been repaired. Arvid was also anxious to meet the two Canadian loggers with whom Hank had become acquainted on a recent trip to Florida. They had given Hank a detailed map showing the exact location of their logging camp. They promised to direct them to a lake which they knew held numerous trophy jacks.

Halfway to Armstrong, on Highway 527, the uneventful trip turned into a nightmare. They had just crossed the Pishidgi River, and a section of road, about one hundred and fifty feet across, was completely submerged in stagnant water. They slowed the F250 to a crawl and cautiously made their way across the impasse, managing to stay on the flooded roadbed. As they approached the far edge of the obstacle and began an assent to dry ground, a menacing, dark object arose from the water, stopping their advance. It was a gigantic bull moose whose morning breakfast on aquatic greens was interrupted by an unknown intruder. Although the moose had lost his rutting antlers, his immense size, well over one thousand two hundred pounds, was intimidating. He lowered his head, charged, and caved in the right front fender of the Ford. Arvid was able to shift the vehicle into reverse to avoid another attack.

However, the moose was relentless in its pursuit of this invader. Finally, Arvid reached the far shore, propelling the vehicle up the bank while implementing a one-hundred, eighty-degree reversal of its path. Completely shaken by the ordeal, he still managed to put the pedal to the metal, leaving the beast shaking his head in utter defiance.

They stopped the vehicle several hundred yards from where the battle had occurred. Removing a set of binoculars from the glove box, they watched the moose for the better part of an hour. Eventually, he regained his composure and wandered west into a thicket of willows and marsh grass. They continued their journey to Armstrong with no other animal encounters.

In Armstrong, they contacted the local police to double check that the bridge across the Ginoozhe River had been repaired and was usable. Unfortunately, the road had suffered numerous complications from recent heavy rains. They were to proceed at their own risk and to exercise extreme caution. The drive to their river destination typically took five hours, but today it took well over seven. Washouts, potholes, and corrugated road surfaces defied description. They arrived at the bridge just before dusk. Following the logger's map, they drove down a two-lane trail that paralleled the river and located the camp. Jean and Jullian were eating dinner in a rustic log enclosure covered with a bright blue plastic tarp. Mosquitoes and black flies were everywhere, creating an ominous hum as they searched for carbon dioxide and a warm blood source. Jullian invited them to join in a meal of black bear steaks and fried Klondike potatoes. After stuffing themselves and consuming several shots of Canadian Club as a fitting nightcap, the loggers suggested they sleep in their twenty-seven-foot Mini-Winnie and forget about setting up a tent so late. They explained that they slept in a bone-canvas outfitter tent during the logging season, keeping the motor home in pristine condition, awaiting another late fall trip to Florida. Hank and Arvid readily accepted the offer. They pulled out their sleeping bags and retired to the comfort of a warm and dry RV.

The smell of coffee and bacon filled the crisp morning air. They quickly dressed and scented their way to the cook shack and found Jullian busy at the stove and Jean setting the table.

Sunrise was still at least an hour away, but Jullian explained, "We must take advantage of the long days of summer. I try to fell at least thirty trees every hour with my chainsaw. Jean operates the skidder, moving my cuts to a staging area to be loaded on a flatbed trailer and hauled to the pulp mill in Thunder Bay."

Jullian was not very tall, probably at most five-foot-seven in height. Still, he had developed muscles in his biceps and legs that gave him the look of an athletic, exaggerated cartoon superhero.

He continued, "Making a living logging pulp has become very difficult. Pulp prices have remained pretty stable, but living costs keep increasing. Diesel and gasoline prices, food expenses, and medical care have crammed operations such as ours."

Hank decided to ask an obvious question, "How do you make more money to cover the increased costs?"

To which Jullian replied, "Simple, I cut more trees!"

He then discussed other problems like equipment breaking down, isolation, loneliness, and vandalism. He finally caught Hank's attention and asked, "What kind of vandalism could occur in these remote areas?"

Jullian explained, "Last fall, two American hunters shot a bull several miles off the nearest trail during moose season. We had taken the day off to make a supply run into Thunder Bay. The hunters, trying to find their way back to their camp, stumbled on our skidder sitting at our latest cut area. With no one around, they decided to start the skidder and use it to retrieve the downed moose. With the animal loaded on the skidder, they worked the machine as hard as possible, ripping through the woods at an unsafe speed. Unfortunately, they had not checked the oil supply in the 353 Detroit engine, and it seized up and died. They abandoned the rig and the moose and quickly returned to their camp on foot."

Upon returning to the work site, Jean discovered the skidder was missing. They quickly followed the trail to the river's edge and surmised what had happened from the blood and gut pile. They again began following the tracks of the skidder and found it and the moose both in an expired condition. They drove into Armstrong and contacted the Canadian Mounties, requesting help. The hunters were arrested and charged with various crimes. But Jullian concluded the story by saying, "We were satisfied to see justice served, but it cost us over one hundred thousand dollars to have an engine helicoptered into the isolated skidder, along with a mechanic and all the necessary tools to complete the repair. All of our profit, for the entire year, was lost to this one act of malicious mischief."

They finished their hearty breakfast, changing the previous discussion to a happier subject; fishing. The loggers showed them where they could launch their boat and explained that river water appeared deceptively calm but was rushing toward a nearby waterfall. They suggested starting the outboard motor before setting it afloat into the river.

Once launched and secured to the shoreline with bow and stern ropes, they could safely load their gear, board the craft, and set sail.

Jullian added, "Although several smaller lakes and streams are part of this river system, I suggest you journey approximately forty-two miles upriver to a lake called Keezheekoni. The lake is about three miles in length and about one mile wide. It contains many shallow back bays and sharp drop-offs along the high, almost mountainous, south shoreline. I will also mark a map of the hidden rock structures submerged in the springtime but can raise hell on boat props as you enter the warmer months. Be careful!"

This lake was originally only accessible by floatplane. Still, as the logging industry infiltrated the wilderness, the remoteness gradually ended, and fishermen and explorers could reach this area without the services of a flying outfitter. Jean pointed out a good camping spot on the East side of the lake. It had a good source of year-round spring water for drinking and a lovely sandy beach to set up camp. They both offered encouragement and asked them to return and spend another night on the return trip.

They cast off from the river's edge, keeping the boat midstream. Evidence of remaining flooding debris was everywhere. Hank kept the motor at a slow idle, and the lockdown latch was in the release position in case they encountered a submerged rock or log. Several times during this snail-paced trip, they had to don their rubber waders, exit the boat and slowly scuttle the craft across almost impassable, shallow water. Every bay was teaming with wildlife. Common green-headed mergansers, gadwalls, northern pintails, and mallards seemed surprised to see a foreign visitor enter their bit of solitude. They also caught glimpses of several black bears out scavenging for an easy meal and a plumped cow moose with her young calf, gingerly feeding on succulent lily pads. Finally, eight non-stop hours of travel brought them to the lake's southern entrance. It was a spectacular and welcoming sight, one that brought goose bumps to Hank's arms.

Jullian and Jean had been spot-on with their description. They journeyed up the east side of the lake, searching for a campsite that the loggers had marked on the map. For the first four hundred yards, the shoreline proved impenetrable with heavy brush and gnarly limbs of red cedar poking out over the water.

Then, around the first protruding rock point, they discovered the secluded, sandy beach. Arvid jumped from the boat and pulled it securely onto the glistening white sediment. Next, they unloaded their gear, including the bone canvas, Wenzel four-person tent, down-filled sleeping bags, and a Coleman two-burner cook stove. Although they had packed light for this voyage, Hank had insisted they bring a canopy tent with screen sides for shelter from bugs and weather. They would also cook under this canopy, using a flimsy, fold-up table to support the stove. After they set the camp, they located the spring that provided fresh water and gathered a large pile of dry cedar driftwood, which they would use for an evening fire.

Sunset was rapidly advancing, and they decided to forgo any fishing endeavors. Instead, they would cook up some beans and brats, settle back around a campfire and enjoy some badly needed, adult-liquid refreshments.

Dawn came early, and the lake was dead calm. Reflections of trees and the high hills surrounding Keezheekoni produced breathtaking atmosphere. Exploration was the watchword of the day. They loaded the fishing gear, placed the Lowrance depth finder on the rear seat mount, and affixed the transducer to the lower stern of the boat with a suction cup. Hank sketched an outline of the lake on a piece of cardboard. They would record lake depths as they circumvented the body of water and identify the most promising pike haunts. Hank tested a new rod and reel developed by the Shimano Corporation, the new Hi-Power x-rod, and the Titanos reel series that utilized carbon fiber with potassium whisker reinforcements. He would compare this test with the English Delmar products recently added to FishNautic's lineup.

They trolled slowly, going south from the camp, and were amazed at how the lake bottom evolved from a shallow, sandy base to a thirty-yard section of thick, green cabbage weeds with a water depth of six to twenty feet. Beyond the outer edge of the weed line, the lake floor dropped dramatically to depths that exceeded ninety feet. Lake trout and walleye/pickerel used these deeper waters for security and isolation from the marauding northern pike who inhabited the weedy arena.

During daylight, the walleye stayed submerged, only venturing to the shallow water at dusk to feed on minnows, bugs, frogs, and the occasional rusty crayfish. When they ventured into the danger zone, the pike would lie in ambush and gorge themselves on these unsuspecting victims. Glacial shield lakes had existed for fifteen thousand years, and prey and predator scenarios were part of daily life.

The survey took up most of the day. Finally, close to sundown, they decided to see if the feeding theory would unfold into a successful walleye meal. They anchored their boat on the edge of the weed line and cast small, feathered ¼ oz jigs toward deep water. They were not disappointed. They had caught six walleyes within fifteen minutes, weighing two to three pounds. It was the perfect size for their cast-iron frying pan. Returning to camp, they filleted the fish, and with some fried potatoes and onions, the walleye became a feast they would long remember.

Day three became pike intensified. The weather had changed, and a cold north wind was blowing in from the Northwest Territories, bringing the possibility of an early snowstorm. They fought the onslaught of white caps and waves approaching two feet, forcing them to retreat to the north section of the lake and out of the direct wind. Finally, they could anchor in the weeds and began throwing red and white Daredevil lures with flashing copper bottoms. Keeping the lures weed-free became a real challenge, but they soon worked out a rapid, surface-hugging retrieve that kept them relatively clean. The change in weather and barometric pressure forced the pike into a feeding frenzy. They were catching aggressive small males on almost every cast. After landing and releasing over fifty small pike (commonly called snakes) and fighting numbing temperatures that hovered just above the freezing mark, they withdrew from the battle and returned to their quarters.

Rain quickly changed to frozen pellets and then into full-blown snowflakes, which began quickly accumulating on the ground. First, they tightened the tent lines and gave each anchor stake a whack with the hammer. Next, they wrapped a tarp over the food supply in the canopy tent and zippered the screen covers to the bottom. Then, grabbing a few sticks of beef jerky and a six-pack of blue, they withdrew to their canvas shelter to weather the storm.

Morning came with snow chunks tumbling off the tent's roof. Arvid opened his eyes and said, "Look at the hoar frost clinging to the support poles and canvas seams. It looks like a white, poorly groomed Santa Claus beard. I wonder how cold it got last night?" Hank methodically rolled out of his bag, put on his clothes, and unzipped the front entrance covers. Then, stepping outside, he yelled, "We have over twelve inches of snow on the ground, but it is no longer coming down. I'll gather some dry firewood from under the canopy and make a fire on the beach."

The sun broke through the heavy clouds as they warmed themselves with the blazing driftwood. Hank started removing snow from the boat while Arvid cooked a hearty bacon and egg breakfast. After boiling some water, they enjoyed a cup of Colombian/Kona blend. They realized the air temperature was rising, and the snow cover was morphing into a dank, saturated mess across the campsite. Besides going back to bed, fishing was the only other enticing activity. They bailed out a few cans of water from the bottom of the boat and shoved off. They each attached a yellow, five-of-diamond spoon-lure and started trolling slowly along the weed edge. Working the metal bait with several intense jerks, Arvid experienced a violent attack that felt like a ton of bricks on the end of his pole. Hank stopped the motor and immediately grabbed the large landing net. He exclaimed, "I am ready with the net. Be sure your drag will allow for some vicious runs."

The monster stayed deep, trying desperately to get into the underwater jungle. Arvid worked the fish perfectly, and after several tremendous surface rolls, he guided the pike portside into the submerged landing net. Lifting the pike into the boat was a challenge. Snapping jaws and inch-long teeth, combined with over four feet of solid body muscle, forced Hank to subdue it by straddling the catch with both knees, keeping it on the bottom of the boat. Arvid found his fish scale and slipped a razor-sharp "S" hook through its bottom lip. Raising the scale with pike affixed, it read a whopping thirty-nine pounds. Next, Hank pulled out a Stanley Leverlock tapeline and was amazed to see a measurement of fifty-six inches, nose to tail. They took several photos of the massive pike and gently released her into the lake, grasping her tail and delicately pulling her body back and forth, forcing fresh water over her oxygen-starved gills. The fish gave one slap of her tail and disappeared into the abyss. When reality sunk in, Arvid became weak and slumped into the front seat of the boat and experienced what it was like to come down from an intense, adrenaline high. Hank realized they had discovered the treasure they had been seeking in this paradise called Keezheekoni.

The sunlight that had revealed itself in the early moments of the day was now engulfed and hidden by foreboding clouds growing on the northwest horizon. With it, the winds were increasing, and several flakes of white stuff began falling. Unprepared for another night of frigid, arctic temperatures, the fishermen decided to break camp and head down the river. After spending the night in the serenity of the logger's RV, they loaded their snow-covered gear, shifted the F250 into four-wheel drive, high range, and carefully made it back to Armstrong and south on 527. They cranked up the truck's eight-track player, spilling country western tunes from the likes of George Jones and Johnny Paycheck while downing several bottles of Labatt Blue on their way to a hot shower and warm bed at the Valhalla Inn. Even though they cut their trip short, the two brothers reveled in the unforgettable memories they had made, and the anticipation of their next trip, promptly lulled them into pike dreams.

CHAPTER 14

Hank arrived at his office on Monday morning, full of piss and vinegar. A crowd gathered around him as he related stories of the recent trip to Ontario. Charles Davis, a smart-ass designer from the marketing department, subtly accused him of stretching the truth and telling tall tales. Hank produced four rolls of Kodak film and said, "Charles, you'll eat those words when the developed photos come back."

Hank exhibited a conquering smile as Rose Climber walked into the room. He asked if she would drop the rolls off at the local Fotomat. Hank would have proof to back up his entire story in twenty-four hours. Hank did not realize the film he used on the trip was 35mm, an Ekatachrome slide film. On Wednesday morning, Rose met him at the main entrance and escorted him to the company theater. The room was packed. They gave Hank a microphone, and Rose had the slide projector cartridge filled with over one hundred slides. She managed to keep them in sequential order, and Hank relived the entire trip during the next hour. After the presentation, an impromptu question-and-answer session ensued. He thoroughly responded to each question, but when one came up concerning the name of the lake and its location, he politely declined to answer. If the whereabouts of this lake became public knowledge, there would be no pike left within a couple of seasons.

When Hank returned to his office, he was surprised to see Mark Branigan sitting on his leather Turri-Gucci sofa that filled the entire west wall of his office. Mark complimented him on his morning presentation but said, "Please tell Rose that we are not to be disturbed or interrupted for the next hour and then close the door. We have a company mole!"

Mark explained that important information was leaked to our competitors. Several advertising campaigns scheduled for release in November and December have been nullified or significantly impaired by pretentious ads from two of our primary competitors.

Mark continued, "I've hired an outside security firm, and they're currently examining our entire computer and personnel system. In addition, I'm requesting all company executives to review their current department rosters and see if they can identify any potential moles. Everything must be kept confidential. No one, and I mean no one outside our executive team, is to know what's taking place."

Hank asked, "When was the problem first discovered, and who reported it to you?"

Mark answered, "Eldon Vatsaas, VP of Marketing, reported finding the first competitive ad about three weeks ago. It will run in sixteen major markets, with about fifteen million printed impressions and numerous radio and TV spots. These ads cite our newest products, including the entire Delmar line. In addition, they have introduced cheaper knockoffs that definitely will impact our sales. We need to get to the bottom of this onslaught now!"

Hank mentally reviewed all team members while Mark continued to express his immediate distress, interjecting cuss words uncharacteristic of Mark's standard vocabulary.

After more than an hour of discussion, Mark said a meeting would occur with the security firm and all executives next Wednesday morning. Hank would present a thorough vetting report on his entire team. In addition, a classified letter would be forthcoming, identifying a secure, off-campus meeting place and an exact time for the event. The meeting ended, and Hank remained isolated in his office, overloaded with thoughts of doubt epitomized as "stinkin' thinkin'." As always, Hank trusted people and found it difficult even to consider disloyalty among his troops. He had built his organization from the bottom up and experienced no personnel turnover. He was confident there was no mole in his department, but grudgingly he would review each team member, visually witness their current behavior and report his findings next week.

The following Monday, Mark Branigan's personnel secretary hand-delivered the letter that spelled out the meeting specifics. It was to be held at the contracted security company's home office, in Anoka, at ten a.m. Hank would thoroughly review and rehearse his presentation by Tuesday afternoon. He is the first person to speak at the assembly. His report went off without a hitch. His attention to detail was appreciated by all attendees, setting the tone for the remaining dissertations. Because the leak was more closely related to the marketing activities, Eldon Vatsaas was the last executive to make his delivery. His team consisted of over forty employees, and he vetted and ranked them using performance and behavior criteria. As in a cesspool, several individuals quickly floated to the surface. They included one individual whom Hank recognized: Charles Davis. Hank found him very intelligent but overly opinionated and prone to spreading rumors at any opportunity. As the meeting wrapped-up, he kept quiet about his assumptions and speculations.

Within several days, the security company compiled results from the previous exercise. Tension among department heads was ever-increasing. There was a low cloud permeating the entire corporate office. Scuttlebutt from the rank and file appeared in the cafeteria, hallways, or anywhere employees interacted with each other. They advised the managers not to respond to questions or comments because it only fueled the fire. They sensed something was wrong, and rumors grew like skyscrapers as time progressed.

Of his own volition, Hank decided to meet with his team to mitigate and defuse the situation without divulging the actual cause. The uneasiness was apparent as Hank closed the conference room door. Everyone on his team had signed a non-compete and confidentiality agreement. He began by explaining how policy and procedure within any organization are its backbone.

He added, "Without this structure, companies cannot survive. They would operate like a ship without a rudder or a plane without a propeller. So, examining these guidelines and how they are implemented and followed is a normal, periodic activity to ensure the organization is on course."

He went on to say how proud he was of each team member, and he commended their stiff-upper-lip attitude and how they had managed to avoid the rampant gossip mill that had exploded in many departments. Hank asked them to set their worries and concerns aside and continue performing at their current high level. He opened the session for questions, but no one raised a hand. Hank, again, thanked everyone, and he returned to his office.

Still feeling uneasy, he decided to phone his friend Winston Farrell. Winnie answered the phone on the second ring, and Hank said, "Winnie, it's Hank. Could you meet me at Nye's Polonaise Room on East Hennepin for a beer around seven? I have some off-the-record stuff to mull over, and I can't think of anyone more qualified to listen than you."

Hank showed up a few minutes early, but Winnie, dressed to the hilt in a gray Kingsridge Herringbone Tweed, was already seated in a back booth and had two cold Leinies waiting on the table. After a bit of small talk and several healthy swigs of beer, Hank related the story that was taking place at work. Winnie, a pretty sharp attorney, listened carefully, formulated the facts, and then asked some poignant and leading questions.

He asked, "Hank, are you guilty of any wrongdoings?"

"Do you suspect any members of your team?"

"What's the name of the investigating firm?"

"How will the mole be found?"

Winnie continued his line of questioning for the better part of an hour. They consumed several more brews and finally concluded that Hank had done everything according to Hoyle and should remain patient and begin practicing what he had told his team to do.

Winnie changed the subject and asked how Hank was doing with his fish identification software project. He said he had run into Arnie Morgan at a meeting in St. Paul. Arnie briefly described his progress and the tests conducted on many fish finder products. Arnie wanted to see if the new software would damage or alter the existing functions. Winnie was extremely high on this invention and hinted that he might be interested in becoming financially involved if the testing proved positive. Hank said he would keep him posted as results materialized. They ordered bar food and capped off the evening with a robust double espresso. Hank appreciated Winnie's advice, and they walked to the parking lot, avoiding two drunks arguing about Governor Al Quie's tax plan. Winnie said, "Let's do this again, real soon. I have good vibes about a future business venture that might work well for both of us."

Hank was an early riser, but today, he arrived at the office just after five a.m. The armed security guard met him in the front foyer and asked, "What the heck are you doing here this early? The entrance alarm went off, and I thought some unhappy Packers Fans were invading us."

On Sunday, the Vikings had beaten the Green Bay Packers thirty to thirteen.

Hank responded, "Nope, it's just me trying to get a jump start on what should be a hectic day."

He walked the dark hallway down to the break area. He was dumbfounded when he smelled freshly brewed coffee.

Who would have prepared coffee at this ungodly hour?

As he strolled toward his office, he saw a light in Mark Branigan's office. It answered his coffee preparation question. He coughed and shuffled his feet to alert Mark to his presence. Mark's desk, usually as neat as a pin, was cluttered with several huge stacks of paper. First, he asked Hank to have a seat. Then, after several uncomfortable minutes of silence, he looked over his half-rim glasses and said, "We got him!"

Hank knew what the statement meant and warily asked, "Who is it?"

Mark fervently replied, "It was that sonofabitch, Charles Davis, in Marketing. He's the mole." Hank was not surprised. His intuition had once again prevailed, but the relief he felt for his team members overwhelmed him with exhaustion, and he felt tears welling up inside as he struggled to gain composure.

The immediate termination of Mr. Davis would happen in a few short hours. Unfortunately, HR discovered he had not signed a confidentiality and non-compete agreement. Mark stated emphatically, "This fiasco will be one of the main topics of a mandatory meeting for all personnel this afternoon."

Specific details of the termination were understandably kept confidential. FishNautics would take no legal action against Charles Davis. However, he may find it difficult to secure a marketing position with another company.

CHAPTER 15

Hank worked through the winter months, trying to undo all the problems caused by the mole and regain lost market share. Legal sent several letters to competitors who appeared to be receiving this confidential data. Ads were canceled, and competitors removed knockoffs from their stores. Not all the damage could be controlled, but Christmas sales for FishNautics were again on track, and the projected spring and summer sales for 1982 appeared to be on target.

Hank began planning several test trips, feeling somewhat confined and claustrophobic in the office setting. First, he would schedule an outing to Whitehorse in the Yukon. Hank had an old college friend who gave up the corporate climb and became a mid-life crisis bush pilot, flying for Garrison Outfitters on Schwatka Lake, a widened part of the Yukon River flowage. He swore he could take Hank into waters that contained monster pike. Jimmy Allbrow purchased a used 1967 De Havilland DHC-2 Beaver. It was one of the last planes produced before the company went out of business. The aircraft was described as the best bush plane ever built. It could easily carry up to two thousand pounds of payload when equipped with floats and a four-hundred-and-fifty-horsepower Pratt & Whitney R-985 Wasp Radial Engine. In addition, it was a very forgiving aircraft.

First, as an independent bush pilot, Jimmy found his customer base needed to be improved, and he needed to find a better cash-flow source. So, he teamed up with Garrison as an independent contractor. Garrison provided all the customers he could handle, and even during the harsh winter months, he had contracts to fly freight and medical supplies to many remote villages. As a result, his plane was now producing a livable income, and the stress of being grounded was gone for the foreseeable future.

Second, Hank was interested in lures manufactured by the Nilsson Company, now corporately located in Germany. Its founder, Anders Nilsson, grew up north of Stockholm. He developed a plastic lure, resembling a fish, that rolled in the water when cast or troweled. He christened his lure Gigant— which is Swedish for a giant. Pike, larger than forty pounds, had been caught on this lure, and throughout Scandinavia, this device became known as the go-to, big-predator lure. Nilsson's legacy continued with an ever-growing lineup of fantastic hooks and lures. Hank arranged to fly into Stockholm later, and be met by several of Nilsson's management team members. They would journey north to the small Swedish town of Skutskar, wedged between the Baltic Sea and the River Dalalven. The village consisted of roughly six thousand residents, all avid pike enthusiasts. The Nilsson team related many stories of enormous pike taken in the brackish waters near Skutskar, and he could not wait to take the plunge.

One evening, the week after Easter, Hank drove down to the Schwarz Woods Inn on East 26th Street for some good German beer, live Bavarian music, deep-fried spaetzle, and a big plate of wiener schnitzel. As he entered the restaurant, he saw Mark Branigan sitting alone at the bar. He had made reservations, and the manager recognized him and escorted him to a booth. They exchanged pleasantries, and the manager departed.

Hank got up, walked up to the bar where Mark was seated,

and asked if he would like to join him for dinner.

Mark graciously accepted. He ordered a stein of red Salvator, and Hank followed with a liter of dark Weltenburger doppelbock. They ordered pickled herring and deep-fried spaetzle as appetizers and sucked down two more German beers. For the main, Hank ordered his favorite, wiener schnitzel. He joked with the waitress by saying,

"I relish very tender veal. When I bite into it, I like to have milk running down both sides of my mouth."

Mark almost choked. When he settled down from his fit of laughter, he ordered the sauerbraten with brown gravy and red cabbage.

After the meal, Hank ordered three fingers of Drambuie, neat, for each of them. Then, he told Mark of his planned excursions to the Yukon and Sweden later in the summer. Mark said he would look at his schedule, and if time allowed, he would be very interested in accompanying him on the Scandinavian trip. Hank was thrilled. Mark always had a full plate of activities on the table, but by accompanying him to Sweden, Hank would have an opportunity to show off his fishing skills and hopefully impress the old man. Mark promised to let him know next week if the trip would fit into his assiduous schedule.

In the meantime, Hank phoned one of the regional managers with HookSet USA, based in St. Cloud. He was immediately transferred to Clint O'Brien's voicemail. Hank left a message, explaining his proposed trip to the Yukon in early June and asking if he would be interested in making the trip, bringing the new lineup of HookSet lures for field testing. Unfortunately, several days passed, and Hank had heard nothing from him. He called the headquarters and asked to speak with Clint. They told him he had undergone prostate surgery and was recovering at home in Ham Lake. So, Hank decided, rather than call his home, he would take the short jaunt to Clint's house, just off Lexington Avenue. Clint answered the door after several knocks and rings. He was moving slowly, but he ensured Hank the worst was over. Clint invited him into the kitchen, offered a variety of Keurig coffee pods, and made two cups of fresh brew. Hank explained the Yukon specifics and apprehensively asked him if he was interested in making the journey.

He joyfully answered, "Hell yes, I want to go! After my last checkup, the Doc gave me the green light and said I could return to work within a week. I'll clear things in Minnetonka, so please put me on the docket. I can't wait!"

Clint was tall, standing over six foot five, and always dressed like he was about to trek into the wilderness. He loved wearing lightweight woolen shirts, summer or winter, and blue denim Levi's, held up by a pair of red Carhartt suspenders. It was his mantra, and it made him unique and memorable. It didn't matter if he was going to work, church, or out for an evening with his lovely wife Janet; this was what he wore. He also was a practicing Jehovah's Witness but never let a good time stand in his religious way. He never smoked or used tobacco products but always enjoyed good Scotch or porter beer and was one helluva pike fisherman.

The first week in May, Hank contacted Jimmy Allbrow and asked him to specifically pick the most promising pike lake in their service area. He should be prepared to haul ass in his float plane the minute their Alaskan Air flight from Vancouver landed in Whitehorse. Jimmy would round up all the food supplies and ample liquid refreshments. He picked a lake named Seagraves because it had abundant pike and a comfortable cabin remodeled only two years ago. Jimmy said they could pick up their fishing licenses and any necessities they forgot to pack, at Smithy's Sports Lodge on Main Street, downtown Whitehorse, on their way to board the Beaver. He would pick them up at the airport to avoid renting an overpriced vehicle. They wouldn't be landing until mid-afternoon but getting to their outpost before dark would not be a problem. Whitehorse had over nineteen hours of daylight in early June, and when the sun sank below the horizon, it never really got dark.

CHAPTER 16

He spent the next few weeks visiting stores, doing competitive shopping, and preparing the office staff for his absence. He would be out of direct communication for just over three weeks. He reviewed, with the team, operating procedures and contingency plans that would be into effect when he was gone.

He reiterated, "We can't afford unhappy clients, customer service breakdowns, or mice playing when the cats are away."

They all nodded in agreement, like the Rod Carew Bobblehead Doll that someone had stuck on the dash of his car. Murphy's Law would undoubtedly rear its ugly head a time or two while he was gone, but for now, he felt he had covered his bases, and the team was focused and re-energized. So, Hank reasoned: *I'll pick up a big box of Hans Bakery donuts in Anoka and drop them off at the office on departure day. A sugar high would enable a clean and diverted getaway.*

FishNautics offered company-leased vehicles to each member of the senior staff. Hank bargained for a Chevrolet Suburban, arguing that many field activities required four-wheel drive, extra seating, and storage capacity to transport clients and stow gear. However, he still owned the 1964 Corvair, primarily used as an errand car on weekends. Winter street salt for gradually consuming the vehicle. Rust holes and flaking paint were appearing everywhere on the car. He had recently moved into a large rental home near the office. The new house had a heated, three-car garage.

He mused: *What an opportunity to check off another item on his bucket list and own a Porsche 930 Turbo.*

He checked the want ads and made numerous phone calls. Finally, he found a one-year-old 930 in Wayzata. A local doctor passed away, and his wife tried to sell it. She could not master the four-speed, manual transmission, so she wanted it to go to a good home. Hank did not hesitate. He left work at two p.m. and drove to the seller's home. She met him in the driveway and directed him to a large, free-standing pole barn at the rear of the property.

Hank followed and was blown away by what he saw. It was a car nut's heaven. He counted eight vehicles positioned along one wall. Each one was encased in a custom car cover, making it almost impossible to identify the contents. A twenty-foot, well-lighted work bench with numerous drawers and cabinets graced the wall nearest the entrance. The rest of the shop contained several large, movable tool chests, air compressors and welders, and two professional car lifts at the end of the building. The floor was concrete but was coated with a gun-metal, epoxy finish that gave it the appearance of a hospital operating room. There was also a mini apartment in one corner, with a pull-out leather couch, recliner, big screen tv, and a complete kitchen. Next to the kitchen was a full bathroom and shower. If you loved cars, this would be the ultimate escape to revel in your passion completely. What a shame he wouldn't be around to enjoy it.

Margaret Winslow preferred to be called Maggie. She was beautiful with short, dishwater-blond hair and striking blue eyes. Although Maggie was a highly skilled pediatrician, she could have easily passed as a professional model, with long, magnificent legs, perky breasts, a tight ass, and a narrow waist.

The lady was well over six feet tall and dressed in loose-fitting sweats, but it was impossible to hide her angelic figure.

She went to the second vehicle in the lineup and asked for help removing the car cover. Carefully unfolding it to the back of the car revealed the coveted 930. The exterior finish was Indischrot Red, with a buckskin leather interior. The car appeared to be in showroom condition. Hank thoroughly examined the vehicle and asked her if they could do a test drive. She returned to the house, retrieved the keys, found a pair of sunglasses, and returned to the garage. He put the key in the ignition, and the car started with a roar and then settled into a clocklike idle. He could feel the pulsing horsepower. Nestled into the passenger seat, Maggie buckled up and gave him the thumbs up. She reached up on the visor and pushed a button that opened a sixteen-foot sectional garage door. Hank carefully shifted the four-speed beast into first gear, and they were off. Forty-five minutes later, they returned to the garage. He shut the engine off and gave Maggie a satisfied smile.

She had the Minnesota vehicle title and a complete set of manuals on her office conference table. On the test drive, they had agreed on a purchase price of thirty-two thousand dollars. Hank would handle the registration, title transfer fees, and sales tax. She signed the title, and he wrote her a check for the total amount; the car was his. He told Maggie he was donating his Corvair to a local trade school and would return in a few hours to pick up the Porsche if that was okay with her. She said she would be home all afternoon and evening, so that would not be a problem.

CHAPTER 17

Hank left the Porsche in his garage the next day and drove the Suburban to work. The Chevy was a great vehicle, but he couldn't stop thinking about the adrenaline rush he experienced behind the wheel of the Porsche. He would check the forecast and find a warm sunny day to take the car out on some backroads and test its capabilities and limits.

He arrived at the office and noticed two vehicles in the parking lot that belonged to lure manufacturers. The Eppinger logo appeared on the side panels of a Mercedes cargo van, and Thomas Fishing Lures insignia on both front doors of a new Ford F150. Hank checked his appointment scheduler, and sure as shit, he had forgotten this was new-product introduction day.

He ingeniously set up two days a month for manufacturers to come in and present new additions to their product line. Fortunately, this stopped most sales reps from dropping by unannounced, hoping for a chance to make a quick sales pitch.

He would drive around to the rear entrance, go into his office and pull and review the files on both companies before calling them in for a session. He had only himself to blame for his forgetfulness. He chuckled to himself and called it the Porsche virus.

It was almost ten o'clock before he asked Rose to bring in the first presenter. Rose stepped into the office and quietly said, "I suggest you make these sessions relatively short because nine more reps waiting in the lobby."

Hank thanked her for the prudent advice, took a deep breath, and with a half-hearted smile, welcomed the first peddler. It was an exciting, long day, and he was exhausted. Nevertheless, he was impressed by all of the product introductions. Possibly by having the reps stacked in the lobby like cordwood, it ushered in a spirit of competition, forcing them to put their best foot forward. Hank committed to over nine new lures, twelve reels, six rods, and other diverse fishing products.

He planned to go home, grab a cold one, and venture into his garage to view and admire his newly acquired work of art. But unfortunately, these plans were destroyed when Eldon Vatsaas, out of breath, barged into his office, asking for help. Eldon cleared his throat and said, "The boss is putting pressure on me to find a replacement for Charles Davis. He wants someone on board before the end of the week. The quantity of applicants who responded to the ad has been outstanding, but their quality was another matter. So, I have been interviewing well into the evening hours for the past week to accommodate currently employed applicants. Eventually, I narrowed it down to three finalists patiently waiting in my outer office."

Hank knew what he was going to ask. He sat unresponsive for several seconds to see if he could find an excuse to relieve him of the looming night duty. Sadly, nothing jumped out at him, and he reticently asked, "What can I do to help?" Eldon handed him copies of three resumes. He said, "Take fifteen minutes to review them and then make a beeline to my office. I was hoping you could sit in on all three interviews, ask questions, take notes, and help me decide on the best candidate. The security firm vetted and approved the applicants. Human Resources checked their references and administered confidentiality and non-compete agreements." He could feel the intense pressure exuded by Eldon. He did not want to make another mistake as he did with the mole. Even though much of this anxiety was unsubstantiated, Eldon did feel his job was in jeopardy if he didn't perform to expectations. Hank said he would be there in fifteen minutes.

The interviews went exceedingly well, each taking one full hour. One candidate certainly stood out from the other two.

For the past five years, she worked for a large outdoor clothing manufacturer but needed to be more challenged and utilize the marketing skills she had mastered. Angie Martinson had a master's degree in Marketing from Vanderbilt. In addition, she completed two internship programs, one with a food manufacturer and the other with a clothing designer, while completing her degrees. Angie received accolades from all her listed references, personal and professional, emphasizing her competitive spirit, intelligence, and extreme loyalty. Physically, he could tell she was an athlete. There was not one ounce of visible fat on her entire body, and the proof was in the pudding with a tight-fitting, red Dolce & Gabbana sleeveless dress. Hank would not decide for Eldon, but if asked, he had mentally prepared a list of Angie's attributes that would leave no doubt.

After the last interview, Hank suggested they run over to Harvey's Pub on Central Avenue and discuss each candidate in detail. They arrived at the pub and ordered two mugs of porter. Eldon grabbed his beer without discussion or fanfare and proposed a toast, saying, "Here's to Angie, my new recruit."

Hank, overwhelmingly pleased, complimented him for making this excellent choice and said, "It was a pleasure to see how thoroughly you conducted the week-long interview process, weeding out applicants who didn't meet the job criteria. I am glad I could assist you with the interviews, but the final decision was yours and yours alone. Great job!" Hank said all this to bolster

Eldon's confidence and to help get his head screwed on straight. After several more beverages, it was evident Eldon was back to his prior self and could put all the paranoia and delusions in the rearview mirror.

CHAPTER 18

May 1982 was ending, and the Yukon trip was only days away. Hank contacted Clint O'Brien, his friend from the HookSet Company, to see if he had healed from his recent surgery and to confirm the dates for the trip to Whitehorse. Everything was a go. They would leave Minneapolis on Saturday morning, flying into Vancouver, BC, and then catch a non-stop Alaskan Air flight to Whitehorse. They carefully packed their gear, anticipating every possible need, including updated passports and insurance policies. On Friday morning, he brought donuts from Hans Bakery and took his team to lunch at the Green Mill in Blaine. They reviewed all planned activities in the next two weeks and reexamined office contingency plans. He was excited to travel again after being cooped up in the office for the past eight months.

When they arrived in Whitehorse late Saturday afternoon, Jimmy Allbrow was waiting at the luggage carousel. He has dressed like a WWI flying ace; a brown bomber jacket, white silk scarf, multi-zippered flight pants, eight-inch high Altama-Foxhound boots, and a leather flying helmet with goggles. He had a big smile, greeted Hank and Clint with a hearty handshake, and said, "The Beaver is ready to fly, fueled up and loaded with grub and other supplies. Seagraves is a mere two-hour flight. First, we'll stop downtown for the fishing licenses, and then we'll blast off for pike waters!"

Hank and Clint had used an old checklist from many similar

outings to ensure all their necessities were listed, inspected, and packed. They were confident that no stone had been left unturned.

Arriving at the Garrison departure dock on Schwatka Lake, they quickly stowed their gear while Jimmy performed a pre-flight check of the plane before takeoff. Finally, the engine on Beaver came to life, and they pushed off from the pier. Jimmy requested clearance for takeoff and slowly taxied out to the lake's departure area. In a few moments, the floats broke free from their watery grip, and they were airborne, heading due north to their final destination.

It was perfect flying weather as they climbed to cruising altitude. Hank could not believe the number of lakes, streams, and rivers dotting the landscape. So many of these isolated bodies of water had never seen a fisherman, and Hank's enthusasm grew with each passing mile. Clint had his 35mm Nikon out and was shooting a multitude of photos as he, too, was mesmerized by the vastness of the wilderness.

Finally, just short of two hours of flying time, they descended into Seagraves. They circled the lake twice, and Jimmy announced they would land on the next pass. He pointed out the cabin on the east shore as they gently touched down. The wooden dock stood solid in shallow waters, and as they floated in, Jimmy cut the engine and asked Hank to open the door, jump out, use the affixed ropes, and tie and secure the plane to the dock.

They unloaded the plane's gear and supplies and carried everything to the cabin. The cabin, as promised, was in excellent condition, with many unexpected, modern conveniences like an electric generator, a well-equipped kitchen with a refrigerator and stove, comfortable beds, and a freshly painted outdoor biffy.

Jimmy gave them a complete tour of the facility, pointing out extra propane tanks to power the generator and several dozen jerry cans of outboard motor gas placed neatly in a metal storage barn directly behind the cabin. He then took them to the dock and introduced them to two fully equipped aluminum fishing boats, harnessed to fifteen horsepower Johnson outboard motors.

It was now around nine o'clock in the evening, and the sun made no move to disappear. Jimmy explained, "This far north, you will not experience total darkness, and it can be a bitch to try and get a good night's sleep. However, the cabin has black curtains, which will help when you want to nap."

He then went on to talk about being careful with food storage and garbage. He said, "Seven to eight thousand grizzly bears live in the Yukon, and although they prefer no contact with humans, sometimes it happens. You don't want to provide an open invitation to these unwanted guests by being stupid with food storage and not properly disposing of garbage and fish guts away from your living quarters. A small landfill area on the far south end of the lake has been trenched and is ready to take your waste. The trench is well over six feet deep, so be careful not to fall in. We placed several shovels at the site, so dump your garbage and cover it with soil up to the existing ground level. Anything buried shallower than six feet is subject to being uncovered by wildlife.

"It is about a sixty-minute boat ride from here, so I expect you to make the run only a few times a week. However, there is a small cave, with a heavy locking door on the high-walled bank, just down from the dock. Store your garbage there until you are ready to haul it away."

Jimmy added, "Next Saturday, I will be transporting another party to a lake about thirty miles west of Seagraves. After dropping the party off, I will fly over here and make a pass around the lake. If you need some help of any kind, take the large red flag stored in the barn and place it into the metal flag holder at the end of the dock. If I don't see a flag, I will pick you up two weeks from today."

He wished them good luck, while scrambling into the plane and taking off. His departure left them in silence, except for an occasional, detached, and mysterious sound from nature.

Clint was so excited about catching a giant pike that he yelled at Hank, "Get your butt down here. The fish are waiting, and I've already started the engine on boat number one. It purrs like a kitten. So, forget about dinner. Let's go!"

Hank grabbed his favorite rod and reel, located his tackle box, and lumbered down the hill to the dock, saying,

"What a perfect evening for fishing! No worries about darkness and getting lost in this huge body of water. I noticed several bays and small islands on the western shore when we flew over the lake. That certainly looks like prime pike country to me. You drive, and I will navigate. Take it real easy until we get familiar with our surroundings."

They were amazed at the water's clarity and could see clearly down to depths well over twenty feet. They both experienced a feeling of weightlessness, floating on air instead of the liquid surface that suspended the boat. Moving carefully in the first weed-infested bay, Hank whispered, "Turn off the motor and let the boat drift. Then, I will drop the anchor, and we'll start casting our lures in a clockwise pattern and see if we can stir up some action."

Hungry pike attacked their lures on every cast. They were mainly small, hormone-filled males awaiting the arrival of their unhurried girlfriends for the late spring spawn.

At just after midnight, dog-tired and drained from reeling in dozens of aggressive snakes, Hank pulled anchor, and they returned to the cabin. They would try fishing further south on their next outing, near an incoming creek. The sun had dipped below the horizon but would soon reappear. They decided to cook bacon and eggs and then hit the rack for a few hours of well-deserved slumber.

Nearly eight hours later, they were rousted from their sleep by the sound of an intruder. Something was trying to enter the storage barn at the back of the property. They had stored some foodstuffs in the structure, attracting unwanted interest. A fully loaded Sig Sauer P220 combat pistol and a Remington 30-06 rifle were on a wooden rack near the back door. Hank snatched the pistol and handed the gun to Clint. They both stood by the rear door and slowly turned the handle.

Hank mouthed, "Stand back! I will fire two shots just over the top of the barn. Keep the rifle ready if the intruder is not scared off and decides to check us out."

Hank pointed the gun and squeezed off two deafening rounds, with the door now open about four inches. Even with the unbelievable ringing in his ears, he could close the door and shove the barricade bar into the jamb brackets without losing his balance. They both listened intently for sounds but could hear nothing. The rummaging and banging had ceased altogether. Checking the kitchen clock, they decided to wait at least thirty minutes before venturing outside. The seconds clicked like hours, but they made no movement to the door. While waiting, they quietly dressed and made a welcoming pot of coffee.

Still clutching their guns and hairs standing up on the back of their necks, they moved out onto the wooden porch. Scanning through the thick brush and trees, they could see no sign of motion or activity. Guardedly they progressed down the path and made the first angled turn to the right. The barn came into view and was still standing in one piece. One of the front windows sustained damage, but grated window bars had prevented entry into the facility. Pieces of glass and pools of fresh blood were visible from twenty yards away.

Hank whispered, "Clint, position yourself by that large white spruce and have your weapon at the ready."

Clint stationed himself, and Hank finally used baby steps to reach the front door. The intruder was readily identified by the deep jagged claw marks on the front door, conservatively measuring about eight inches across, belonging to a giant grizzly bear. They surmised the bear was hungry after six to seven months of winter hibernation and was wandering and searching for an unexpected meal. After receiving some pretty punishing injuries on his front paws and legs, being shot at, and acquiring no nourishment, they felt the bear had probably learned a good lesson and would not be back to bother them again. However, Hank emphatically stated, "We'll not venture out of this cabin without carrying at least one of the guns, including taking it in the boat with us while we fish."

Hank unlocked the barn door and found a broom, dustpan, and one worn-out, emaciated mop. After they swept the walkway, they threw the debris in the garbage cave by the dock. Clint prepared a quick lunch, and Hank filled the stainless Thermos with fresh-brewed coffee. Then, finally, they made their way to the boat and chugged over to the next fishing spot.

Fishing hard for the next five hours, they continued to pull in only small male pike. Hank initially thought they were in pre-spawn waters due to the late ice breakup on these northern lakes. But he changed his mind. They were fishing in a post-spawn period, and the big females were dormant and recovering from spawning their eggs. He determined this by observing large pike in deep, clear water, aligned, side by side, in groups of four or five individuals.

The females were resting and recuperating after depositing their eggs. Hank sensed that this trip might become a complete bust.

He had no way of knowing how long the females had been in repose, but once they regained their strength, they would become more active and aggressive.

After several more days of utter disappointment, Hank suggested they take some time to explore the lake's southern end, which they had not fished. They found a detailed map of the lake in one of the bedroom closets and discovered two bays that appeared to be relatively shallow and were adjacent to where the river exited Seagraves. A glimmer of hope surfaced in Hank's demeanor, and he even cracked a smile as he uttered, "Clint, I know you are as disappointed as I am, but this southern possibility may produce some great results. I checked the dock's water temperature this morning; it was almost fifty-five degrees. If the southern bays are near sixty degrees, the pike will become active and start feeding again, attempting to regain some of the weight they lost in the spawn. We can also load up a week's worth of cave garbage and take it to the landfill. Two birds with one stone. How about that?"

Clint cheerfully responded, "You've got that right! We'll get an early start tomorrow morning, dump the garbage, and work out of those two bays. Your point about the rising water temperatures sure makes good sense. I feel it in my water! We are overdue for a fucking good day!"

Neither slept well that night, and both were up making breakfast, preparing lunch, and brewing coffee at four in the morning. Finally, they went to the cave, loaded two black contractor bags filled with waste, and threw them into the front of the boat. Hank stowed five gallons of gas in the stern and strapped it securely with a bungee cord. Clint shouted as they were about to leave,

"Hold on a minute. We forgot something."

He raced up the bank and disappeared into the cabin. A few seconds later, he emerged, yelling, "We forgot the pistol, and I found an additional ammo clip. We may not need it, but I'm not taking any chances!"

He handed Hank the pistol and extra clip and leaped into the boat. It took them a full hour to reach the landfill. Although not marked, the hand-dug trench was visible from the water.

They pulled the boat onto the pebbled beach and tied it to a fallen tree limb. Hank spotted a pair of shovels standing erect, embedded into the soil on each side of the trench. They looked like two soldiers pulling essential guard duty. Clint tossed one of the bags to Hank and struggled to lift the heavier one out of the boat. Hank opened his bag and dumped the contents into the far end of the trench. He watched as Clint awkwardly dragged the other plastic sack to the opposite side and vigorously shook the contents into the depression. They each retrieved a shovel and began covering their deposit, one scoop at a time. Almost finished with their unpleasant task, they were interrupted by a loud, threatening scream. They both dropped to their knees, desperately trying to figure out what it was and where the sound originated. Hank gathered his senses and rushed to the boat. He plucked the pistol from his Osprey Day pack and scampered back to where Clint was kneeling, glassing the surroundings with his Occer compact binoculars. He suddenly grasped Hank's arm and handed him the glasses, murmuring, "Look to the left of that lodge-pole pine. Do you see the white spruce directly behind it?"

Hank answered with an affirmative nod.

"Now, look up about twenty feet from the ground and tell me what you see nestled on the first big branch?"

Hank couldn't believe his eyes. It was an enormous mountain lion or cougar, baring its teeth and looking directly at them. Documented cougar sightings in the Yukon were scarce, but with the return of deer and elk to the Territory, it only made sense that cougars had followed the prey. He returned the binoculars to Clint as the cougar leaped from the tree. The pair turned in unison, ran to the boat, untied the line, and launched it in one fluid motion. Hank gave one mighty pull to the starter cord, and the engine sparked to life. He twisted the throttle to wide-open, and the vessel thrust away from land. The cougar burst through the brush at the end of the clearing, waving its right paw and razor-sharp claws at them while continuing its ominous growl. Now sitting in the relative safety of the lake, they realized that they were in the wilderness and were considered trespassers by many permanent residents. The cougar finally gave up its thunder and slinked back into the woods.

Hank located a hidden pint of Canadian Club, Black Label, in the bottom of his tackle box, unscrewed the cap, took one gigantic swig, and passed the bottle to Clint. They emptied the pint with a couple more exchanges and seemed to recapture their sanity.

Hank breathed a sigh of relief and remarked, "That was a close one! But Christ, if we had not moved when we did, the beast would have been on us, for sure! So, let's get back to fishing and put this drama behind us."

Clint placed the first cast near the edge of a well-constructed beaver house that jutted out from the corner of the bay as though it were an island. The floating lure hit with gripping jaws and a set of deadly teeth. It was an impressive female. She made several long runs and put the drag setting on the Abu Garcia pike reel to a strenuous test. After several more futile attempts to free herself, she gave in and floated to the side of the boat and into the partially submerged net. They simultaneously gave a loud cheer and then silently stared at the prize. The pike reacquired some strength and mustered a vicious twist of her head, hurling the lure from her mouth. Now totally depleted, she settled into the net and remained stationary. Clint did not want to weigh or handle the fish, in any way, for fear of damaging the creature. They estimated her length at over forty-seven inches and probably weighed twenty-eight pounds post-spawn. What a beauty. They tipped the net downward, and the fish gently wiggled its way back to deep water and freedom.

The final seven days flew by without a hitch—no more bears or cougars and more nice-sized pike, but nothing close to record range. Jimmy had passed over the lake the previous Saturday, but seeing no red flag on the dock, he tipped his wings and returned to home base. With all their gear packed and loaded and placed on the dock, they sat quietly, straining to hear the roar of the Beaver. Jimmy was supposed to arrive at noonish, but it was now well after three in the afternoon. Hank finally broke the silence by saying, "You think he could have had a plane problem? Even in college, Jimmy was always a stickler for being on time. We'll give him a few more hours, and if he hasn't shown up, we better move our gear back to the cabin and get set for another night in the Yukon. While waiting, let's unpack our rods, grab a few spoons and take the boat to the first bay we fished last week. The water has warmed, and maybe we can hook into a big one? If he shows up, we can make it back to the dock before he lands."

Clint responded, "This reminds me of the old army saying, hurry up and wait. With the rising temperatures, that bay may have morphed into pig heaven. Let's give it a whirl."

They fished until the sun was dipping below the tree line. There was still no sign of Jimmy, and they caught no big pike. Disappointed on both counts, they motored back to the dock, and once again, lugged their gear to the cabin. They wanted to avoid unpacking anything and start cooking, so they found a six-pack of beer in one of the coolers and a large bag of Old Dutch potato chips in one of the duffel bags. That became dinner.

They awoke early the next day to find the weather had changed dramatically. First, they were treated to sunshine daily for almost two weeks, with little or no wind. Then, it blew out of the north, bringing cold temperatures and a few snowflakes mixed in with driving rain.

There was no point in moving anything to the dock, so they unpacked their food supply and began making breakfast.

They cooked the last of the bacon and eggs, rustled up some ground coffee, and proceeded to stuff themselves royally, not leaving a single crumb to waste. Then, finally, they retreated to the two easy chairs in the front room and enjoyed their hot brew when reality sunk in.

"If the weather stays nasty and we're stuck here for several more days, conserving the remaining food supply might be prudent and wise," said Clint, speculating about their future.

Hank concurred as he got up and put another log in the pot-bellied wood burner. With the temperature now hovering around freezing, they checked the split-wood supply on the front porch and were relieved to see at least a cord of neatly stacked pieces. They played cards and took several naps during the day while keeping an ear for any mechanized sounds.

Sunday turned into Monday, and still no Jimmy. The constant bad weather had not diminished in intensity. They were trying to remain optimistic but gloomy, *"what if"* thinking was making itself known. Finally, the weather broke late Monday afternoon, and sunshine appeared briefly with several patches of blue sky. The wind settled down, and the outside temperature warmed considerably.

Early Tuesday morning, they heard the sound of the Beaver

as its floats kissed the water, and the plane made its way to the dock. They secured the aircraft and were surprised when Jimmy did not emerge from the cockpit. Instead, a young lady introduced herself as Baylee and jumped from the float to the dock in one easy motion. While she helped load the gear into the plane, she explained that Jimmy had suffered a fatal crash while attempting an emergency landing. She explained, "Jimmy took off from our home base on Saturday morning in deplorable weather conditions. He was headed north to pick you up when icing started forming on his wings, and he crashed into a heavily forested area along the Yukon River. He radioed a mayday call before the plane crashed but could not give a specific location. His plane probably would not have been found for several days or weeks without some gold miners going upriver to their camp. They saw the plane go down. I'm sorry to be the bearer of bad news, but we have another weather system coming in. Let's get loaded, close up the cabin, and like a duck, get the flock out of here."

They landed safely back in Whitehorse. They checked into the Paddle Steamer Hotel and decided to stay several days and attend Jimmy's funeral. He had no immediate family, but the bush pilot community and all the friends he had made in town would pack the Sacred Heart Cathedral with standing room only. It would be a vivid reminder of how precious life can be and how it can be extinguished, in a flash, without any warning. God rest his soul.

Hank made a phone call to his office, and Clint did likewise. Clint also remembered to call Janet his wife. They explained what had happened and would phone again when they had confirmation of their return flight, dates, and times. Everyone was happy they were safe and sound but wanted them home as soon as possible.

They decided to walk to the downtown 98 Hotel Lounge for

some brewskis. The establishment claimed to be the oldest, most active Canadian lounge west of Winnipeg.

After an hour of frosty refills, Hank reminisced, "I never made it to Alaska on the big trip I had planned after graduating high school. So instead, I want to rent a vehicle, drive south to Skagway, and maybe even take a ferry down to Haines. Who knows when an opportunity like this will come up again." Clint loved the idea. So, after the funeral, they rented a Chevy Blazer and began preparing for the trip.

CHAPTER 19

Alaska Airlines contacted them with a new itinerary. They would leave Whitehorse in three days on an early-morning flight to Vancouver. It gave them plenty of time to make the trip to Alaska without being rushed. They left the Sternwheeler early in the morning after consuming a hearty Yukon breakfast; eggs over-easy, a stack of pancakes smothered in maple syrup, and a generous serving of caribou and moose sausage paddies. They made their first stop at a warning sign not far from Whitehorse. The sign emphasized the need to watch for wild horses on the roadway. These horses were feral offspring of those used to transport fortune seekers during the Yukon gold rush of the late 1800s. So many people seeking gold failed miserably or died trying to find the elusive mineral. When faced with catastrophe defeat, they abandoned their claims and personal belongings and attempted to return home, wherever that might have been. The horses that had provided transportation were now of no use or value. They were released into the wild to fend for themselves. *Hank reflected briefly on the absurdity of it all.*

As they continued driving, they talked openly about their feelings and impressions of the past two weeks. Finally, they better understood this beautiful country and what made people settle in these surroundings. While at the cabin, they had read several of Jack London's tales that reflected on the beauty of this part of the world and the harsh and often deadly consequences of living in the wilderness. They concluded that Jimmy died doing what he loved doing; flying the bush. This thought provided the closure they had sought, and a cloud of mild depression gradually lifted.

Their next stop was a small community called Carcross. This area was part of the Chilkoot trail that prospectors used to get to the Yukon. It was also home to a series of sand dunes. It was named the smallest desert in the world at one time, but it wasn't a desert at all. It was about one square mile in size, and the impressive dunes were kept dry by the rain shadow effects of the mountains in this region. Carcross received too much rainfall to meet the scientific definition of an arid desert. The dunes were fed and maintained by sand blowing up from the beaches of nearby Lake Bennett.

All in all, it was a most impressive freak of nature. Clint suddenly suggested, "Hank, why don't you put the Blazer in four-wheel drive and see if you can climb a couple of dunes? I'll set up the video camera to capture all the action."

Hank reluctantly drove onto the first dune and made it about halfway up the intimidating slope. He then realized the Blazer was losing traction and sinking in the sand. He quickly turned the vehicle around, and gravity helped propel him to terra firma. It was Hank's only attempt at climbing the dunes, and Clint had captured it on tape.

They rolled on to Skagway, crossing the border into Alaska at Fraser. The entire journey from Whitehorse to Skagway was only about ninety-eight miles. Clint had phoned his wife Janet while they were still in Whitehorse. She told him she had a cousin named Marty Wilburn living in Skagway. She gave him Marty's last known address and telephone number and thought it would be nice if they could visit.

Upon their arrival in the town, Clint made a phone call from the Corner Gas Station to Marty, and he answered on the first ring. After explaining who he was, Marty invited them over to his house for lunch. They had a terrific visit, and Marty suggested they drive out Dyea Road, past the airport, and then north up the coastline of Nahku Bay. They could see some wildlife along the trail while avoiding the countless tourists who had invaded their fair city at this time of the year. They followed the windy road and circled back down through an adjacent peninsula to Dyea Point. They parked the Blazer and began walking along the water's edge. It was low tide, and Hank noticed a dead seal on the lower portion of an exposed rock formation. Clint pulled out his binoculars and examined the distant seal when suddenly, a bald eagle landed next to the animal and began pulling and tugging at it with his beak and talons. He was trying to move the seal from its current location to a much higher point on the slab. This relocation would ensure the meal was safe when high tide arrived. But try as he might, the eagle could not move the carcass. Unexpectantly, another eagle landed and offered help. Then a third and fourth bird arrived, and in a team effort, they could pull the seal to a secure spot on the rock. Hank, continually seeking ways to make a point, would use this orchestrated thing of beauty to exemplify how teamwork could accomplish a seemingly impossible task.

  They decided not to take the ferry down to Haines. Rain was in the forecast, and they could see dark clouds forming as the winds began increasing out of the northwest. The two-and-one-half hour drive back to Whitehorse quickly passed as they considered the perils the gold diggers went through at the turn of the century. Completely mesmerized by the thought of striking it rich, they were mentally and physically unprepared for what Mother Nature would throw at them.

Hank muttered, "Here we are, cruising in the comfort of a modern vehicle. Eating up the miles as we sit in air-conditioned comfort. Just consider walking along a fully loaded pack horse with a light jacket, a pair of faded jeans, and a worn-out pair of cowboy boots when a fast-moving storm hits you in the face with howling winds and wet snowflakes the size of pancakes. If you weathered that ordeal, you then had the Chilkoot Pass, at over four thousand feet, rivers to ford, bandits to avoid, and health problems that could kibosh your dreams in a hurry. Finally, if you were lucky, you arrived in the desolate Yukon Territory, worn-out and nearly starving. You had to find some food, eventually, stake a claim, and build a shelter for protection against the elements before you could dip your first pan into the murky water or load your first shovel of river bottom into a sluice box."

Clint retorted, "And if you were fortunate enough to find some gold, you had to protect it from roaming thieves who were not beyond using violent means to get their hands on the riches. As a result, many prospectors who struck gold were threatened and driven off their sites by claim jumpers or killed while traveling to register their claim." They both agreed that being part of the Yukon Gold Rush was not for the faint of heart.

Arriving in Whitehorse, just as the predicted storm hit, they skipped dinner and retired to their rooms in the Paddle Steamer. Hank called his office, and Rose Climber answered the phone. She was working late because of an extensive product order from Delmar Industries that disappeared in a terminal on the Jersey shore.

Rose further explained, "The dock workers think they found the shipping containers but cannot confirm it until the terminal manager arrives in the morning to break the seals. Besides this minor hiccup, the office is running smoothly, sales are way up for the quarter, and we have had nothing but sunshine and blue skies since you left."

Hank was relieved and pleased. He verbally gave her his flight itinerary and asked if she could drive his Suburban to the airport on Wednesday afternoon to pick them up. He had parked the vehicle in the east lot, and the keys were in the middle drawer of the office desk. She agreed and would park in the short-term ramp and meet them at the baggage carousel precisely at three o'clock. With this good news, Hank knocked on Clint's door and invited him to the bar for a nightcap.

They slept in the next day and met for lunch at the Chalet Bakery on Alexander Street. It was one of the oldest food establishments in Whitehorse, and its reputation was outstanding. They both ordered a soup & sandwich special and some of the best-tasting coffee they had had in weeks. After the meal, they wandered around the streets of Whitehorse in the rain, purchasing a few souvenirs to take back with them. They also visited the MacBride Museum, the oldest museum in the Yukon, housing a wonderful collection of indigenous artifacts, wildlife, and Klondike gold-rush history. Then they returned to the hotel late in the afternoon and decided to pack their gear, order a room-service meal and get ready to catch their early-morning flight to BC. Alaska Air was on time for takeoff in the morning and arrived in Vancouver on schedule. However, being somewhat rushed to make their Minneapolis connection, they hired a golf cart taxi to drive them to their gate. Hopefully, their gear made it onboard, but they were on the final leg home.

CHAPTER 20

It was good to look out the aircraft's windows and see miles of green fields, interrupted by splashes of sky-blue water as the plane made its final approach to the Twin Cities. Rose was standing by carousel five and had pulled two of Hank's bags off the conveyor. They were easy to spot, with FishNautics logos printed on all sides. She hugged him, then looked at Clint and said, "You must be HookSet, Clint? I've heard a lot about you, and I'm so glad to finally meet you in person."

Clint extended his hand and declared, "I've also heard a lot about you, mostly good stuff! Hank tells me you have taken a shine to your new job. If you are ever looking to make a change, say the word, and I'll immediately find a position for you." Clint chuckled.

Somewhat embarrassed and not knowing what to say, Rose grabbed one of Hank's bags and said, "We best be going. I'm in the short-term lot, and we only have another twenty minutes."

Hank smiled and jabbed Clint, saying, "Leave poor Rose alone! She has FishNautics in her veins and wouldn't consider jumping ship! Right, Rose?"

Walking in front of them, she masked a big, beaming grin and felt like she was floating on a cloud as she briskly picked up the pace. Rose drove Clint to his home in Ham Lake. His wife Janet was waiting on the front porch with open arms. He knew she was worried about Clint taking an arduous trip like this so soon after surgery. She had mentioned to Hank that she didn't want him to go. But it was all forgiven when she put her arms around her hubby. They drove back to the office, and Clint reiterated how much he appreciated her several times. He was incredibly proud that she had assumed ownership of all office responsibilities while he was away. Knowing she was at the helm would make his future travels more manageable and less problematic. Hank dropped Rose off at her car and decided not to go into the office. It was late, and he just wanted to get home. But as he drove up the long driveway to his house, he noticed a car was parked in front of the garage, blocking the entrance. Hank walked slowly alongside the vehicle and realized someone was sitting in the driver's seat. The door opened, and the driver got out. Hank immediately recognized Winnie as he approached the Suburban.

He said, "I called your office this afternoon, and the receptionist said you'd be back from a trip this evening. So, I decided to come over and be entertained by your tall tales. I've only been waiting about ten minutes, but I'm drier than a popcorn fart and can't wait to consume some of your expensive German brews."

Winnie moved his car, and Hank opened his double-wide garage door and pulled the Suburban inside. He saw Winnie glance into the attached single garage, noticing the canvas-covered vehicle positioned in the stall's center.

He asked, "Is that yours? Where the hell did the Corvair go?"

Hank responded, "You knew the Corvair was on its last leg, right? So, I searched for my dream car and found it in Minnetonka about four weeks ago."

Winnie said, "You don't mean you bought a Porsche 930?"

Hank walked into the smaller garage and asked Winnie to help remove the covering. His jaw dropped about a foot when he saw the package unwrapped, and his eyes became big as saucers. Being a lawyer, he was never at a loss for words, but the Porsche caused him to stammer, drool out of both sides of his mouth and remain speechless. Finally, Hank asked him to jump in, and they would go for a ride. Still tongue-tied, he got in, buckled up, and waited to hear the engine ignite. His complexion was as red as the car's exterior, but his breathing returned to normal, and his hands stopped shaking. All he could say was, "What a car! What a car!"

Hank drove out on Lexington Avenue and proceeded to put the hammer down. The Porsche responded like a lightning bolt, even surprising Hank with unexpected torque. It was a dark, moonless night, and he was aware of the large deer population in the area, so he let up on the accelerator and cruised reasonably back home.

Winnie wanted the full scoop as to how he had acquired this treasure. They sat at the kitchen table, and Hank told the story, leaving nothing out. Finally, at midnight, they decided to call it a night. Winnie couldn't get enough of the car story and never asked one question about Hank's trip to the Yukon.

CHAPTER 21

Hank slept most of the weekend. He didn't fully understand how much energy the past three weeks had taken out of him. Around noon on Sunday, Hank drove to Central Avenue and picked up some groceries and a Sunday edition of the *Star Tribune*. He looked at the headlines and began carefully reviewing the inch-thick ads section. He was elated to see a two-page spread on FishNautics products emphasizing Delmar's latest additions.

He would meet with Eldon Vatsaas on Monday morning and congratulate him on starting the impressive summer ad campaign. After eating a bite, he settled into his favorite recliner, opened a beer, and dozed through a boring Twins game. *He found out later that they won, 1–0.*

Hank jumped out of bed on Monday morning at five. He showered, microwaved a Jimmy Dean egg sandwich, and rushed out the door with sixteen ounces of Kona in a bright, blue thermal cup. Walking through the parking lot, he met Mark Branigan, who said, "It's the early bird that gets the worm; glad to see you made it back in one piece."

Hank recapped the trip highlights and agreed to meet later to chronicle the story. His desk looked like an overrun battlefield, with post-it notes and paperwork assembled in hastily formed bundles over the entire work surface. But taking one pile at a time, he made tremendous progress before anyone else arrived for work. As the team members arrived, each one welcomed him back. He appreciated the gesture but suggested an office meeting at around nine, so he wouldn't have to tell his Yukon tale more than once. Hank called the meeting to order and gave each team member a condensed report of their activities during his absence. He was impressed. Hank then delivered his rendition of the trip, focusing on the dramatic highlights. The group was fascinated and hung on his every word. Finally, after the last storyline, he presented a collection of various lures and fishing tackle that he had tested in the Yukon. Hank compiled a test checklist for each item evaluated, noting the current weather, water temperatures, water depth, time of day, species caught, size of the catch, and many other conditions that could impact the item's final grade. But he stressed, "Less than twenty percent of products tested ever make it to a stocking status in the stores. So, we cast aside the bad apples and concentrate on those that produce juice. Do you get my drift?"

He was thrilled to see everyone taking notes. They would likely use this information to promote the approved products when conducting training classes at the store level. When the meeting concluded, Hank gathered his test results and went to marketing to present the Yukon data.

Eldon's door was open, and Hank poked his head in and said, "Could I take a few minutes and congratulate your team on the first impressive summer ads run in Minneapolis and our seven other outlet cities? We can then analyze my test conclusions and proceed with a few new entrees."

Eldon reviewed the early sales figures but not shared any results with his team. Finally, he jumped up from his desk and exclaimed, "Come on, Hank, let's do this together. You can thank them for their amazing job in producing the ads, and I will share some early sales numbers that will blow their minds!"

Hank had never seen Eldon so enthused and animated. It was truly miraculous to witness how he and his team had evolved since the mole incident. After the rousing marketing session ended, Hank strolled down to Mark Branigan's office to thoroughly brief him on his trip and update him on company news. Mark had just returned from a luncheon with the board of directors. He, too, was in great spirits, probably due to the company's growth numbers but also from consuming several glasses of admirable wine. However, he listened as Hank spilled the details of the Yukon adventure. Finally, Hank concluded the meeting with his new product recommendations. They included several lures from HookSet, which would put a big feather in Clint's cap. Mark mentioned several personnel changes, but none directly impacted Hank. He also laid out plans for future expansion into the Northwest, specifically Boise and Portland, with the possibility of a smaller unit in Spokane. Mark suggested that Hank consider visiting each location as part of the preliminary crew. Mark concluded the meeting by thanking Hank for the assistance and direction he had given Eldon in Marketing. He truly felt that Eldon would not have survived at FishNautics without it.

Hank responded, "Eldon has more marketing talent in his little finger than any other hawker I have ever met. However, he needs some time in grade to develop critical leadership and business skills. I just came from a meeting with his team; believe me, he's definitely on the right track."

As Hank left the office, Mark declared, "Don't forget to include me in your upcoming trek to Sweden. I have cleared my calendar for the first two weeks of September. I'm ready to rock and roll!" Hank openly smiled as he made his way down the hallway.

CHAPTER 22

July was approaching an accelerated end when two board members, Harry Ensrud and William Campbell, wanted Hank to accompany them on a spur-of-the-moment trip out west.

The expansion was on their minds, and they wanted to visit at least three cities that held immediate interest. Naturally, Hank did not want to make this trip, but he realized that when the Board says jump, you ask, how far and how high?

Their first leg of the trip was to Boise, Idaho. They had done some research on the city and had arranged to visit two sites that radiated promise. Two members of the City Council picked them up at the airport and drove them to the properties while listening to their plans. The site, located on the north side of town, bordering the Boise River, was perfect. Boise was hungry for new business. They offered generous tax breaks, inexpensive land, and a viable workforce. After the meeting, the threesome had dinner at the Lock Stock & Barrel on West Jefferson Street. Hank ordered a large portion of pan-fried scallops, while Harry and William each craved a cowboy cut ribeye, medium rare. They discussed what they had seen and learned from their visit during the meal. All three agreed that Boise had risen to the top of the expansion list, and they saluted their decision with three fingers of fifteen-year-old Aberlour single-malt Scotch.

They rented a car the next day and drove the 419 miles to Spokane, Washington. The city was less than two hundred thousand in population, but Spokane County brought that total to around three hundred and fifty thousand. In addition, Coeur d'Alene, Idaho, only forty-one miles away, boasts a population of almost sixty thousand. Lake Coeur d'Alene and the US Navy used Lake Pend Oreille to train sailors during WWII. Hank's favorite uncle, Glen Wesberg, had received training at this facility during the war, often telling stories of his exploits and missions on the Lakes. As a result, the Navy established a permanent base near Bayview, on the shores of Lake Pend Oreille, to test submarines. The lake was bowl-shaped and had a depth of almost twelve hundred feet and some of the most transparent waters. What a perfect setting to secretly assess the Navy's fleet of E-Class submarines. The sailors called them *pig boats* because of the deplorable living conditions inside.

Hank also knew about the northern pike population in Coeur d'Alene. Pike were illegally introduced to this lake in the 1970s and voraciously fed on the lake's cutthroat trout and bass populations. As a result, they increased prolifically, and several pike had been caught, well over thirty pounds. Hank would put this area on his testing schedule and try to arrange a trip late next Spring.

Boating and fishing were essential to the community; seemingly, everyone owned a boat. The outdoor spirit was alive and well in this community, and they recommend moving forward with a store-site selection in the Spokane Coeur d'Alene area. They drove back to Spokane and checked into the historic Chesterfield Hotel. In the morning, they met with two commercial realtors who presented several options for possible store sites. Unfortunately, they could not meet with any city officials, but they would stay in touch with the realtors, who assured them that the mayor and his staff would be present at any future get-together.

They left Spokane the following day and drove 351 miles to Portland. It was a monotonous drive south to Interstate 84, but that all changed when they got on the Interstate and were treated to many spectacular sights along the Columbia River as it meandered west. Unfortunately, they arrived right in rush hour, and it became evident that Portland's highway infrastructure could not support the number of vehicles attempting to flee the city. Luckily, they could get to the Hartman Hotel on Broadway before dark. Harry had stayed at this hotel on previous visits, and booked three rooms with a late arrival guarantee before they left Spokane. He knew what Portland was all about but kept his mouth shut and prayed for a real estate miracle.

They spent two full days viewing potential building sites while getting to know the city.

Traffic congestion continued to plague them at every turn. Building sites near the city center did not exist. Instead, they had to consider areas currently under development, miles away from any concentrated population. As they drove to the airport on the final day to drop off their rental and catch a flight back to the Twin Cities, they all agreed that Portland was a nonentity for the time being.

CHAPTER 23

As he finished his second cup of coffee, Boise and Spokane were on his mind. Hank called a mandatory meeting for all department heads at ten o'clock in the main conference room. He had received an urgent email from Mr. Branigan, asking him to present data they had compiled on their fact-finding mission. He replied to Mark, requesting that both board members, who went on the trip, be present at the meeting to help answer questions and ensure they overlooked no details. Mark replied in the affirmative.

The meeting came to order, and Mark gave an enthusiastic synopsis of the company's expansion plans and reiterated the need for total confidentiality. He then introduced the two board members and asked them to highlight their backgrounds, as several managers had never met them.

Hank joined them at center stage, and they each took turns explaining what they had uncovered. Then, Rose presented the facts in a bulleted format using the overhead projector. They then opened the meeting for questions and answers. Hank was quite impressed with the insightful questions and the vitality that emerged from the group. After the meeting, Mark vigorously shook their hands and congratulated them on the results. He would take their findings to the next Board meeting, and finishing plans for Boise and Spokane would be underway. Finally, Hank was able to get Mark aside and respectfully told him, "Please don't include me in any more trips of this nature. I need to spend some serious office time analyzing the results of the recent product tests and formulating concrete objectives and projections for the next quarter before I leave for Sweden. In other words, I need to do my job!"

Mark nodded and said, "I knew I was pushing it when I recommended you for the trip. You were barely back in the office from the Yukon, and I had you back on the road again. However, with your ability to think outside the box and to readily see the big picture, I knew you were the only choice I could make. Unfortunately, God love 'em, the two board members don't have your field instincts. Thanks for being a tremendous team player, and your wish to be office-bound until September, is granted." He walked back to his office with a slight skip in his step.

Rose was worried and concerned when she saw him in a private discussion with Mark after the meeting. She needed him in the office to catch up on his growing workload and provide her with some necessary guidance and training to feel more confident in performing her duties and responsibilities. She was relieved when Hank told her he would be in the office for five to six weeks. He didn't comprehend how much his team missed and needed him when he was gone. Leadership has to be employed and exercised to make it work effectively. Hank would try to sit with each team member to review their progress. He would identify their strengths and weaknesses and implement a plan of action to keep them growing and excited about their career and future with FishNautics. A sense of guilt overcame him when Hank realized how easy it was to lose focus. He vowed not to let that happen again.

It took most of the week to get his office back in order. Then, with Rose's help, he set long overdue vendor appointments, conducted several training classes, and arranged company-wide department meetings to get feedback on how new products affected their performance. He also began practicing MBWA (*management by wandering around*) and was astounded at how much he learned by keeping his eyes and ears open while encouraging conversation and open dialogue. Hank didn't know it then, but he set the foundation for a day when he would lead his own company.

CHAPTER 24

One evening, while he was out in the garage, putting a coat of polish on his Porsche, he received a phone call from Arnie Morgan. Arnie had worked on Hank's fish identification software for the past few years and had finally achieved a breakthrough. He had overcome an application bug that had thwarted his efforts for some time. Arnie explained in great technical detail what had transpired and how he accidentally discovered the problem. Since that discovery, he installed the new software in over sixty fish finders and locators with zero failures. In addition, the software identified each fish species by name, eliminating guesswork when a blip appeared on the screen.

Hank had to find a place to sit down. His legs had turned to jelly, and his blood pressure soared. He could not speak for a moment, and then he let out a scream of joy that undoubtedly startled his slumbering neighbors. He wanted to see the results with his own eyes and asked Arnie, "When can we get together for a demonstration? I will contact Winnie, and we will come over whenever you are ready."

Arnie replied, "Regrettably, I will be out of town for five days. My company is expanding into Chicago, and they need my expertise in setting up a new computer system at that facility. I will phone you when I get back home to set a time to meet. Sorry, that's the best I can do right now."

Hank took a deep breath and said, "I understand. But please phone me the minute you get back home. I won't contact Winnie until I hear from you."

They hung up, and Hank eventually got partial control of his body. He awkwardly stumbled into the house and poured himself an entire beaker of Drambuie to brace himself.

Hank entered the office after suffering through an anxious and sleepless night, but his thoughts were not on FishNautics. Instead, he found he couldn't curb his excitement. He got up from his desk, closed the office door, and telephoned Winnie. "Winnie... Winnie, I received a call from Arnie Morgan last night. He said he had accidentally uncovered the bug stifling his software progress for the past two years. He has installed the new application on over sixty devices with no failures. The bad news is that he will be out of town for five days, but he'll contact me when he gets home, and we'll set up a meeting time. Christ, I can barely contain myself."

Winnie found the enthusiasm contagious and said, "Hank, that's fantastic news! Let's get together this evening to discuss how we should proceed. What if I come over to your house around seven-ish? I have a late court date, but I'll stop by Ham Lake Liquor and pick up some refreshments. I feel like we just won the lottery!"

Hank agreed, and he hung up the phone, took several deep breaths, and stared at the wall for over ten minutes. When Rose tapped on the door and stepped in, and jolted him back to reality.

"Are you okay, Hank?" she asked.

He regained his composure and assured her everything was hunky dory. But then, seeing the immense grin on his face, she wondered what the heck was going on with the boss.

Hank remained busy for the rest of the day. Before noon, he had two vendors scheduled to review their product sales for the second quarter. The first review lasted well over an hour, and by the time Galen Greene from Hot Lures, Inc. entered the conference room, it was lunchtime. Galen suggested they go for lunch at the Sea Maid on Central Avenue; he would buy it. Returning to the office, he finished with Galen and went down to Mark Branigan's office to confirm he was still on board for the trip to Sweden. Everything was a go, so Hank said, "I'll contact Nilsson's office in Stockholm and clear the dates with them. They volunteered to provide transportation, fishing gear, and a local guide in exchange for some additional lure facings in our stores. They also want us to test three new lures still in prototype design and provide detailed feedback to their R&D department before we return to the States."

Mark gave his blessing and told Hank not to worry about making flight arrangements. He added, "Just give my secretary the departure and return dates, and she will get the tickets."

Hank knew he wanted the flight points put into his airline account.

Finally, Hank drove to the U of M Bookstore on Washington Avenue. He explained to the clerk that he wanted to purchase a roadmap of Sweden that included most lakes and rivers. The clerk disappeared into the back room and returned with a plastic-coated, fold-up map that contained all the details Hank wanted and would fit nicely into his carry-on bag. He gasped when he saw the sticker price but still forked over the forty dollars to complete the purchase.

CHAPTER 25

He arrived home just as Winnie roared in with a new red Ferrari Testarossa. After Hank purchased his Porsche 930, he knew that competitive Winnie would somehow try to outdo him. So, when he phoned Hank and told him what he had purchased, Hank immediately ran a comparison spreadsheet. The Ferrari was most impressive, with a top speed of 176 mph, compared to Porsche's meager 156. However, the Porsche was faster from naught to sixty at only 4.9 seconds. Hank made sure he mentioned that fact to Winnie as he slowly walked around and examined the Italian Stallion. Then, Hank drove his Suburban into the garage and suggested Winnie pull in next to him.

Rain was in the forecast, and Winnie had packed an overnight bag prepared for a long evening. He drove the car into the slot and revealed a case of Einbecker Ur-Bock Dunkel in the passenger seat, accompanied by a liter of Killepitsch Schnapps with an already broken seal. Winnie then carefully opened the rear engine hood and unveiled an all-aluminum, mid-engine V12 with double overhead cams and twenty-four valves, putting out about 380 hp. The engine was mated to a synchronized five-speed transmission and completed the quarter mile in 13.3 seconds at 107 mph, compared to the Porsche's best time of 14.6 seconds at 110.6 mph. The heated Porsche vs. Ferrari dialogue continued in the garage for another hour while they consumed several Dunkels. Finally, their debate ended in a draw, and they decided the only way to determine a winner was to put their cars in a head-to-head contest on some deserted section of the road.

They retreated to the kitchen to discuss the startling progress that Arnie had made with the software. Hank explained in detail everything Arnie had verbalized. Solving the persistent bug problem in all the previous efforts was an absolute miracle. Winnie put on his lawyer persona and began spewing out legal steps they should take if all of Arnie's work could be verified and documented. He mentioned the word patent and how important it would be to protect this creation. Winnie did not have a background in patent law but knew of a reputable firm in Edina that he would approach when they were ready. Hank had come up with a company name and had applied for an LLC with the State of Minnesota. The name he chose was VisualFish. Winnie thought this was a little premature but bit his tongue and went with the flow. While pouring two flutes of schnapps, Hank mentioned that he had located an abandoned warehouse, with office space, in Spring Lake Park, just off Highway 65. Unfortunately, the builder had gone bankrupt, and the local bank wanted to dump it for a song. He had met twice with the bank president, and they had signed a purchase agreement. Hank would use most of his savings to complete the transaction but still need a small business loan. He felt this was a no-brainer but wanted Winnie's legal opinion on the deal. He said, "Even if VisualFish doesn't materialize into anything, I'll finish the offices, put in a proper loading dock, and complete a generic warehouse layout. Then I will hire a leasing company to find a long-term client. After that, I'll recoup my investment in five years and own the property at current lease rates, free and clear."

Winnie said, "It sounds like a helluva deal. I'll take the package back to my office and examine it. I should have an answer, with any suggestions, back to you by the weekend."

They felt they could only do something with the software dilemma once Arnie was back in town. Winnie would keep his schedule highly flexible for the next two weeks, but he wanted Hank to call him as soon as they set a date and time for the meeting. So, with the rain coming down in wind-driven sheets and lightning and thunder enacting an unsettling and noisy display, they toasted the day's events and called it a night.

CHAPTER 26

The morning broke with blue skies and sunshine. Hank knocked on Winnie's bedroom door and said, "I have an early meeting with my team. There's cereal and fruit on the table, and I just made a pot of Kona coffee. Take your time, but remember to close the garage door and lock the front entrance when you leave. Think about coming over on Saturday morning. You can give me the lowdown on the warehouse purchase agreement, and maybe we can arrange a back-roads cruise over to Wisconsin in our newly acquired works of art?"

Winnie sleepily replied, "Sounds like a plan."

When Hank arrived at the office, his team was in the conference room with a box of fresh bagels and enough crème cheese to coat the entire conference table. After they consumed the bagels and everyone had a second cup of coffee, he asked Rose to pass out a tablet and pen to each member. He explained that training sessions would now be part of their weekly routine.

He went to the whiteboard and wrote down a list of subjects he wished to cover in the next twelve weeks. Hank would teach the first session, covering communication skills. He stressed that taking notes was extremely important because there would be an open-book quiz at the end of each class. He asked for volunteers to teach the subsequent eleven sessions and provided a list of books and articles supporting each presentation. It took only ten minutes to fill the training slots, and Thursday became FishNautic's official training day. Hank realized that not every team member could be an effective teacher, but he appreciated their zeal and eagerness to help make this a successful endeavor. Hank then recanted a story about when he was sitting at a waterfront bar in San Francisco. A well-dressed, scholarly-looking gentleman with a distinctive handlebar mustache sat beside him. He turned out to be a visiting professor who was giving a series of business lectures at Berkeley on how education can play an enormous role in the success of any business. After two quick shots of Johnny Walker Black, he exclaimed, "I'm pissed off! At the end of my first presentation, a student stood up and yelled these words from George Bernard Shaw's play: *Those who can do; those who can't, teach.* I was caught off-guard, and the loud ringing bell ended the session before I could respond. Probably it was for the best because I didn't have a proper rebuttal."

At that moment, inspiration hit him right between the eyes, and he told the professor, "The next time you encounter that nondescript, pithy remark, you might hit back with, *Those who can, were taught by doers; those who can't, were never taught.*"

The professor smiled, took out his notebook, and asked, "Do you mind if I copy down those lines?"

Hank concluded, "Don't ever sell education short! Formal or informal, education plays a major role in our lives."

He would send company-wide invitations to anyone wanting to attend the planned sessions, regardless of position or department. Hank's presentation lasted about an hour. As promised, he gave a written quiz at the end of his talk. All attendees passed with flying colors, primarily because of due-diligent notetaking. He thanked everyone for attending and reminded them of next week's topic: selling features and benefits. Hank was pleased.

When he returned to his office, he found Mark Branigan and Eldon Vatsaas seated in front of his desk. The word spread rapidly about the new training program, and they congratulated him. They thought he should consider using the auditorium for future sessions because the posted sign-up sheet had already captured over seventy-five names. Hank was speechless, and Eldon thought he saw tears of joy run down his cheeks. However, he couldn't confirm it because Hank quickly turned around and vaulted through the office door, murmuring, "I need to go to the bathroom."

When he returned, only his team remained in place. Eldon and Mark had disappeared, and he could reflect on what had just happened this morning. He was thrilled about the interest in his program and realized how dedicated the entire company was to making measurable improvements through training.

Rose popped in and said, "Are you okay?"

Hank replied, "If I were any happier, there would have to be two of us!"

She continued, "I just wanted to express how much we all appreciate your dedication and passion in implementing a training program that breaks down department barriers and brings all of us together as one big team. So, thanks!"

Hank said, "You're welcome. Progress starts taking hold when we recognize how vital everyone is in the company. You can have the most advanced equipment and surroundings but fail without dedicated people. So, I'm just happy to be an outspoken catalyst."

CHAPTER 27

On Saturday morning, Hank was up bright and early. While he was making coffee, he heard a knock on the door. When he answered it, Winnie was standing there with a wide grin.

He said, "You didn't think lawyers could get up this early, did you?"

Hank opened the door and said, "Come on in, you rascal you."

Winnie had a large envelope in his hand, and immediately threw it on the kitchen table. He said, "Last night, I had an uninterrupted evening at home and spent several hours reviewing the bank's purchase agreement file. I have to agree with you; this is one fantastic deal. Nevertheless, only one major concern keeps returning to haunt me: your weakened position when all is said and done. You are drawing out all your savings and will still need a business loan to purchase and finish the property. Do you see where I'm coming from?"

Hank confessed, "I know what you're saying about using all my savings. The loan I am taking out will cover the cost of bringing the property to a leasable state. Still, if unexpected expenses materialize, they probably will, or if my realtor can't find a qualified candidate to lease the property, I am in deep shit! You know I am only doing this because I wholeheartedly believe in the future of VisualFish."

Winnie stood up from the table and said, "I think there is another way to make this happen. I, too, believe in the company, and if we can secure the patents on the software Arnie has written, the shape of things to come is very bright. Therefore, I want to make a credible investment in your company and become an active partner. It would forgo the need for a loan, and you would not deplete your savings. We would own the property outright. With my investment, we could address unexpected financial issues as they arise, allowing us to concentrate on developing a solid business plan. We both know we must continue working with our current employers for at least three to five years. Leasing the property for that time frame makes good horse sense. We will save the lease income and only touch it once we open VisualFish as a viable business. Now, what do you think of my proposal?"

Hank just smiled and said, "Welcome aboard, partner."

They would draft and present a new purchase agreement to the bank on Monday. Winnie would finalize the LLC structure of VisualFish, giving Hank fifty-one percent ownership, thirty-nine percent for himself, and they would offer ten percent to Arnie. VisualFish would only be a holding company until they started producing their software and related products.

Hank had developed an appetite and decided to prepare a full English breakfast consisting of fried eggs, sausages, back bacon, tomatoes, beans, mushrooms, fried bread, a slice of black pudding, and several pieces of buttered toast. He had to thank Elaine Edwards from Delmar Industries for the introduction to this very British morning feast. Winnie ground the beans and made coffee but watched in awe as Chef Hank delivered the goods. Neither man could completely clean his plate, but they gave it a college try. Now fully stuffed, they grabbed a mug of coffee and retreated to the garage to formulate a driving adventure. Hank had suggested a trip to Western Wisconsin because of the abundance of well-maintained, curvy back roads. Winnie uttered, "I would love to make that excursion, but not today. I have a date with a Mexican senorita I met on my last trip to Oaxaca. She decided to fly into Minneapolis and surprise me. I can't wait to see Camila tonight."

Hank agreed and said, "Postponing the drive is the right thing to do, but I want a complete recap of the date on Monday morning!"

Winnie responded, "A gentleman never tells secrets out of school, so don't hold your breath!"

Then, he jumped in his car, smoked the tires, and headed down Lexington Avenue with a fading melody that only a Ferrari could sing.

CHAPTER 28

Hank had never taken a sick day in his entire life, but today he called Rose and feigned a raspy throat. Concerned, she asked, "Is there anything I can do for you? Do you need any medicine from the pharmacy?"

Hank responded in a deep voice, "No, it's probably just allergies. I'll be all right tomorrow. Just hold down the fort."

He hung up, feeling incredibly guilty and ashamed when his phone rang.

Winnie, sounding excited, said, "What time should we meet at the bank? I have prepared the paperwork; we need a signature to start the ball rolling. But first, you should call the bank and confirm the time."

Hank responded, "Winnie, slow down! I have already called the bank president, who will meet us at ten o'clock in his office. I informed him about the changes we made to the purchase agreement. He is okay with everything. However, he wants us to bring our checkbooks. The board of directors is very anxious to get this bankruptcy off their books. See you at ten sharp. Bye!"

Hank was about to take a shower when the phone startled him again. This time it was Arnie Morgan. He would be back in town this afternoon and wanted to know if he could present his findings on Tuesday evening in Dinkytown. Hank said that he and Winnie would be at his apartment around seven. How much more good news could he handle?

He finished a light breakfast and took the Porsche to the

meeting. He wanted to avoid driving his company vehicle while conducting personal business. However, as he approached the bank in Spring Lake Park, he saw Winnie's red beast parked in a visitor's stall. Hank parked the Porsche and walked over to the Ferrari. He got in on the passenger side and suggested they chat before entering the bank. He quickly reviewed Winnie's paperwork and was delighted at the results. The Bank President, Leonard Cromwell, met them at the door and ushered them into his office. He offered them coffee, water, or tea.

Within minutes, his secretary appeared with two black coffees, served in special bank tankards, which they could keep. Winnie presented the purchase agreement, and they reviewed each page with a fine-tooth comb. Leonard then produced all the additional bank and government documents to give them complete and sole property ownership once their checks cleared. Next, he suggested they go over to the property, do a final inspection, and complete an inventory of everything included in the sale. They returned with the signed documents, and Leonard presented them with the keys to the facility. Finally, they wrote the checks and became the new owners. Leonard said their copies of the entire transaction would be available in a few days. As they departed, he invited them to set up a business account with his bank and establish a line of credit that could be useful in the future. They agreed and said they would return on Friday. It was hard to believe it had taken a whole day to complete the property purchase. Leonard had offered to take them to lunch, but they declined. Now they were both as hungry as springtime bears, and Winnie suggested they leave the Porsche in the bank parking lot and drive the Ferrari to his favorite restaurant in Anoka, The Vineyard. They had a fantastic meal and ended the evening, toasting the new partnership with two healthy shots of Drambuie.

As they were leaving the restaurant, he had forgotten to tell Winnie of the scheduled meeting with Arnie tomorrow night. It had completely slipped his mind. They did an immediate turnabout, went up to the bar, ordered two more shots, and drank to the promising future of VisualFish.

Hank arrived at the office on Tuesday morning with a pounding headache. He skirted his desk, plastered with post-it notes. As he glanced at the yellow labyrinth, he knew it was punishment for taking off one undeserved day. Rose, dressed in a perfectly fitted Calvin Klein pantsuit, coasted into his office with two steaming cups of coffee. Uncharacteristically, she said, "You look like warmed-over death! Why are you here?"

Hank desperately reached for one of the coffees and said, "I don't feel as bad as I look! It must be the twenty-four-hour bug that's going around."

He took a huge gulp of the hot brew and knew it was a mistake as the caffeinated liquid scourged down his throat. Not commenting, Rose shook her head and quietly retreated to her cubicle.

By mid-morning, Hank shed most of his headache and prioritized the numerous jaundiced jottings. Two of them caught his attention, both from the Nilsson office in Sweden. First, they wanted to confirm the flight information for their arrival in Stockholm. Second, they wanted him to review the list of gear and provisions they were supplying and make deletions or additions. He looked at his watch, calculated the seven-hour time difference, and decided not to return their calls until early Wednesday morning. It would give him time to review the list and to contact Mark's secretary for the flight schedule. He then saw a message from Arnie Morgan asking him to call him at his office in St. Paul asap. Hank dialed his direct number, and Arnie answered, "Hank, I have been trying to reach you. Can we delay tonight's meeting until eight? My boss has me working late again, and there is no way I'll be home by seven."

Hank responded in the affirmative and told him he would call Winnie and inform him of the time change. He took a quick lunch break in the cafeteria as two overzealous sales reps from Hot Lures approached him. They had found out, through the grapevine, about his upcoming trip to Sweden. They wanted him to take two of their newest pike lures and have him test them in Baltic waters. He listened to their sales pitch and asked, "Has Galen Greene approved the products you just presented to me?"

They looked at each other, hung their heads, and said, "Nope, but I know he wants you to consider them."

Hank clutched the two boxed lures and said, "Have Galen phone me. Then, in the future, you call and make an appointment. I never want to be subjected to these dogface tactics again! Are we clear?"

Their heads drooped, and they sheepishly said they were sorry and that it would not happen again.

Hank reasoned: *It was a lesson they both needed to learn.*

On his way back to the office, Rose met him in the hallway and said Galen Greene had called and wanted Hank to contact him the minute he returned from lunch. She paused and said, "He sounded distraught and would remain in his office until he hears from you."

Hank briefly explained to Rose what had happened in the cafeteria, returned to his office, and firmly closed the door. He took a few minutes to digest the events that had just taken place and then dialed Galen's number. Immediately Galen picked up the phone and started whining, "I'm so sorry! I had no idea they would show up unannounced at FishNautics. One had just graduated from college, and I teamed him up with an old pro I hired away from one of our competitors. I thought he knew proper sales etiquette, but boy, was I wrong!"

As Galen took a breath, Hank finally said, "I accept your apology, and I think they learned a good lesson today. They caught me off guard, but I must say, in retrospect, they made a good presentation. They were excited and hungry, but we both knew the importance of following proper protocol. First, give them a swift kick in the butt and then pat them on their backs. I think they'll make you proud in days to come. Second, tell them I will test both lures when I get to Sweden."

Hank had a passing thought: *I wonder how they found out I was going overseas?*

CHAPTER 29

Hank was about to leave the office when Winnie called and said he received the voicemail about the time change for the meeting. He then asked if Hank would like to join him for a light dinner and a cold one at around six in Nye's Polonaise Room. He agreed, but he first wanted to go home for a quick shower and change of clothes.

The room was tranquil for a Tuesday evening, so they chose glittering booths. A small polka band was performing on a small stage, but no one was dancing. They settled into their leather cubbyhole and ordered a pair of frigid Leinies. Hank took a long pull on the beverage and spouted, "Do you think he's mastered the bug? How many years has it been? If it's true, this certainly changes our tomorrow."

Winnie rubbed his grizzled chin and said, "I'm confident in Arnie's abilities, but we both need convincing that he has hit the elusive jackpot."

He added, "We must also consider how Arnie will fit into the company. I know you legally own and control anything he develops, but do you think ten percent ownership will keep him loyal and motivated?"

Hank replied, "Let's wait for his presentation, and then we can decide on the final steps. I don't want to mention formally making VisualFish a Minnesota LLC. Further, I don't think we should discuss our warehouse purchase now. Let's play it by ear. We're in no real hurry."

Winnie concurred and then interjected, "I think I've found a patent attorney that will be a perfect fit for us. She works for Strighton and Williams in Edina and manages their law firm's patent division. If everything goes well this evening, we must move on to a patent application as quickly as possible. I'll contact her to schedule a meeting as soon as we feel ready."

They drove to Dinkytown, with a plan in hand and a goodly amount of apprehension and excitement. Arnie met them at the door, and they could tell by his demeanor that he was beside himself with enthusiasm. Arnie took them through the entire process that evolved into his success. The bug he uncovered was a temporary file he had written as a coding roadblock when he first experimented with the software. Unbeknownst to him, it had stifled his progress for over three years. With the bug removed, he demonstrated the successful installation of the program into several top-selling fish finder units. They were amazed to see how easily the software loaded into each device. He had documented numerous trials conducted in nearby Minnesota lakes and had even ventured out on Lake Superior to put the software to the test. It correctly identified: lake trout, walleyes, large-mouth bass, white fish, northern pike, muskellunge, burbot, yellow perch, small-mouth bass, suckers, rock bass, crappies, sunfish, and many other species. Unfortunately, he had not been able to complete any salt-water testing for obvious reasons but would welcome the opportunity when it developed. He finished the presentation by giving them the complete and only copy of his work and findings, referring to the non-disclosure and confidentiality agreements he had signed when he took on the challenge.

Hank had purchased all the equipment for the project, including the latest computers from Apple and IBM, which now housed their critical software. He had also compensated Arnie with monetary gifts over the past several years, none of which were taxable. Arnie suggested they rent a trailer or a U-Haul truck to remove the equipment from his apartment as soon as possible. He had made an offer on a house in White Bear Lake, and if it all went as planned, he would finalize the purchase before the end of the month. Hank said, "I'll rent a truck, and Winnie and I will be over tomorrow evening to load everything. We want to discuss a proposal involving your future with VisualFish. Maybe we could meet for dinner on Saturday night to talk about it?"

Arnie replied, "You tell me where and when, and I'll be there!"

Hank and Winnie arrived with a truck at his apartment around five-thirty the following evening. Parking a large vehicle on 13th Avenue was a real pain in the ass, but Arnie directed them into an alleyway that gave them a reprieve from rush-hour traffic. In addition, he had enlisted two burly friends from work to help with the loading. Thirty minutes later, the two headed up Interstate 94 to the new warehouse. When they drove into the warehouse parking lot, they proceeded directly to the loading dock at the rear of the building. Because they had placed the equipment on wooden pallets in the truck, Hank opened one of the overhead doors and approached the back of the U-Haul with a bright yellow Hyster forklift. Within ten minutes, he had removed all five loaded pallets and placed them in one of the locked storage areas within the warehouse.

Hank extended his hand and shook Winnie's with such a vice-like grip that Winnie shrieked and withdrew in pain.

Hank gasped, "Sorry, I didn't know my strength! I am so excited and relieved to see how far we have come in such a short time frame."

Winnie, shaking off the numbness in his fingers, said, "Let's get this truck back to the rental center in Blaine and find the nearest bar to celebrate."

They went to Nystrom's Bar in North St. Paul, arriving just after eight. They ordered beef tacos and two bottles of Hamm's beer because Nystrom's didn't stock their Wisconsin favorite. They began discussing their plans and decided to proceed with their offer to Arnie. They agreed that he would receive ten percent ownership in the company. They also expected him to contribute his computer expertise and be subject to the non-disclosure and confidentiality agreements already in effect. He could maintain outside employment with his current or future employer as long as he wished. However, as an active owner of the LLC, he would be expected to partake in scheduled meetings and accept one of the officer positions within VisualFish. Winnie would have the full-binding agreement drawn up before the dinner on the weekend.

That Saturday night, the Schwarz Woods Inn only admitted bar stool customers. It was a standing room only. Thank God they had made reservations because it seemed like every Tom, Dick, and Harry was out on the town. When Winnie arrived early, he slipped the head waiter a folded *Jackson* to get a private booth at the rear of the dining room. Arnie came next, followed two minutes later by Hank. Winnie ordered a liter of Spaten lager. Hank and Arnie settled for a pint each of dark Hacker-Pschorr. They briefed Arnie on the events that had recently taken place; the purchase of the warehouse and the formation of VisualFish as a registered LLC. Winnie extracted three copies of the Arnie agreement from his hand-stitched leather satchel propped against the booth's far side. He briefly disclosed the document's main points and waited for a definitive response from Arnie. His rosy complexion and the massive smile on his face were all Winnie needed to proceed. They examined, in detail, each of the ten pages that comprised the agreement. Arnie asked a couple of clarification questions and then requested a pen. In unison, they raised their mugs and shouted, "Prosit." The new company was now official.

CHAPTER 30

Hank couldn't believe August had come and gone, and the trip to Sweden was only two days away. He and Mark Branigan would leave on Saturday and be gone for two weeks. The fully equipped Nilsson Team met them at Arlanda Airport, the largest international facility, twenty miles north of Stockholm in the small town of Marsta. Because of their early morning arrival, the group would immediately take the seventy-mile drive north to their final destination of Skutskar. They would check into the Buffalo Hotel and Steakhouse, their home base for the next few weeks, giving them easy access to the Dalalven and the brackish waters of the Baltic Sea. When they arrived, Kennet Gustavsson, Sales Manager for Nilsson, who would be their guide on this trip, declared, *"gadda himlen" (translated: pike heaven).*

As they boarded the Marcraft-Tomasco Pike Master boat, harnessed to a 115 hp Evinrude, Kennet hollered, "Put on your life jackets. She's pretty rough today."

Mark asked, "What about our rain outfits? The sky looks menacing, and I sure as hell don't want to get soaked!"

Kennet opened a storage bin behind his seat and handed them two complete sets of Grunden's rain gear.

He said, "They'll keep you warm and dry. You better put them on now, or you'll pay hell trying to do it out in the rouge waves."

They headed southeast on the Dalalven River, past Myrholmen Island, and then turned east toward Lundvistsholmen

Bay. They would start fishing the brackish waters in this area because Kennet wanted to stay within the safety of the islands. However, he said, "Red flag warnings have been issued, with wind gusts above forty knots."

Hank opened his rod case and pulled out two Shimano Beast Master rods. He handed one to Mark and said, "We'll start with these rods. I have a Shimano BBX 2500 EV reel that I want to test, and I would like you to use this Shimano Quick Fire II FX-300 spinning reel. I spooled the reels with a heavy-duty line, and we'll use fifty-pound steel leaders, so we won't have any bite-offs from big-toothy pike."

They began a slow drift to the west and cast various lures ranging from tumbling shad to Heddon Torpedos. They even tried the two lures the overzealous, Hot Lure salespeople had left with him. Within an hour, they hooked and landed several impressive pike, one weighing almost twenty-one pounds. Then, they backtracked to the river and started a slow troll back to home base. Luckily, the rain had held off, but the steady high wind zapped their energy, and by mid-afternoon, they decided to hang it up for the day. Heavy rain started in the early evening and would continue for several days. They took the next day and documented and reviewed the gear they had used on day one. Then, they treated themselves to rib-eye steaks at the Buffalo Steak House and thoroughly enjoyed several bottles of Fagerhult Export Beer in the bar.

CHAPTER 31

Sunshine and calm winds arrived on day three. Mark started feeling claustrophobic and was relieved to see the blue, cloudless skies. Kennet suggested they travel southwest, down the Dalalven, to a broad section of the river near the city of Marma. They fished the bays and around dozens of small islands in this vast expanse of the river. It was a pike fisherman's dream come true. They were successful with every lure they had squeezed into the six drawers of the large My Buddy Tackle Box. By early evening, they were exhausted from casting and catching, pike after pike, although none had exceeded the twenty-pound mark. During the remaining days of the trip, they focused on only the productive, brackish waters right on the Baltic shoreline. They were often the only boat on the water with cooler nights and shorter days.

The weather had been perfect for nine days in a row as they headed east on Friday morning, the last fishing day of the excursion. It was overcast, with only a slight breeze. With a front moving in, the fish became active and hungry. No one had checked their fuel supply when they left the dock that morning, and when the motor started to shutter, backfire and quit running, they looked at each other in disbelief. The boat was adrift with one sun-rotted emergency paddle and a southeast wind pushing it toward the craggy shoreline. The first submerged rock they encountered lifted them to a pivotal point, utterly free of the dreadful abyss. The boat teetered in mid-air for a moment and then was flung off the lofty summit with such force that it nearly capsized. Hank and Mark used a rusted piss can and a discarded Tupperware bowl to bail the salty sea brine from the bottom of the vessel. Their efforts were futile. It was like digging a grave using only a teaspoon as a tool.

The billowing rollers were approaching five feet in height, and Kennet was still trying to control the boat with the lifeless keel. Somehow, while frantically scooping water, they lost their useless paddle to one of the towering waves that leaped over the gunwales. The sleet-infused rain had joined the gale-force winds. They could barely see the shoreline when Mark screamed, "Brace yourselves; we're going to hit that big boulder in front of us! Be sure your lifejackets are secure because bigger than shit, and we're about to take a cold dousing!"

The craft was hurled sideways into the jagged rock and crumbled like aluminum foil. A Baltic black hole devoured the boat. All three men were tossed into the icy waters and then violently thrust onto a flat slab of an igneous outcropping.

Hank, gasping for breath, shouted, "Is anyone injured? Let's get the fuck up to higher ground and safety before the next big breaker hits!"

They scampered up the glacial boulders, escaping the giant sea swells that now roared in defeat from several feet below. Then, staying at least a hundred feet from the shoreline, they carved their way through eight kilometers of thick pine forest into Skutskar. Finally, they reported the incident to the Swedish Coast Guard and the local authorities. The Guard would send out a patrol boat when the storm subsided, but they gave no hope for a recovery of the vessel or its contents. Still shaken from yesterday's trauma, they met for breakfast and began making afternoon plans to get to a hotel near the Arlanda Airport on

Saturday. They had a Sunday afternoon departure for the Twin Cities. So, sleeping in on Sunday morning and being close to the airport made good sense. They returned to their rooms and packed the remains of their gear and the data they had compiled. Hank went down the hallway to Mark's room with a liter of Canadian Club-Black Label. He knocked loudly on the door and startled Mark, who was in the middle of a brief catnap.

He eventually opened the door and smiled when he saw what Hank was holding. He poured two generous shots of the whiskey, and Hank stretched out on the big Natuzzi leather sofa while Mark settled into a comfy Fjords recliner.

Neither man spoke for several minutes. Then, like a failed dam, they both developed severe diarrhea of the mouth and began recapping the events, often talking over each other as the alcohol took command. They laughed until tears flooded their eyes and then sobbed with the same amount of salty discharge. Life was good, and they were exceedingly grateful for everything as they fell into a gentle sleep.

The lime-green phone on the nightstand began an obnoxious ring in the late afternoon. Mark stumbled to the bedside and picked up the intruder. It was Kennet, and he said he was waiting in the parking lot to transport them south. They were down in the lobby in ten minutes and ushered into a large Volvo transport van while Kennet and the driver loaded their luggage. Arriving at the hotel, they said their farewells and voiced their appreciation for the memorable Swedish hospitality. Mark said that anyone from the Nilsson Company who wished to visit Minnesota would be subject to the same friendship they received in Sweden. On that note, they boarded their NWA flight early Sunday morning and departed without a hitch.

CHAPTER 32

The flight landed in Minneapolis, on time, at nine-forty-five a.m., the same day. It's incredible how gaining seven hours in time zones and flying more than four hundred miles per hour equated to a mere three-hour flight. Hank thought, *Screw jet lag!*

Mark had deposited his Mercedes wagon in the long-term parking lot when they left for Sweden. After collecting their luggage from the baggage carousel, he left Hank with their belongings outside the terminal and procured his vehicle.

Traffic was light, and they arrived at the office in Forest Lake a little before noon. They slept soundly on the return flight, so they decided to venture into their offices and get caught up on the waiting workload. It was almost dark when Mark slipped into Hank's office and said, "It's time to quit. Let's pack it up and go home. My wife telephoned several times and informed me that I promised, when we got married, not to become a workaholic. I pleaded my case, but her last words were: *Get your ass home, and I mean now!* Hank, I sometimes envy you for being single."

Hank walked into the office on Monday and felt he had not been away for two weeks. Rose was utterly baffled when she saw his empty desk. She distinctly remembered what it looked like on Friday afternoon as she locked up the office. She asked Hank, "Did you come in over the weekend, or am I dreaming?"

He told Rose to sit and said, "I'll be back in a few of minutes. Just sit tight."

When he returned, he had a large black coffee in each hand.

He gave one to Rose and then began telling her the entire Swedish story, leaving out no details. He then asked her to highlight what had taken place at FishNautics while he was gone and to clarify several notes she had written that he did not understand. Delighted with her explanations and progress, he entered the main office and invited the entire team to a noon luncheon.

He said he wanted a brief team meeting right after they finished eating, which meant each member would recap what they had accomplished while he was gone. But little did he know, they had grown accustomed to his M.O. and had already devised a comprehensive summary.

Early in the afternoon, Hank visited each department head. They each gave an updated state of the state recap for their areas of responsibility. The company was multiplying, and everyone was in high spirits. When he asked, "What else can my team do to make your life better?"

The answer was unanimous, "Just keep doing what you're doing." He was about to leave for home when his phone line lit up. Winnie wanted to meet briefly to fill him in on the progress of the patent plan. He was already one beer ahead of him at the Polonaise room, and Hank responded, "I'll be there in twenty minutes, barring any traffic problems on 35W. Bye."

Hank got off the freeway and motored down East Hennepin, arriving at Nye's in just over twenty minutes. As he entered the Bar, Winnie stood up and barked, "Get your butt over here, and let's get down to some serious drinking, you hardheaded Norwegian."

Hank laughed out loud as he slid into the booth. He asked, "How was your trip to the land of spectacular tall blondes with small brains and big bosoms?" He filled him in on the details while slurping down a cold Leinie.

With Sweden out of the way, he asked for the patent update that Winnie had promised. Hank said, "I had an introductory meeting with Lydia Tribeck at her office in Edina. I must say, she's extremely knowledgeable in every area of patent law. I gave her a brief description of the software and how it works. She was intrigued and wanted to set up a formal meeting at our convenience. I told her you were out of town, but I'd get back to her sometime this week. As an aside, she's an absolute knock-out, brains, and beauty."

Hank asked if they could arrange an evening meeting because his daily calendar at work was booked solid for the next two weeks.

Winnie emphasized, "Thursday evening would work best for me. Will that work for you?"

Hank, checking his pocket calendar, said, "That's perfect. It's a date, and I'll meet you at Lydia's office around seven."

Winnie then began telling about his recent exploits in the Ferrari. He had a good friend who worked at Brainerd International Raceway and invited him to the facility last weekend. Although the Raceway had been running for five years, bookings were light, and nothing was scheduled for Saturday morning. He asked Winnie if he would like to put the Ferrari on the track and run some laps. Naturally, he jumped at the chance and said he would drive up early Saturday morning. His friend told him he would have to sign the paperwork, receive a briefing on the track rules, and be issued a helmet and some safety apparel. They would also perform a complete safety check on his car, including wheels, tires, brakes, lights, seat belts, etc."

He said, "When I arrived in Brainerd, my heart was pounding in my chest, and I was sweating like a stuck pig!

Finally, after completing the preliminaries, they ushered me down to the track entrance, and I was set free! I took it easy for the first two laps around the three-mile track. I cautiously approached each of the ten turns in the course, learning the lay of the land and improving my track confidence as I maneuvered my way around. By the third lap, I was hitting close to the red line and topping over 150 mph on the straightaway. The Ferrari performed flawlessly. Having sucked my adrenal glands dry, I pulled off the track after twelve laps and shut the engine down, as well as my body. What an absolute thrill! Hank, if you are interested, I'll see if I can arrange some track time for you and the 930."

Hank replied, "You say the word, and I'll be there with bells on my toes." They ordered two more Leinies, toasted their automobiles, and said goodnight.

CHAPTER 33

Thursday rolled around, and Hank found himself daydreaming short vignettes throughout the day about what lies ahead for VisualFish. However, he couldn't wait for the evening meeting with Lydia Tribeck to place the significant component of his company into the patent application process. Winnie had telephoned earlier in the day and told Hank he could not attend the meeting in Edina. His only cousin was involved in a head-on crash near Duluth, and they didn't expect him to live. Winnie was his closest living relative and executor of his will. One of the partners in the law firm where Winnie worked was a private pilot and suggested they head to the Crystal Airport and use his twin-engine Cessna to get to Duluth in about an hour. Knowing the situation's urgency, Winnie took him up on his offer.

Hank drove to Edina with a heavy heart. He knew how close Winnie was to his cousin. Hank also knew his cousin was the last surviving relative on either side of his family. *He whispered a little prayer for the two of them.* Hank arrived in Edina, and due to road construction, he was forced into unfamiliar territory and was lost. He finally pulled into a convenience store on France Avenue and went inside. The clerk behind a heavily barred window barely spoke English, and when Hank showed him the address of the law firm, neatly written on a legal pad, he started giving directions by waving his arms and pointing his fingers. His theatrics reminded him of the semaphore lessons he received in the Army, which proved to be about as useless. Hank, now thoroughly frustrated, was standing outside on the sidewalk when a well-dress woman, driving a crystal-white Corvette with the top down, stopped directly in front of him. He slowly walked to the driver's side and politely said, "Are you from Edina? I need directions to the law office of Strighton and Williams on West 66th Street. Can you direct me?"

She smiled and calmly replied, "Make a right on France and go four blocks to the next traffic light. That will be 66th Street. Take a right turn and then another immediate right into the law office parking lot."

He thanked her and said, "How did you know the firm's location precisely?"

She giggled, "I'm the office manager, and you must be Hank Walhberg. Lydia is anxiously awaiting your arrival."

Hank sheepishly walked into the reception area almost forty-five minutes late. Lydia emerged from one of the large conference rooms and curtly said, "You must be Hank, and you're late!" Hank followed her into the room and remained quiet as he watched the most beautiful lady he had ever seen ask him to have a seat. Winnie had understated her physical beauty, and he hoped he had not underestimated her intelligence. First, Lydia gave a lengthy history of the firm and carefully presented her experience and credentials. Then, she was all business as she began explaining the patent process and what steps would be necessary if they chose their firm for the project. Hank had already decided, but he kept her in suspense like a good poker player. As a course of due diligence, he and Winnie had compiled questions that needed to be addressed and answered. She skillfully surmounted each question and articulated answers that left Hank awestruck. After the presentation, Hank started making small talk. He had noticed she was not wearing a wedding band

and asked if she knew of a nearby restaurant where he could buy her dinner. She said she had several more hours of urgent work that needed to be completed before morning and graciously declined the offer but left the door open for a rain check. Hank shook her hand and thanked her for the time she had afforded him.

He stared into her deep blue eyes and thought he was in a hypnotic state. He almost yelled out his decision to go with her firm but caught himself in the nick of time. He selfishly wanted another opportunity to meet with her before he divulged the good news. She started to hand him her business card but paused and then scribbled her home phone number on the back. She said, "Call me any time with your decision."

As he drove home, he knew that something extraordinary had just happened. He felt like he was floating several inches above the car seat as he raced up 35W. Hank trusted his intuition, and his intuition was screaming: *Don't screw this up; she might be the real thing.* When he drove into his driveway, he stopped the car in front of the garage door. Hank exited the vehicle, drifted to his favorite chaise lounge, and unceremoniously collapsed. It was a fantastic night with a clear sky, and he gazed up at the millions of flickering stars and concluded that he was close to capturing one.

CHAPTER 34

The Board of Directors wanted Hank and Mark to deliver a formal oration on their recent trip to Sweden. They had been highly impressed with the solid relationship developed with Delmar in England and expected similar results from Nilsson in Scandinavia. They also wanted a detailed breakdown of the various products they field-tested on this excursion. Hank had prepared a slide presentation and carried the Kodak-carousel slide tray to Mark's office. Mark had drawn the office curtains, and Hank began loading one hundred and forty slides. He had inserted them in chronological order, so they could review, comment, and make notes on each slide as they relived each day of the trip. Mark turned on the lights when the last slide was ejected, and said, "Hank, I can't believe you could capture so much of action, and I especially appreciate the photos showing product close-ups. I think the Board will be notably impressed."

Hank replied, "It sure makes it easy to weed out the losers when you can see them in honest test conditions. By the way, I did shoot most of the photos myself, but I bribed Kennet with a bottle of Drambuie, to continue shooting pictures when you and I were onstage."

They scheduled the presentation for Friday afternoon in the main auditorium. They could use the high-powered projector, the massive movie screen, and the newly purchased Bose sound system to help tell their story.

Several times during the show, unexpected applause and

cheering erupted from the board members, who appeared to be overwhelmed with the projected realism in many of the slides.

After the program, they rifled question after question for almost an hour. Two members of the board were avid fishermen and were planning to visit this part of northern Europe. Each left with a list of products that made the grade and would become part of FishNautic's fortuitous inventory. Mark excused himself while Hank sank into one of the leather movie recliners and mentally wandered and digressed through this two-week adventure. Mark quietly slipped back into the auditorium and slammed a liter of twenty-five-year-old Macallan Sherry Oak Scotch on the display table. Hank vaulted from his slumber, wondering what was happening. Mark held up two Waterford Crystal tumblers and said, "I think we earned this! Come on and join me!"

Hank approached the table, staring at the bottle, and said, "Where did you find the money to purchase Scottish perfection? This shit sells for well over a thousand dollars a bottle if you can find it! I'm afraid to pour it, fearing I might spill a drop."

They did break the seal and toasted several neat pours of the smoothest whiskey that had ever numbed their tonsils. Mark, usually not a very demonstrative fellow, walked over to Hank, gave him an imposing hug of gratitude, and said, "This was the best excursion I have ever been on, and I want to thank you from the bottom of my heart. Let's hope we can do this again sometime!"

After releasing him from a crushing clinch, Hank managed to expend a husky, "You're welcome."

As they departed the facility, he saw that Mark struggled to keep his balance and could not drive anywhere. He politely asked, "Are you sure you're okay to drive home?"

He replied, "No, I am not! My wife will be here shortly to cart me down the freeway."

Hank had a much higher tolerance for liquor because he felt sober enough to drive home, taking some little-known backroads that were presumably never patrolled. He was almost home. About a mile from his driveway, Hank momentarily closed his wearied eyes, and when they reopened, the car was heading toward an ugly, water-filled ditch. He swerved the vehicle off the gravel shoulder, hit the brakes, and stopped in the middle of the roadway. It scared the crap out of him. However, he was now wide awake and cautiously maneuvered the last mile. Hank took a deep breath as he safely entered the garage. Then, not moving a muscle, he turned off the ignition and solemnly promised himself never to do anything that foolish again.

CHAPTER 35

It was Saturday morning, and Hank was busy polishing his 930 in the garage. He hadn't driven the car for several weeks, and as he rubbed out the last powdered streaks of polish, he decided to go for a spin.

He drove north on Lexington Avenue, heading for Coon Lake. The road had recently been seal-coated, and it was in prime condition. He leaned into the curves and rapidly moved through all five gears on the straightaways, surpassing one hundred miles per hour on at least three occasions. No one was on the road at this hour, but animals, primarily white-tailed deer, posed a potentially dangerous threat. Hitting a two-hundred-pound buck at high speed could mean certain death for both parties. Hank slowed down as he made the turn into the village of Coon Lake. White sugar sand streets forced him to crawl slowly in the Porsche toward a collection of small businesses. There was a small convenience store boasting a bright orange Union 76 sign. Across the street was the Ramblers Inn. It was an old-fashioned bar and dance hall. He remembered his Uncle Glen telling stories of how gangsters from Chicago would come to this area when the heat was on in the Windy City. He and his wife enjoyed coming to the Ramblers on weekends to enjoy live music, good booze, and the vast planked dance floor in the main hall.

Hank drove slowly down the hill to the shoreline of Coon Lake, named for the raccoon hunters who would descend on the area to hunt the elusive bandit. He followed Lakeshore Drive and was amazed at the beauty of this one-thousand-five-hundred-acre lake.

All along the shoreline, dozens of weathered and peeling boat houses perched above the waterline, containing hidden treasures with names like Starcraft and Chris Craft. Up the high bank bordering the water were quaint, little cabins nestled on tiny lots, probably no more than four hundred square feet.

Weekend getaways for the urban yuppies who needed a break from the rat race.

The road made an abrupt pivot, and before he knew it, he was back on Lexington Avenue, heading south. He met several fishermen towing boats and trailers on his way back home. He had been thinking about purchasing a fishing boat for some time, and begging to borrow one of his supplier's boats every time he wanted to get out on the water was starting to be a real drag. But storing a boat at his home meant it would sit outside, constantly exposed to the malicious Minnesota climate.

However, with the warehouse purchase in Spring Lake Park, indoor storage for a new boat was a real possibility. He'd eagerly bring the proposition to his partners at their next meeting.

He had conceivably solved his boat dilemma, but now a new subject wormed its way into his mind, women. Finally, Hank's particular case boiled down to one woman: *Lydia*.

He twisted the cap off a cold beer and absorbed twelve ounces without putting the bottle down. He was hoping to find courage in the amber brew. But unfortunately, one dead soldier did not produce the desired effect, so he chugged another and felt a sudden burst of confidence, grabbing him by the short hairs. He picked up the phone and started to dial her number. He quickly slammed the phone back into its cradle before punching the last digit.

What am I going to say? What if I sound like a babbling idiot? I don't want to blow my chances. Maybe I'll forget about making the call. She probably has already made plans for tonight.

Hank took a deep breath and once again picked up the handset. He stared at it as though it were some strange entity he could not control. Finally, he moved his fingers to the dial pad, forcing them to depress each memorized number.

The phone started to ring on the other end. It had rung five consecutive ringlets, and there was no answer. Hank was just about to hang up when suddenly he heard her say, "Hello! Hello! Is anybody there?"

He choked up, and all he could come up with was, "It's Hank! What're you doing tonight?"

There was total silence as Lydia gathered her thoughts. She had been pruning roses on the far side of her garden and felt like she had completed a hundred-yard dash in under ten seconds to get to the phone.

Still trying to catch her breath, she replied, "Nothing! Do you want to get together?"

He said, "How about a movie? *Risky Business* is playing at the *Lake Theater*, and we could have dinner before the show. But if you don't like Tom Cruise, I could find something else downtown."

She smiled and said, "No, that's a great idea. It's a date! Why don't you pick me up around five-ish?"

Hank agreed and was about to hang up the phone when he realized he didn't have her address. She laughed loudly and slowly verbalized her location, sensing his nervousness. He was pleased that the *Porsche* was ready to go. He took a quick shower; before he knew it, he was motoring south on the

Interstate. As it turned out, Lydia's home was less than a mile from her office. He exited the freeway and pulled into her driveway at precisely five o'clock. She had a beautiful home that fits nicely into the upscale Edina neighborhood. He approached the towering twelve-foot entrance door and lifted and dropped the arm of the ornate doorknocker to announce his arrival. She answered the door, and Hank grew weak in the knees. Lydia wore a tight-fitting, black pair of Levi jeans, topped with a crisp, white cotton shirt and an emerald-green cashmere sweater that thoroughly embraced her perfect-ten body. He managed a pathetic hug as Lydia led him into the foyer. She excused herself and told him to make himself comfortable in the adjacent great room. As he entered the room, he was astounded by its size but was even more amazed by the collection of stuffed animals and fish that ingratiated much of the wall space.

She probably had a previous relationship with an outdoorsman, or she's my kind of gal! It was simply too good to be true. *I'll keep my questions to myself for the time being.*

She returned to the foyer and asked, "Are you ready to go?"

Hank jumped from the couch and said, "Yes, we better get going. The movie starts in thirty minutes, and we'll cut it pretty close when we find a parking space."

She said, "I've read a couple of reviews of the movie, and most critics felt the acting was so-so. But as a *Porsche* enthusiast, you will enjoy the scenes when a beautiful *928* takes center stage."

She was right. As they departed the theater, Hank inquired, "Have you ever eaten at the Vineyard Restaurant in Anoka? I took the liberty to make reservations if you are up for it?"

They arrived at the Vineyard and were seated in his favorite booth. Hank ordered a bottle of Italian pinot grigio. Lydia ordered fresh ricotta cheese with white truffle honey as an appetizer. Then, the conversation started, and they discovered their backgrounds were similar. They both were born in rural, small-town settings, although Lydia was not a native Minnesotan. She was born and raised in the remote town of Park Falls, Wisconsin, where her father owned a professional dry cleaning and laundry facility.

She spent many hours with her father, fishing for pike and muskies on the nearby Flambeau River. Her father, Roy Tribeck, used his fishing talents to become a field tester for a local fishing rod manufacturer. He received no monetary compensation for the testing he did, but he was allowed to keep the new creations once the results of the tests were verified and recorded.

He had amassed quite a collection of fishing rods in all shapes and sizes. Roy was also an amateur taxidermist, which answered Hank's question about how she acquired her collection of wildlife mounts. When Roy passed away, Lydia inherited the whole kit and caboodle. She said she often felt like a hoarder but could not part with his accouterments.

Adding all of this interest in the outdoors to the fact they were both excellent cooks, absolutely loved country music, and cherished romantic weekends only fostered Hank's belief in their bright future. Hank also shared much of his background with her, and as the evening progressed, he could candidly slip in the fact that he had chosen her firm to represent VisualFish with the patent project. He told her about Winnie's unfortunate loss of his only cousin and that he would be unavailable to meet for at least two weeks. He had discussed his decision with Arnie and Winnie by telephone, and they enthusiastically endorsed and approved it. They were about to toast the new business relationship when the lights in the restaurant flickered on and off. Hank ignored the interruption, but when it happened several more times, he looked around the facility and was surprised to see all the empty booths and tables.

He blinked and focused on the entire restaurant staff, lined up against a far wall. They all had smiles on their faces and were listening intently to the private conversation that was taking place. Finally, the manager flipped the light switch and declared, "It's closing time, but my team just wanted to hear the end of the story."

It was well after two in the morning when they returned to Edina. He walked Lydia to the door and smoothly placed an anticipated kiss on her lips. She pulled back slightly and thanked him for the beautiful evening. Then, she asked him to phone her and let her know he had made it safely home. Before she closed the door, she turned and whispered, "I have never had a more perfect date. So, let's keep a good thing going. Nighty night."

Hank had been taught not to mix business and pleasure, but he had never felt this way about anyone in his life, and he sure as hell would not give it up for some corny cliché.

When he arrived home, he ran to the telephone and made the call like there was no tomorrow.

He was thrilled when Lydia picked up the phone on the first ring and said, "Thanks for calling to let me know you got home okay. I can't wait to see you again! What if I drive to your place tomorrow, and we hang out and get to know each other?"

Hank thought, what a perfect segue, and he replied, "That's a great idea! Come over anytime you like. I'll be counting the minutes. Have a dreamy night. I know I will."

CHAPTER 36

Hank woke up on Sunday morning with an unfettered smile on his face. He hadn't slept better in years. Then, glancing at the silent alarm clock perched on the nightstand, it hit him like a ton of bricks; it was almost noon. Never in his life had he stayed in bed this long. He rolled out of bed, ran into the bathroom, and peered out the small vent window to see if she had arrived. No one was in the driveway, and he morphed into a *shit, shower, and shaving machine*, and in less than fifteen minutes, he was presentable and had coffee brewing in his French Press.

Lydia arrived fifteen minutes later, presenting a warm and passionate embrace as he invited her in. She said, "You truly live in the boonies. I've been driving around for over an hour to find your hermitage." Hank apologized and asked if she would like a cup of coffee. She nodded, curled up on the living room couch, and said, "I take mine black."

Hank joined her, and an afternoon of small talk ensued. He was genuinely amazed at how much they had in common. A few times, she artfully posed questions that made him feel like he was in a courtroom, but she laughed out loud and exclaimed, "Sometimes, I just can't take off the lawyer cap."

They wandered outside, and he gave her a tour of the property. Then, he said, "Lydia, this is only a rental, but I love living out here. I find the peace and solitude refreshing and rejuvenating after spending hours in corporate warfare. I contacted a local realtor and told him to keep his eyes open for any unique properties that might come on the market. I want to design and build my own home without any compromises."

She reflected, "Dreams are what makes the world go around. However, living in a secluded area does not mean living a secluded life. Recently, I've found myself engulfed in claustrophobia as I stand in my rose garden and feel the frigid fingers of the city closing in on me. I'm a country girl at heart, but I squelched that thinking by telling myself what a beautiful home I own and its proximity to work and shopping. But little by little, I seemed to be losing the debate with myself, and the rebuttals had no substance. Maybe someday I'll be able to break free."

The setting sun was forcing its final rays through the tree line as they retreated to the house. Hank suggested they delve into the refrigerator and pantry to see if they could create something resembling a dinner. She uncovered a frozen tray of Italian ziti while Hank found an unopened bag of mixed salad greens and some garlic-flavored croutons. She preheated the oven as he found a salad bowl and started cutting tomatoes and deli-fresh olives to add to the crisp greens. He thought about opening a bottle of wine, but as he glanced at the empty, dust-covered wine rack, he knew he needed a plan B. He suggested, "How about a cold beer to make our taste buds pop as we feast on the ziti?"

She had already noticed the sorely depleted rack and responded, "Beer would be great as long as it's served above thirty-eight degrees and has a head of at least one-half inch."

Hank was bowled over and speechless. The woman kept surprising him at every turn in their new relationship. She's a real beer connoisseur; how much better can it get?

After dinner, Hank suggested they retire to the living room. He said, "I purchased the new John Denver album, *It's About*

Time. Would you like to hear it?"

She purred, "Perfect."

He clicked on his Pioneer PL400, dropped the needle, and snuggled beside her on the couch. The first three songs set the mood, and they melted into each other's arms, and the kisses became more intense with each new note. Finally, she softly reached up, touched his lips, and murmured, "I decided to take tomorrow off from work. Would you like to have a willing bedmate tonight?"

Try as he might, words would not come out. So, all he could do was hold Lydia even closer and pray she got the message.

CHAPTER 37

As dawn broke on Monday morning, he glanced over at Lydia. Her naked body was covered only by a thin sheet that left nothing to the imagination. He had an important meeting, and quietly slid out of bed, trying hard not to wake her. He took care of bathroom business, stepped out, and silently padded his way to the walk-in closet. But he stopped in his tracks and was suspended by a fantastic smile and a sexy pointer finger, inviting him back to the lair. Hank, still unclothed, couldn't resist. He sprung back under the covers and resigned himself to the fact that he would be late for the meeting.

Mid-morning, he called the office and told Rose he had overslept. She said, "Don't worry about the meeting with the Ranger Boat people. A severe thunderstorm in Arkansas grounded Sunday flights, and they would not arrive until Tuesday morning. So, they wanted to reschedule the meeting for one o'clock Tuesday afternoon. I checked your planner, which was wide open, so I committed to the change."

Hank thanked her and said he would be in the office by eleven. Then, fully dressed, he returned to the bedroom and kissed Lydia lightly. She opened her eyes, and he said, "Sleep as long as you like. I cut up some fruit, cereal, and bread on the table. I won't be back until late this afternoon, so if you're not here, I'll call you when I get home." He whispered sincerely, "Don't take this the wrong way, but I think I love you." She looked him in the eyes and silently mouthed, "I think I love you, too."

Hank had tears of joy as he made his way to the office. He had to pinch himself to appreciate what had just taken place fully. His whole world was changing; he could only hang on for dear life.

He was getting out of the Suburban at his reserved parking lot when Eldon from marketing pulled in next to him. He said, "I just returned from a follow-up trip to Idaho and Washington. We will be breaking ground on both new stores in October. Thank you for blazing the trail for this fabulous expansion."

Hank humbly replied, "I was just the catalyst. The Board Members pushed for this new growth, and we will all reap the rewards of this impressive move. I want to hear your ideas about how marketing will support these stores, but I need to get to my office. Why don't we set up a meeting later this week? Must run. Call me!"

Rose greeted him at the door and intuitively thought something was different, but she couldn't put her finger on it. Unlike most Monday mornings, Hank was smiling, joking with his team, and apologizing for being late. When he finally entered his office, Rose followed and gently closed the door.

She said, "Okay, tell me what's going on! I know it must be positive to elevate your spirits to this height. But you know me, I can keep a secret!"

He looked at her; unable to keep his emotions in check, he burst out with, "I finally found a special lady, and I think I want to spend the rest of my life with her."

He filled her in on most details, repeating and emphasizing how unbelievably happy he was to have found Lydia.

She pondered briefly and said, "I am so pleased you finally found that special someone. At least now I know why you were acting so out of character this morning, and don't worry, mum's the word. My lips are sealed."

She was delighted and very disappointed at the same time. Hank had never shown romantic inclinations toward her, but as the tears welled up inside, she could only say, "Can you believe I'm crying! I must go to the lady's room and fix my makeup."

CHAPTER 38

Hank spent the rest of the week conducting vendor meetings. He even squeezed in an afternoon with Eldon to get in sync with his plans for the new northwest stores.

He was tempted to call Lydia during the day but was content with phone pillow talk in the evening. He couldn't wait for the weekend. She invited him to come to her home on Friday night and spend a few days and nights, adding more substance to their relationship.

She, too, had been married to her job for too long. Life was passing her by, and Hank was a welcomed slap upside her head, putting some real meaning back into her mundane existence. She was in love.

Winnie called on Friday evening just as Hank was leaving the house. He wanted to inform him that he was back in the Metro area. His cousin's funeral occurred at the First Lutheran Church in Hibbing. He wanted to be buried next to his parents. Unfortunately, he had been away from Hibbing for many years, and few people attended the funeral. Winnie said, "It is sad to see how quickly we are forgotten when ties are broken."

Hank briefly explained that he was busy for the rest of the weekend, but they should plan an evening meeting early next week. He did not say anything about his new relationship with Lydia. That could wait for another time. Winnie suggested they should meet at the new warehouse. He had found a potential lessee interested in the facility and would like to take a tour as soon as possible. Hank agreed and told him to set it up.

He arrived in Edina at just after seven. She had made reservations at the Pracna Café on the historic riverfront in Minneapolis. It was one of her favorite dining places. In addition, she had invited the two founding partners of the law firm and their wives to join them for dinner.

She thought it was important that he meet them to solidify their alliance. Lydia said she would drive her Lexus as she knew all the shortcuts in the downtown area, and the Porsche could take the evening off.

He was impressed with both gentlemen, but especially with John Williams. He had personally been part of many successful patent applications and offered to lend his expertise. But first, he wanted to clarify that Lydia was in charge and would only intervene if she requested help or advice. Hank smiled with admiration and very discretely patted one of her sinuous legs.

After dinner, John suggested they all go down to the warehouse district for a nightcap. The Monte Carlo was his favorite haunt and was still warm enough to sit outside on their extensive patio. They spent two hours sipping wine and enjoying some great conversation. Even the reserved Harry Strighton loosened his tie and became entirely animated. As the evening progressed, his wife, Marilyn, joined in the frivolity, but her voice carried like a banshee cry with each glass of port. Harry tried to tone her down but knew how futile it was when she reached that liquored state. Hank didn't know how to leave the party politely. Lydia caught his anxiety and artfully stood up from the table and announced, "Thanks for the fabulous evening, but I think Hank and I will bid you a fond farewell, wishing you pleasant dreams."

She collected his hand and gracefully led him out of the

establishment and into the freedom of the street. They returned to the 9th Street parking lot and started their journey home. Lydia had nursed only one glass of wine all evening. Hank was in no condition to be driving, and he called her his *taxi angel* while exploding in laughter.

CHAPTER 39

Sunday morning arrived with the smell of bacon frying and aromatic coffee percolating. Hank tried to raise his head to check the time, but the throbbing was so intense he thought he might suffer a stroke if he forced the movement. Settling back into the down-filled pillow, he took several deep breaths and turned his head slowly toward the bedside clock.

Both eyes seemed to be operating separately, but finally, he could focus; at seven o'clock. Then the bed started spinning violently, and he firmly planted his right foot on the cherry wood floor, momentarily stopping the wheel of fortune or unfortune as was the case. He laggardly lifted his body to a sitting position on the edge of the mattress. Confronted with his reflection in the tall dressing mirror affixed to the wall before him, he didn't recognize himself. He asked: *What did I do to deserve this kind of punishment?*

He closed his eyes tightly and felt his way to the en suite entrance. After splashing several handfuls of cold water on his face, he made it to the doorless shower and turned on the enormous rainfall shower head. He didn't wait for the water to warm but stepped straight into an arctic blast. His heart pounded frantically for a few seconds, and then his body adjusted, and the throbbing in his head started to withdraw. He finished his bathroom ritual, grabbed an attractive white, terry cloth robe, and gingerly went to the kitchen.

Lydia looked up from her culinary undertaking and said, "You look like warmed-over death. Living proof that the dead do rise!"

She told him to sit down before he fell. She poured him a steaming black coffee and waited for a metamorphosis.

Finally, he spoke, "I have never felt so hungover in my entire life. What did I ingest last night that brought me to this unbelievable point? Don't answer that question. Just don't let me do it again!"

He was unable to eat any of Lydia's cooking. She understood but was disappointed. She suggested they go for a long walk through a nearby park. Lydia was sure the fresh air would help, and plenty of wild vegetation would conceal any nasty occurrence if he vomited.

By mid-afternoon, Hank could eat some solid food, crack a smile and carry on a meaningful conversation. He profusely apologized and made a sincere vow to her, stating that this would never happen again. She hoped Hank had learned his lesson and gave him a generous and warm hug of forgiveness. She hinted that it would probably be best if he drove home in daylight and took advantage of a good night's sleep. He agreed and sadly waved to her as the Porsche reached France Avenue.

Thirty minutes later, as he entered his driveway, he was met by his landlord. Peter Olmstead asked, "Hank, do you have a few minutes? I need to discuss an important issue with you."

"No problem. Just let me park my car in the garage and then come up to the front door," he replied.

He invited Peter in and said, "It must be important for you to come out on a Sunday afternoon. What's up?"

Peter explained that he had received an incredible offer for this house and the adjoining eighty acres that surrounded it. A developer was putting a package together to rezone the property from agricultural to residential and would start the approval process with the government agencies for a new subdivision. The sale of the property would take place within the next few weeks. He assured Hank that the new owners would honor the twelve months remaining on his lease agreement. However, the construction process would begin on the eighty acres after the project was approved. It could mean some minor inconveniences, including noise from construction equipment.

He thanked Peter for the visit and wished him good luck, but his mind was already fluttering with the thought of buying some land and bringing his dream home to fruition.

These thoughts wholly erased the remains of the hangover, and that evening he slept soundly, dreaming about becoming a first-time homeowner.

CHAPTER 40

Hank whistled into the office just after six a.m. After getting his morning Java fix, he heard a conversation in the board room. Hank wandered down the hallway and almost collided with Harry Ensrud. Like a bloodhound on a trail, he smelled fresh brew and was not to be denied. Unscathed from the near collision, Harry yelled, "Go on in and have a seat. The entire board is meeting this morning to discuss the new store progress, and we'd appreciate your input."

Hank slowly made his way into the room and was instantly recognized by the Chairman of the Board, William Campbell. They shook hands, and Bill turned to the group and said,

"For those who don't know this gentleman, he's Hank Walhberg, VP of Product Development. He traveled with Harry and me on our first fact-finding excursion to the Northwest. Hank gave us excellent insight and played a significant role in picking Boise and Spokane. Please join us. We'll get started as soon as Harry returns."

Hank found a chair at the far end of the big oak table and calmly sipped his coffee, not uttering a word. Harry came back with a large platter of Krispy Kreme Donuts. He entered the room with Mark Branigan, who toted two large decanters of coffee. Everyone copped a donut, and the Chairman called the meeting to order.

He was elated by the positive remarks that came out of the meeting. The board saw these two new stores as the beginning of their optimistic expansion plans. The meeting ended, and Hank casually mingled with the members and briefly said hello to Mark, explaining how he ended up attending this meeting, in case he wondered.

Hank returned to his office, and no one, not even Rose, had arrived. He picked up the phone and hoped to catch Lydia before she left for work. No answer.

He would call her later and tell her about the landlord meeting. In the meantime, he flipped through his Rolodex and found his realtor's number. Dennis Chambers of PrimeView Realty answered with a gruff hello. He explained to Dennis what had happened over the weekend. His need to find a property had escalated from speculation status to finding me something now! It certainly wasn't Dennis's first rodeo, and he assured Hank he would have a list of potential parcels by the end of the week.

They would meet at PrimeView's office mid-morning on Saturday to kick off the search.

He later telephoned Lydia's direct line but was immediately directed to voice mail. He briefly told her what was happening and asked her to call him back when she found time. Two minutes later, she was on the line asking many questions.

Hank responded, "I want you to be with me on Saturday. Why don't you come over on Friday evening, and we can explore the lineup of properties that Dennis is currently preparing? I can't tell you how much I need your input. Please say yes!"

"Of course, I'll come over," she replied. "I want you to find the perfect setting for your dream home."

Hank murmured as he hung up, "Our dream home."

Friday evening, Lydia arrived with another barrage of questions that Hank, quite frankly, couldn't answer. He told her about several properties Dennis had previously recommended, but nothing ever came of it because he needed to be more severe in his search.

They carefully examined the updated list of properties that Dennis had couriered over to them. Two parcels of land caught Hank's attention. They were both located along Lexington Avenue, one was eighty acres in size, and the other was thirty-eight. Lydia found aerial photos of both properties, astounded at the detail and clarity. The eighty-acre parcel contained a vast swampy low land and still needed to finish the road into the property. However, the other parcel appeared much higher in elevation, with no visible wetland.

They also notice a finished black-topped, circular driveway extending well into the center of the acreage.

Lydia said, "It looks like someone was going to build a home right about here." She pointed at a cleared-out area with metal utility boxes already in place."

Hank sputtered, "If that's what it is, we'll have to dig deeper and discover why no construction had ever occurred here. Having the utilities on the property would save me a ton of money, but if the current owner couldn't get a building permit, all is for naught."

They motored to the PrimeView office on Saturday morning and arrived as Dennis unlocked the front door. He motioned for them to come in. Hank introduced Lydia, and they were seated in the conference room. Dennis said he had only prepared one detailed packet of information on the selected properties, so they would have to share. But first, Dennis would make some coffee, and then they could get to business. After he left the room, Lydia fumbled through the packet, pulled out the details on the thirty-eight acres, and laid them out on the table. It became clear that this property was involved in a bankruptcy filing.

Dennis returned with coffee and sweet-smelling pastries he had picked up at Key Café and Bakery in White Bear Lake. Having missed breakfast because they couldn't stop cuddling when the sun roused them from slumber, the sugar and caffeine bestowed a welcomed high.

"This thirty-eight-acre parcel has piqued our interest," said Hank, plopping the segregated information before him.

Dennis replied, "Yes, an interesting story goes with this land. It has been through an unfortunate bankruptcy. This parcel became collateral against a business loan, and now the bank owns it. It is an exceptional piece of land with a much higher elevation than the surrounding area. From what you told me, this property checks everything on your must-have list. So, let's jump in my car and look."

As they drove down the long driveway, Dennis pointed out the nice stand of white pine trees encompassing about ten acres around the entrance. This feature afforded privacy which was high on Hank's checklist. As they entered the cul-de-sac, at the very heart of the parcel, Dennis stopped the car, and they had a wander. First, phone and electricity boxes were placed on concrete slabs, confirming the photos' accuracy. Next, Hank noticed a periscoping gas meter and a locked fill pipe protruding from a buried LP tank, and within twenty feet of the meter was a wooden box covering a good cap. The only thing missing was a septic system, but Dennis pointed out that a permit was issued, but they never completed the drain field. Finally, they walked through a grove of birch trees to get to the first property marker located on the northeast corner of the parcel. Dennis pulled a yellow plastic flag attached to a metal rod and placed it next to the marker. He then suggested they continue west to locate the following tag. When they found it, he repeated the flag placement and said, "When we leave, I'll point out the two remaining markers flagged in the ditch along Lexington Avenue. It will give you a pretty good picture of the rectangular shape of this property."

Both Lydia and Hank loved this parcel. He let them walk alone so they could discuss it without his input. It was less than fifteen minutes from the Interstate and fulfilled their specific expectations.

She said, "Hank, this seems to culminate your dreams. So, I say let's do it!"

Hank looked at Dennis and said, "We can end the search now. Let's return to your office and write an offer."

CHAPTER 41

The title office cleared the land with no hidden issues tied to the bankruptcy. The bank accepted the cash offer, the property would close within a week. About three years prior, Hank met an architectural firm's owner while attending a business luncheon in Minneapolis. He told Larry Lindquist, owner of Lindquist Design, Inc., of his dream-home concept. Unbeknownst to Hank, Larry had prepared a complete set of drawings, asking only that Hank shares some of his secret fishing spots as payment in full. He took the information to the city office and started the building permit process.

Hank called Lydia and asked if she earned any personal days or vacation time at work. He felt overloaded and needed a friend to act as a sounding board to help get his head back on track. The patent process, the purchase of the warehouse, the purchase of the land, and his job responsibilities at FishNautics weighed heavily on his mind. Lydia said she would discuss it with the owners and let him know immediately.

Hank set up a meeting with Rose and Mark Branigan. He wanted to ensure that taking a few weeks off would not cause undue hardship. Rose said she could handle the office, and Mark was pleased to hear that Hank would finally take some personal time off. He said, "You haven't had a vacation since you joined the company, so you have my blessing. Are you planning to travel or go on an elaborate cruise, or what?"

Hank told them both about his land investment and how a

developer has purchased his current rental, and he must be off the premises within twelve months. So, he would spend his vacation securing a building permit and finding a reputable builder to commit to a twelve-month construction project.

Lydia called back and left a voice mail, stating she had been granted two weeks of paid vacation and would join him in Ham Lake this evening.

After listening to the message, he asked Rose to come into his office. He said, "I'll be starting my vacation tomorrow, and I know you'll do a good job while I'm away. However, you always call me if you run into any major problems. Mark also said he'd be available to help in any way."

Rose replied, "Thanks again for your trust and confidence, but I know the whole team will pull together, and you can rest assured we won't be bothering you."

Lydia's car was in the driveway when he got home. She met him in the garage, wrapped her arms around him, and planted a passionate kiss that sent shivers down his spine. Then, she softly uttered, "I'm all yours for the next two weeks. First, I cooked up something special for dinner, and later, over a couple of snifters of Bonnie Prince Charlie's favorite concoction, we'll put a plan together to get the dream home kick-started."

The following two weeks flew by rapidly. The City of Ham Lake approved the impressive building plans and issued a permit. Hank found a respected builder committed to his time frame, and groundbreaking would occur in a few days. He and Lydia spent parts of each day on the property, trying to imagine what the home would look like when completed.

Lydia surprised him by offering her financial help to eliminate the need for a construction loan.

She knew his cash flow was dwindling, and until he finalized the warehouse lease agreement with the new tenant, he needed help. He graciously accepted her offer.

Then he turned the tables on her. He got down on one knee and pulled out a diamond engagement ring his mother had given him on her deathbed. She told him to make sure it goes to someone worthy of it. Hank cleared his throat and chortled, "Lydia, will you marry me?"

All she could do was bob her head in the affirmative.

He said, "Try the ring on. It was originally my grandmother's. If it doesn't fit, we'll take it to the jewelry store and have it sized just for you."

He slipped the ring on her finger. It needed no adjustment.

That afternoon, they talked about setting up the big day. Lydia wanted to be married at Cross View Lutheran Church in Edina, where she was a member. She thought a June wedding would be perfect. Hank agreed wholeheartedly and suggested they contact the Pastor to find out how to secure a date. Lydia couldn't wait. She had a church bulletin folded up in her purse, and she found a phone number and dialed it. A man answered, "Cross View Lutheran Church, how can I help you?"

She recognized his voice and loudly responded, "Pastor Anderson, this is Lydia Tribeck, and I want to get married!"

The Pastor began laughing and then asked for details.

Several minutes later, he said Saturday afternoon, June 9th, was available, and penciled it into his calendar.

CHAPTER 42

The months passed quickly, and the house took shape by the early spring of 1983. The walls were up, and the tiled roof was finished, making the dwelling completely waterproof. The contractor had several building projects canceled over the winter and could bring in extra crews and subcontractors to work on the project. He told Hank he was confident the house would be ready for a final inspection in mid-May, give or take a week or two. Hank relayed the good news to Lydia: "We might have a home to move into when we return from our honeymoon!"

Winnie had finalized the lease agreement on their warehouse with a local snack food company. He approved a two-year lease with two one-year options. Cash was now flowing into the VisualFish bank account.

Lydia had taken advantage of the US Patent and Trademark's *Track One* priority examination process, and it appeared the application would be approved and granted within the next few months.

Once the patent was in place, they could finally begin sourcing manufacturing equipment and material suppliers to move the company into an actual business entity. She had planned and developed the entire strategy for this patent without involving either of the two law firm partners. Hank thought their relationship may have influenced her work, but Lydia, representing the firm, always included billable hours to VisualFish. Her professionalism and loyalty made him immensely proud.

Spring was in the air and also in the stores. After a very wet and snowy winter, the northern half of the country was champing at the bit to shed their sorrels and parkas and hit the open water with a heated vengeance. Sales were going through the roof, and suppliers, caught unaware, had difficulty filling the shelves. Hank was putting out fires and had little time for product testing. The two new stores in Boise and Spokane led the company in sales. Even though it was a small market, lack of competition and solid support from the community had driven sales beyond belief.

Hank had comprised a written proposal, asking for approval to hire an assistant to give him some relief. He was planning his departure from FishNautics in the future, and training a protégé, would be the right thing to do. Hank had not discussed his probable egress with anyone in the company. He was not about to shoot himself in the foot if things did not unfold as planned.

First, he presented his action plan to Human Resources and copied all the department heads, including Mark Branigan. He received written permission to search for a qualified candidate within a few hours. First, HR would place strategic ads in appropriate newspapers and magazines and establish a salary and benefits package for this new position. Then, following the must-haves in Hank's proposed job description, HR would conduct initial phone interviews, separating the wheat from the chaff. Next, he would get a vetted applicants list and interviews scheduled with HR assistance. He also wanted the job posted in-house. He had already identified at least two team members who deserved consideration, and there may be other candidates in other departments who warranted a chance. Hank was adamant about not leaving any rock unturned in his dedicated search.

It was hard to believe how much interest the ad mustered. Good candidates were emerging like dandelions in spring soil. Over twelve candidates came from the in-house invitation, and twenty-three individuals came from the outside. He thoroughly read and reread all applications and resumes. After intensive review, all the candidates remained on the list.

They conducted interviews over the next three weeks. However, Hank wanted to administer up to two or three interviews daily, and HR stuck to that plan. They gave each candidate a fair amount of time to present their case for consideration. In the end, five extraordinary finalists surfaced, each scheduled for a second interview. First, they would conduct background checks on each of the candidates. Next, they had to offer three personal and three business references. These references should know the candidate's intentions and be willing to speak candidly about them when contacted. Hank had encountered several instances where references didn't know the applicant was searching for employment or felt unqualified or uneasy about giving their opinions. On the other hand, open-ended questions posed to a reference often produced insightful answers that directly influenced the hiring process.

Hank told each finalist he would conduct the interviews, and two members of the new product development team would be observers. Even though he would make the final decision, he wanted the team's input after each interview, knowing the candidate would have a *tough row to hoe* without their support.

Dylan Sanders became the new Assistant Vice President. Two competing companies had employed him, and a master's degree in business administration from Stanford University cemented the deal. After the interviews, Hank knew Dylan was the only finalist who checked all the boxes and was unanimously given the green light by the team. However, Dylan wanted to give his current employer four-weeks-notice, so he could assist them in finding his replacement. Hank accepted his terms and informed HR of his official start date.

CHAPTER 43

It was the middle of April, and Hank received a phone call from his builder, asking to meet him Friday afternoon at the site. He said, "We are making serious progress on the house, but I have several issues to discuss with you. They involved kitchen appliances, kitchen and bathroom plumbing fixtures, paint colors, flooring, light fixtures, garage doors, and others. Again, I suggest you bring Lydia so we're all in sync for the final push."

He responded, "I'll phone Lydia right now and call you back with an exact time."

Hank talked to Lydia, and she, too, felt reality had set in around her. The house construction was well ahead of schedule. They could move in before the wedding. Hank could feel the anticipation and excitement in her voice.

They agreed to a two p.m. meeting with the builder, and he brought his contracted interior designer with him. He felt she could provide some exciting interior design possibilities. While Lydia and the designer began looking at options, the builder took Hank outside to the massive garage. The free-standing garage consisted of six single bays and one huge unit accommodating a large motor home. In the six bays, all ceilings were fourteen feet in height, and the builder suggested single metal doors that were nine feet in width and ten feet in height, mated with a faux-cedar exterior finish. On the more oversized RV garage, he thought a twelve by sixteen commercial roll-up door, made of the same material used in the six bays, would work just fine. The smaller two-car garage attached directly to the house would be set with an eight-foot by twenty-two, foot double door, again with a matching exterior finish. All garage doors will be fitted with a shaft-drive Chamberlain opener, requiring no unsightly hardware mounted to the ceiling. All walls were two-by-six construction, fully insulated, and adequately sheet-rocked. The floors would be finished in a gray-speckled, epoxy surface, resisting oil and Minnesota road salt. They would install fluorescent lights in all units, numerous electrical outlets on walls and ceilings, and 110v and 220v service. Several roof-mounted units would supply air conditioning and heat, ducted and zoned into each bay. The entrances to each garage would continue to the existing blacktop, butted right up to the garage foundation. Hank also approved three strategically placed light poles and a camera security system on the property.

Returning to the house, Lydia had decided to pick out three or fewer options for flooring, appliances, paint colors, light fixtures, and many other necessities. Having more than three choices made the decision process too complicated. She took Hank by the arm, asked for his opinion on each tagged selection, and then candidly stated hers. Hank primarily fell in line with her choices, and the ordeal was wrapped-up and finalized in less than an hour. They appreciated the designer's suggestions and valuable insight. The builder was also happy. He could now place orders for the needed products and felt more and more confident about completing the whole project by the end of May.

CHAPTER 44

They wanted a small, intimate wedding, and arrangements still had to be made and invitations sent. Unfortunately, Lydia had lost both her parents, and had no brothers or sisters. Hank's situation was similar, with only one brother in the family tree. The wedding would take place at three p.m., and later a reception would be held at the Lafayette Club on the shores of Lake Minnetonka. Winnie was a member, and he arranged for the reception room, entertainment, open bar, and food catering as a wedding gift for both of them.

Hank had free rein to plan the honeymoon. Lydia wanted it to be a total surprise, and her only stipulation was that it must be somewhere very romantic. He could only think about one place in the world that, in his mind, fit the bill; the Amalfi Coast in Italy. So, starting in Salerno, they would travel down the coast, visiting all thirteen seaside towns and even spend a few days in Sorrento and on the Isles of Capri and Ischia. Thirty days was the perfect amount of time to launch this new chapter of their lives.

Lydia worked twelve-hour days at the law firm and maintained the same schedule at FishNautics. Preparing to be incommunicado for a month was challenging. They treasured their free time on weekends, but even those precious days gave way to wedding and house plans. Loose ends seemed to be cropping up everywhere. As soon as they solved one problem, another would surface. Hank felt like a child playing the infamous *rat game* at the carnival. Nine holes were cut into plywood, each containing a stuffed rodent. When one rat mechanically emerged, you had a wooden mallet to knock it back in the hole. But as soon as you struck that rat, it triggered another one to rise in an adjacent hole. This futile game emulated, metaphorically, what is often called the human rat race.

Hank had always been a master of staying in control when faced with challenges. He only hoped the bright light at the end of this tunnel was not an oncoming freight train.

He telephoned Lydia, and when she answered, he grunted, "How is your day going? Mine is horseshit! Today, I am feeling the pressure that comes from physically going away. My team at work always seems to ascend when I'll be out of the office for an extended period of time. Today, even Rose was unsure of herself, and her demeanor spread like a virus throughout the office. Maybe it all centers around Dylan Sanders, the new AVP, who is coming on board just as we leave for Italy? I don't know what the hell to do!"

She waited until the venting subsided and calmly replied, "It seems like you have your *knickers in a twist*. Of course, we all have bad days, but as a friend in law school said, in times of trouble, *illegitimus non-carborundum*, don't let the bastards grind you down. What you need is an attitude adjustment. I am leaving the office in ten minutes, stopping by my house to pick up a nice bottle of wine, and I will be at your doorstep before you know it. It will be you and me only weekend, I promise!"

The minute Hank came through the doorway, she said, "I disconnected your home phones, and we're going to act like a couple of late-season bears and go into hibernation. We're not going to the property. We're not going out for dinner. But I want you to know I am all yours for the weekend, so take whatever liberties you want with me."

Hank's bad day instantly disappeared, and work issues only

came up on some weekends. He mentioned that she needed to ensure her passport and insurance information was available and updated for travel outside the country. Lydia didn't pry, and he didn't volunteer any clues regarding the honeymoon. He had used a travel agent, whom Winnie had recommended, for hotels, excursions, and car rentals. He said they would wing it for meals because no one could predict when romance might supersede a preplanned meal. They certainly wouldn't starve.

Lydia told him she asked her office manager to be her maid of honor. She wanted no other bridesmaids and no ring bearer or flower girl. He said he had requested Winnie to be his best man and Arnie Morgan to be the only groomsman.

She added, "That's perfect. I don't think I told you, but Pastor Anderson wants to schedule two meetings with us before the big day. He has a church procedure he must follow, but I think he wants to be sure we understand the sanctity of marriage. Also, since my father died, he had become like a big brother, giving me advice when I asked for it and sometimes when I didn't. He's a good guy."

Hank agreed and noted that evenings would be best for him.

He and Lydia dreamed and speculated about the future for the rest of the weekend. Getting their priorities in order was a godsend. Now they could face the next two weeks without trepidation. They had put their heads together and made collective and definitive decisions on all the essential things affecting their lives. They would stick with their plans and agree to quit micromanaging everything. The thought of casting their fate to the wind was uncomfortable for both of them, but they would press on.

CHAPTER 45

The big day arrived with low humidity and abundant sunshine—most fitting for a day that would change their lives forever.

Hank and Winnie arrived at the church just before three p.m. Arnie stood at the church entrance, diligently handing out the wedding program and ushering guests to open pews. Once everyone was seated, the three boys took their positions at the altar.

Hank was so anxious that his knees shook, and Winnie and Arnie looked like they could use a double shot of something spirited. Three church bells sounded, and Lydia had not appeared. He was worried. *Was there an accident? Did she change her mind? Was she fashionably late?*

Then like a *Siegfried and Roy* magic act in Vegas, she suddenly appeared at the top of the carpeted aisle, dressed like an angel in white. Pastor Anderson escorted her to the front of the church. Hank and Lydia stood staring at each other in disbelief. He could not believe how beautiful she looked; her eyes revealed exactly how she felt about him. They exchanged the vows they had individually created; neither knew what the other would say. The church did not have a dry eye, including Pastor Anderson's.

When the ceremony ended, a chauffeur-driven Rolls Royce transported them to the Minnetonka reception. Winnie had borrowed the Silver Shadow Rolls from a friend. Once inside the Lafayette Club, toasting, dancing, and eating was the natural order. Unfortunately, Winnie had consumed too much champagne, but his *best-man speech* was humorous, filled with gratitude, and tactfully presented. The well-wishers, including the entire team from work, continued their personal and sometimes embarrassing stories about the bride and groom—all in good fun.

Hank kept an eye on the clock. He had booked a first-class flight to Rome, with a departure time of ten p.m. They had packed their suitcases days before but still needed to freshen up and get a change of clothes. Arnie, who had remained quite sober the entire evening, volunteered to drive them to Lydia's home and then to the airport.

Everyone on the plane knew they were newlyweds, and they gave them the *"gold star"* treatment with champagne, caviar, and first-class dinner entrees. All the passengers raised their glasses to toast happiness, love, and good fortune. Then, exhausted from the day's activities, they slept soundly through most of the eleven-hour flight. Finally, they cleared customs, picked up their luggage, rented a Ferrari 288 GTO, and were on the autostrada just after sunset, heading to Salerno.

Hank completed the 167-mile trip in about ninety minutes, arriving at the Hotel Santa Caterina in time for a late dinner.

The hotel opened in 1904 and has been in the Gambardella Family since then. They were ushered to their magnificent suite, threw their luggage on the massive four-poster bed, and rushed down to the ristorante. After a delightful dinner, excellent service, and a terrific bottle of wine, Hank said, "I think it's time to retire to our chambers to appreciate the first night of our honeymoon."

With the curtains drawn open, the view of the Mediterranean Sea was breathtaking. They opened the sliding doors and walked out to the balcony rail. Lydia purred, "Look at the moon. Its reflection on the calm water is truly amazing!"

He softly murmured, "You requested a romantic location. Does this fit the bill?"

He reached out and slowly caressed the lower portion of her back. She pulled him tightly to her waiting body, and their heads spun as their lips met in flaming passion.

They were awakened in the morning by birds chirping and the tangy fragrance of lemon from the trees surrounding their terrace. They both looked at each other and without saying a word, they knew they would be spending the rest of the day in their bower of bliss. Room service became the explicit watchword for the next two days.

The Amalfi coastline mainly had stayed the same since Hank first visited in the 1960s. Oh yes, there were more cars, buses, and wandering tourists, but just a step or two off the main road, they witnessed a much slower pace of life; *dolce vita*. The cliffs rising from the deep blue waters contained impressive and dangerous walking trails used only by the locals and their beasts of burden, donkeys. Some of these quaint villages were only accessible by walking. Hank treated Lydia to her first sip of *limoncello* near the village of Positano. It took place at a rustic *taverna* amid a lemon tree glade. She immediately felt a fervid flush, probably from the 190-proof grain alcohol used in concocting this Italian delight.

They spent another week in the Positano area. Again, they took advantage of the sandy beaches, and their Minnesota pallor disappeared like magic, replaced with the Mediterranean olive glow. Lydia looked like a native as they left their Ferrari in a secure parking lot and grabbed a ferry to the Isle of Capri.

They checked into the fabulous Quisisana Grand Hotel and spent several hours walking around its lush gardens with spirit-stirring sea views. Then, they ventured out, explored the city center, and reserved a gozzo boat with a skipper to explore the Blue Grotto (*Grotto Azzura*) in the morning.

The hotel had three restaurants, all serving special foods related to the Island. So first, they picked the Rendez Vous Ristorante and gorged themselves on freshly caught seafood and a bottle of Caprese White. For dessert, they ate cannolis, joined by two frozen glasses of *Vecchio Amaro del Capo Liquore*. Then, staggering, singing, and dancing back to the hotel, they were accompanied by a small group of Italian singers playing the mandolin and an accordion. Each member believed they were direct decedents of Mario Lanza or Luciano Pavarotti, and they sang their hearts out to prove it!

They returned to the mainland and decided to make the city of Sorrento their final stop in this month-long romantic journey to paradise. They managed a day trip, on an excursion bus, into Napoli and on to Vesuvius and Pompei. They even squeezed in a fast hydrofoil ride out to the Isle of Ischia, where they spent another day sightseeing, visiting Mount Epomeo, the highest point on the Island, and walking the sandy beaches of Spiaggia dei Maronti.

When departure day arrived, Hank drove the *Ferrari* into Napoli and caught the autostrada back to *Rome*. They vowed to return to Italy and the Amalfi Coast someday, probably to celebrate a future anniversary. Then as they boarded their flight, Hank uttered, "You truly made this honeymoon perfect. I think we're genuinely bounded for life." Lydia smiled and kissed him gently on the cheek.

CHAPTER 46

They arrived in Minneapolis and were met at the airport by Winnie. He had driven Hank's Suburban, not knowing how much luggage or souvenirs they might bring back from Italy.

Winnie commented, "It looks like the Mediterranean climate agreed with both of you. Wow! Tanned, rested, and still in love. I take it the honeymoon was a real success?"

Hank replied, "It was the most fantastic thirty days of our lives! The weather was terrific, the people were friendly, the rented Ferrari was most impressive, and our accommodations were superb up and down the Amalfi Coast. Someday, when you get the guts to ask Camila to marry you, Italy would be my only recommendation for a post-nuptial vacation."

Winnie chuckled, "I'll take the matter under advisement."

As they drove up Interstate 35, Winnie said, "I have a bit of a surprise for you. Arnie and I visited your new home and unpacked some of your essential belongings that were boxed up and stored in your garage complex. I hope you don't mind. We felt the property needed to be more inviting when you returned home."

Lydia immediately responded, "As I dozed on the airplane, I had a nightmare about being unable to move into our home for those reasons. So, all I can say is thanks for your thoughtfulness. It is greatly appreciated!"

Turning off Lexington Avenue into their long driveway, they found two immense pillars supporting a split, wrought-iron security gate. Winnie reached up on the visor and pushed a button on the controller, and the gates swung open. Hank was impressed. But even more impressive were the two massive northern pike fish carvings affixed to each gate panel. Winnie had contracted a friend who owns a woodworking business in Maple Grove to produce the sculptures. Hank had tears in his eyes as he asked Winnie to stop the vehicle. But instead, he got out, walked around the pillars, and stood silently staring at the artwork. Winnie and Lydia had to plead with him to get him back in the Suburban. She had never seen him so emotional.

Approaching the house, Hank could see how clean and organized the driveway appeared. The scene was beautiful, with hanging flower baskets on each porch pillar. It produced a spectacular homely feeling. Hank held her hand tightly as they walked to the front door. He turned the key in the lock, swept her into his arms, and carried her across the threshold. It was finally their new home.

Before the wedding, they decided to sell Lydia's home in Edina. She had a good friend who was a realtor at Coldwell Banker's office in Plymouth. They completed an appraisal but told Dennis Morequist not to list the property on MLS. He could do some private showings, but they did not want to entertain offers or answer questions until they returned from their honeymoon. The phone rang before Hank could put Lydia down after entering the house. It was Dennis, and he was so excited he could barely speak. Finally, he blurted out, "I am so glad you're back home. I have three parties interested in purchasing your home. Unfortunately, I am in the middle of a bidding war, and we need to meet as soon as possible to formulate an action plan. All three parties are cash buyers, so it's just a matter of accepting the highest bid, approving any contingencies, and establishing a closing date. You haven't changed your mind about selling, have you?"

She calmly replied, "No, Dennis, I have not changed my mind. But unfortunately, after spending eleven hours on an airplane, we just walked into the house and will not be able to meet with you until tomorrow evening. So please prepare the three offers, and we will meet you at the Plymouth office around seven."

When she hung up, they stared at each other in disbelief. Then, finally, Hank said, "Are you okay with what I just heard?"

"Yes," she said, "I just didn't believe it would happen this quickly."

She had sold or donated many duplicated household items.

Many of her precious keepsakes were already boxed and stacked in her garage. Her father's collection of stuffed wildlife would be individually crated and moved by a specialty packing business. The remainder of the household goods was to be transported by a local company that worked exclusively on short-distance relocations. Naturally, she would miss the convenience of living only a few blocks from her workplace. Still, like a blessing in disguise, it may have removed some workaholic tendencies she had begun to develop at the firm.

After losing her father, the work that went into maintaining a house with over five thousand square feet and a one-acre lot was much more than she could aptly handle. However, good memories would be stored and recalled as needed. After all, it was still just a house; she was now moving into a shared utopia.

They crashed and slept for hours. Then, early the following day, Lydia woke up to some annoying pounding in the great room. She slipped on a white, terry-cloth robe and silently crept down the hallway for a curious look. She found him carefully hanging several small paintings they had brought back from Italy.

She muffled a slight cough and said, "You can't keep a good man down! The paintings look great, but I wonder how we'll effectively fill a sizeable room like this. It must be well over sixty feet long, and with the high ceilings and mammoth beams, it looks like one of the small cathedrals we visited in Sorrento."

He replied, "You bet your sweet patootie it's big, but we'll have a ball, making it work for us!"

That evening they made their way to the realtor's office. Dennis had skillfully prepared the three offers and laid out all the information on a fold-up table. The offers were all well above the appraised property value, and two didn't require a home inspection. They all agreed that the submission from a doctor, moving in from California with his wife and three children, felt best. They could close within two weeks and had no contingencies other than producing a clear title. Lydia signed the purchase agreement.

CHAPTER 47

Hank returned to work at FishNautics, and Lydia adjusted to the long drive into Edina. They were both overjoyed to have settled comfortably into their new home. Coordinating the movement of household goods from her home and his rental was now just a blurred memory. The garage complex on the property proved to be just what the doctor ordered. He had space to store everything from Christmas decorations to his mechanic and woodworking tools.

His prized 930 had a dedicated bay, as did Lydia's Lexus and the company Suburban. Hank dreamed of owning a fishing boat. So, with another waiting bay, he purchased a Lund, Mr. Pike 16 with a 60hp Johnson outboard and a 15hp Johnson kicker. This boat gave him excellent comfort, the newest electronics, and safety, yet still afforded him entrée into smaller pike lakes with often tricky access. He couldn't wait to take it on a maiden voyage into Keezheekoni country.

Fall was a hectic time at all of the company stores. Hank made two separate trips to Spokane and Boise to witness and delight in the tremendous success these stores had experienced. Portland and Seattle had risen to the top of the future expansion list, and he would investigate possible store sites next spring. Dylan Sanders had become a valuable part of the new product team. Hank knew he had made an excellent choice in Dylan for AVP, but he had to pinch himself as he validated and observed the strides Dylan had made in less than six months on the job. He had gained the respect of the team members, and everyone had noticed his innate concern and dedication to the company. Even Rose Climber, who was as skeptical and aporetic as humanly possible, had praise and accolades for this young man. But with his full-patent approval looming on the horizon, he knew it would just be a matter of time before he left the company. When that day arrived, having a replacement, already trained, would be Hank's gift to FishNautics.

Lydia had taken on several new clients at the law firm. She was considered one of the leading patent attorneys in the upper Midwest. She had received the complete patent approval for Hank's invention but kept it a secret until she could arrange an appropriate surprise party. Whenever Hank questioned her about the status of the patent, she would reply, "Oh, you know how slow government agencies can be. Patents take time, so you have to be patient. I'll let you know when I have the official documents."

This approach seemed to satisfy him for the moment, but she knew he would relentlessly bring it up repeatedly.

She called the Vineyard Restaurant in Anoka to see if a large meeting room available the week before Christmas. She knew how busy restaurants were right before the holidays and was elated when they said the most significant room was all hers on Friday night.

She invited Harry and John, and their wives to the event as well as several staff members from the firm. She also called Winnie and Arnie, informed them of the event, and told them to keep it on the Q.T. Then she contacted Hank's brother Arvid and invited him and his wife, Jan, to party. The manager of the restaurant said he would create some appropriate decorations fitting for this special occasion.

He had known Hank for many years and wanted it to be something he would cherish and never forget. Lydia was beside herself. She only hoped she wouldn't slip up and let the cat out of the bag. After digesting what she had just accomplished, she phoned him and said, "How would you like to go on a dinner date with me on Friday night? We have worked hard since returning from Italy, and I thought we deserved a night on the town. What do you think?"

Hank cunningly replied, "Just a minute; I must check my calendar." They both had a good laugh.

Vendors were all in the Christmas spirit. They planned party after party. Hank knew nothing important would take place in the last two weeks of December. At Hot Lures, Galen Greene rented an entire floor at the Radisson Hotel in downtown Minneapolis.

Not to be outdone, Clint O'Brien from HookSet, Inc. managed to obtain a conference room at the Minnesota Viking headquarters in Eagan for their party. His guests included several Viking players who resided in the Twin Cities. Hank enjoyed all the hoopla but kept thinking about Friday night and his mystery date with Lydia.

He left his office early on Friday afternoon. He went to his main garage and checked his winterized 930. He removed the custom car cover and was happy to see the trickle charger was working perfectly, with the battery at full charge. He added a few ounces of STA-BIL 10 to his gas tank to prevent evaporation and to repel moisture formation. Next, he applied a light coat of Simoniz II liquid wax to the body and used a liberal amount of ArmorAll interior detailer spray on the dash and door panels. Finally, he carefully treated the leather seats with a generous coating of Obenauf's leather oil preservative. He stood back and was highly pleased with his efforts as he pulled the fleece-lined cover back over the Porsche and put it back to sleep. Next, he moseyed on over to his new Lund fishing boat. It, too, was draped with a custom, fitted cover. It looked lonely, sitting in its stall, awaiting spring sunshine that would thaw the snow-covered and frozen lakes, turning them back into a receptive, blue liquid. He untied the tarp rope from the bow and judiciously folded the cover back in two-foot increments. The handsome vessel emerged in all its glory, outfitted with all the latest gadgets. It was truly a sight to behold. It even included a fish finder that integrated the beta version of his pending patent. He checked the boat batteries, and the tender chargers were doing their jobs. The boat had not seen its maiden voyage, and Hank couldn't wait for warm weather. He quickly wiped it with a plush bath towel and buttoned the boat back into storage mode.

Only now, in the dead of winter, could Hank appreciate what the massive garage afforded him: security, controlled temperatures, protection from the elements, and the most impressive man cave one could ever imagine. He returned to the house and checked the time. It was almost five o'clock. He was about to call Lydia when he heard the garage door open and saw her snow-covered Lexus enter the bay. She opened her car door and saw him standing in the doorway. She exclaimed, "It is snowing like a banshee out there. Thank God for the all-wheel drive! 35W was like a parking lot from Edina. The good news is the snow has stopped falling, and traffic should loosen up before we leave for dinner."

Hank gave her a tremendous hug and poured two glasses of her favorite chablis. She told him reservations were at the Vineyard for seven. He reached over, kissed her passionately, and said, "My favorite restaurant with my favorite girl; it can't get any better!"

She was right. Traffic conditions had improved as they headed up Highway 10 toward Anoka. She wore an outstanding Nordstrom low-cut, red holiday dress that left nothing to the imagination. He wore a dark blue Ralph Lauren blazer, Haggar gray slacks and a matching Todd Snyder tie.

They found a parking spot near the front door. The manager greeted them outside and escorted them into the restaurant. They checked their coats, and the manager insisted they follow him to the Stardom Room at the rear of the facility. Unfortunately, the room was dark as they opened the door. Suddenly, cheers and flashing cameras erupted from all over. The lights came on, and paper streamers and confetti filled the air. Hank could not believe his eyes. He looked around the room and realized everyone there was an essential thread in his life. Hank looked at Lydia as she pointed to an easel supporting an official-looking document. He walked over for a closer glimpse and realized it was an official document awarding him the fish identification patent. Everyone took a seat while Hank remained standing. A proverbial lump was in his throat as he tried to speak, but quivering lip movement was all he could muster. He took several deep breaths, and finally, the swelling dissipated, and he could once again speak, although he sounded like a scratched-up vinyl record.

He began by emphasizing the fact that this get-to-gather was a complete surprise. Then, he looked at Lydia, smiled, and said, "Thanks for being my best friend, confidant, partner, and lover. You were with me from the beginning, and with your encouragement, due diligence, and dogged work ethic, this patent marks the beginning of a dramatic change in our lives. So, for the record, thanks for all you've done for me and just being you!"

He went around the room and recognized everyone for their role in this achievement, including his brother Arvid, whom he thanked for teaching him the love of fishing at an early age. He praised Winnie and Arnie for all their support in the past and for great expectations in the future. But unfortunately, Hank had not discussed the formation of VisualFish with anyone except Lydia, Winnie, and Arnie and would not divulge it at this patent party.

After dinner and desserts, Hank asked the entire restaurant team to come into the room. He wanted to recognize them for their extraordinary service and for designing the fish decorations covering each wall and ceiling.

"The Vineyard has been my favorite restaurant for years, and you people are what make it so special. Keep doing what you are doing, so we can come back and celebrate many more special occasions," he concluded.

CHAPTER 48

The year-end holidays passed quickly, and the spring of 84 knocked at the door before they knew it. Hank had already been on two fishing trips this winter: one to Lake LBJ in the Texas Hill Country and Lake Okeechobee in Florida. Both trips centered around major bass tournaments that attracted the top bass pros in the country, competing for *beaucoup bucks.* He visited with several contestants and was surprised to see the number of FishNautics product lines used in the competition. Next, he would look closely at company expansion plans to be sure the deep south was on the list.

Lydia ultimately settled into their new home. She had fully adjusted to the daily thirty-mile drive to work. Word spread rapidly about her patent successes, inundating her with new clients. The firm rewarded her with the appointment of a new attorney to assist her with this unexpected growth. Working smarter, not harder, was her new mantra. She planned to take an additional vacation this year, including a long-awaited fishing trip into Ontario with Hank.

Winnie, on the other hand, was spending more and more time in Mexico. His relationship with Camila was starting to take a positive turn. He was pleased to have been formally introduced to her family on his last trip to Oaxaca. His Mexican Spanish had improved immeasurably, and he had made quite an impression on *el padre* and *la mama.* Hank was extremely happy for Winnie, but he sensed changes coming on the horizon.

Arnie Morgan had also found romance in his nerdy world. She was a co-worker representing the same techie and analytical lifestyle that Arnie had adopted. Molly was a match made in heaven. Neither of them wanted to have children, and they both enjoyed traveling when they were not immersed in applied science projects or contemplating the next high-speed CPU (central processing unit). Arnie had proven his loyalty as a minor partner in VisualFish and a trusted friend who always had your back.

The three partners met at the warehouse in Spring Lake Park for their monthly meeting. The tenant was using the facility as they had planned. They were producing a line of healthy snack foods, and two Hayssen packaging machines with nitrogen-flushing capabilities stood ostensibly in the center of the warehouse. The rest of the facility held boxes of the finished product, stacked on pallet racks, awaiting shipment and delivery. The tenant paid all the utilities, so their only overhead was taxes, insurance, and facility repair and upkeep. All three agreed to place the rent revenue directly into the company bank account. They would draw no salary and take out only expenses necessary to keep the warehouse operating. Hank made it clear that he intended to leave his current employer and would spearhead the development of *VisualFish* as his only endeavor. His timing for this move was still in the future, but he clarified to Winnie and Arnie that the two-year warehouse lease would not be extended or renewed. He had discussed this move with Lydia and was thrilled to know she supported and encouraged his plan every step of the way.

Winnie and Arnie would remain silent partners, allowing Hank the opportunity to build the business as he saw fit. When needed, they would undoubtedly be asked to contribute to their areas of expertise but would not be directly involved in the company's day-to-day operations. Hank had begun using an out-of-state marketing firm to test product interest with some of the significant *fish-finder* manufacturers. He was not ready to execute confidentiality agreements with potential clients, so the marketing people had to be extremely careful when conducting their research. Even with the patent granted and positive test results on hundreds of existing fish finders, Hank would move cautiously as the results from the marketing exercise came to fruition.

CHAPTER 49

It was the last week of May, and Hank had been busily planning a working trip to Ontario. The FoldaBoat Company wanted him to test one of their twelve-foot prototype boats equipped with a six-hp outboard motor. This boat is unique because it folds completely flat into the shape of a surfboard, but in less than five minutes of setup time, it becomes a safe, durable, three-seat fishing boat. Hank could see a niche for this type of vessel and was anxious to see how it performed on cold, glacial-shield lakes full of submerged rocks and other hidden dangers. He also wanted to test its stability, with two full-sized adults attempting to boat a monster, northern pike.

Hot Lures also had two new plastic and metal pike lures sliced in segments to produce lifelike movement in the water. Galen Greene brought a box of these lures to Hank's office and pleaded with him to include them in his next trip to Canada. Each lure resembled a pike minnow. Hank remarked that he had never seen a more realistic, true-to-life lure, and they certainly would be included in their next outing.

Hank seldom went on these excursions without a partner. He had offered several invitations to the usual suspects, but could not get a commitment with such short notice.

Dejected, he was sitting in his office when the phone rang. When he picked up the receiver and said hello, he immediately recognized the voice on the other end.

It was Joe Watkins, an old fishing friend from his college days. Hank said, "I haven't seen you in years. How the hell are you?"

Joe explained he had been working in California, and his company transferred him back to Minnesota to set up a new office in the south suburbs. He asked, "Would you like to get together for a beer and bullshit about the good old days? Unfortunately, the new office will not be ready for occupancy until July first, so I have five weeks with nothing to do."

The bells went off in his head, and Hank realized he might have found a partner. They would meet that evening at Nye's.

He phoned Lydia and told her he would not be home for dinner. She wished him luck. After several afternoon meetings, Hank drove home to get a change of clothes and a quick shower. He parked the Suburban and fired up the Porsche. Nye's parking lot was almost empty, unusual for a Thursday night. He parked the 930 and acknowledged the friendly bartender, who said, "Hank, your friend just walked down to the head, but he ordered a Leinie for you. Have a seat!"

Within a few minutes, Joe returned and gave him a bear hug that took his breath away. Joe had put on some weight, primarily muscle. They grabbed their beers from the bar and retreated to a private booth. Swapping stories and reminiscing about past events went on for several hours. They downed several longnecks and were getting somewhat giddy and shitfaced when Hank brought up his planned trip to Canada. He hinted that he needed a partner, and as they walked to their cars, Joe snorted, "Damn right, I'll go. Call me tomorrow, and we'll work out the details."

Hank was relieved as he pulled onto the Interstate. He knew Lydia would also be comforted, knowing he would not be traveling alone.

Hank was at the office early on Friday morning. He had asked Dylan to meet him in the cafeteria. It was the first extended trip he would take while leaving Dylan in charge. Hank wanted to ensure Dylan was comfortable running the office for almost three weeks in his absence. Although Rose would be there to assist with the daily routine, he wanted Dylan to make final management decisions, proving he was up to the task. Their conversation continued, and after consuming two cups of coffee and several sweet rolls, Hank knew the office was now in Dylan's capable hands. He had nothing obvious to worry about while he was gone.

Hank phoned Joe and gave him a list of things he would need for the trip, including a passport (although a valid driver's license would work), Canadian money, warm clothing, a sleeping bag, particular medications, if any, and good pair of boots. In addition, Hank would supply fishing rods and tackle, and they would purchase Canadian fishing licenses, food, and liquid refreshments in Canada to avoid paying any special import taxes.

He said they would depart early Sunday morning, crossing the border mid-afternoon, and spend the first night at the Valhalla Inn in Thunder Bay. Hank was so excited. He had everything packed and his new boat and trailer attached to the Suburban by Saturday afternoon. Hank telephoned Joe and reiterated how important it was for Joe to be at his house by six a.m. at the latest. Joe said he had made a dry run on Saturday morning down Lexington Avenue to be sure he knew precisely where Hank lived, and he arrived on Lombardi Time, fifteen minutes early. When they had loaded Joe's gear, Hank turned to see Lydia's outstretched arms waiting for him at the front doorway. He rushed to her side, embraced her, and whispered sweet nothings in her ear. She wished them a safe journey and emphasized,

"Don't take any foolish chances!"

They crossed the border at Pigeon River and arrived in Thunder Bay just after six p.m. The trip would have been two hours shorter had it not been for a complete search conducted by the Canadian Border Patrol. They had to unload everything packed in the Suburban and boat while a driving Lake Superior thunderstorm completely soaked all their belongings.

The Patrol inspection found nothing unusual or illegal in their search, and they were allowed to proceed into Canada. However, the officers offered no assistance repacking the vehicles and casually returned to their office. Hank knew it could take days for items like sleeping bags to dry out completely, but hopefully, the weather would be more hospitable at Keezheekoni. However, predicted low humidity, a brisk west wind, and a white-hot driftwood campfire would readily transform their moisture-laden gear.

They rose early the following day but lost an hour because they were now in the Eastern time zone. They had a quick breakfast at the Inn and picked up fishing licenses and extra gas at the Canadian Tire Store. They purchased food at the Safeway on Dawson Road, and they made their last stop, after ten a.m., at the LCBO on Arthur Street to pick up some spirits and a few cases of beer. They passed the Terry Fox Monument on the Queen's Highway and then turned north on Highway 527 toward Armstrong. As was forecasted, the weather cleared, and blue skies accompanied them on their journey north. Arriving in Armstrong, they gassed up at the Can-Op and drove directly to Victor Lowbranch's home. An abandoned outfitters cabin on Keezheekoni had recently been claimed and remodeled by a local Indian family. The cabin was not an approved provincial rental, but Victor secured permission for them to use the place for their three-week visit. But a minor problem had just occurred. Charlie Chubbuck, the new owner of the cabin, had been detained while on a trip to Thunder Bay. He would not be back in Armstrong until tomorrow and had the only keys to the dwelling. Victor felt terrible about the circumstances and invited them to stay at a summer cabin he had recently purchased on a lake just west of Armstrong.

Victor had winterized the cabin, and no electricity or running water was available on-site.

Victor said, "This cabin still beats sleeping in your vehicle or renting a marginal hotel room. The only thing I ask is one small favor. I need to move a refrigerator to the premises, and I would appreciate some help lifting it out of my pickup and moving it into the cabin."

They followed Victor for about ten miles and finally arrived at a secluded lake. As they pulled up in front of the cabin, Hank asked Victor, "Why are we seeing so many black bears along the roadways? On our drive up from Thunder Bay, we spotted well over fifty bears in the ditches along Highway 527. I know the Armstrong area has a large bear population, but isn't it unusual to have this number of sightings?"

Victor answered, "The Ontario Progressive Conservatives and the DNR decided to close the season for a two-year study. Reports of abandoned bear cubs during the hunting season prompted this closure. The net effect was that the bear population had grown unchecked to numbers never before realized. The bears have become aggressive and are extremely hungry. At night, they enter the city limits, break into houses, and open and destroy any reeking garbage containers. It's a mess! I know it will be only a matter of time before we experience human injury or death from a bear attack. Therefore, I caution you to take great care in handling or storing food items in the bush, and for God's sake, don't leave any garbage or fish guts near your campsite. You're only asking for trouble!"

Victor opened the cabin and gave them a quick tour. He pointed out an outdoor biffy they could use if nature calls. As he drove away, he wound down his window and said, "Be sure to lock up the cabin when you leave in the morning. Charlie will return to Armstrong later tonight, so drop by my house, and I will have the Keezheekoni keys waiting for you. Pleasant dreams."

They unloaded fishing gear and brought in a fifth of Drambuie, and vinegar-flavored potato chips. This combination would be their evening meal. They settled into two old, stained, and frayed recliners in the front sunroom of the cabin. As they sipped their honey-infused nectar, they saw movement at the far end of a three-acre clearing. Joe grabbed a pair of binoculars from an open tackle box and adjusted the focal point to reveal three black bears in the field. It appeared to be one good-sized sow with two yearlings in tow. Joe handed Hank the glasses and told him to take a look. Hank propped his elbows on the window ledge to steady the view.

Then, he exclaimed, "They're hungry, all right. The bears are gorging themselves on a buffet of newly blossomed dandelions."

They watched the threesome move along the edge of the field and eventually lost sight of them as they disappeared behind the cabin. Hank removed his 35mm Nikon from his backpack and told Joe he was going out on the porch to get a photo of the bears as they emerged from the back of the cabin. The porch, protected on two sides with a plastic tarp, kept drifting snow from accumulating against the doorway. He quietly moved down the three wooden steps and made a ninety-degree pivot to open ground. The sow saw him first and gave a danger growl to the two cubs. They scrambled up a weather-beaten, black spruce tree. She double-checked to ensure the cubs were safe, and then, with hackled hair rising on her shoulders and her black eyes bulging out of their sockets, she charged from a low stance. Suddenly, she stopped and retreated. She had been only about ten feet from where Hank stood.

He had the camera ready and photographed much of the first attack. He stood almost frozen to the ground as the old girl again attended to her babies. Then without warning, she turned on all fours and stormed at him like an out-of-control freight train. Hank, realizing what was happening, spontaneously jumped for the first step on the porch. Unfortunately, the bear caught his left leg with her extended claws, shredded a large piece of nylon from his pant leg, and left three deep gashes gushing with adrenaline-infused blood. Standing in the doorway, Joe reached out and forcibly jerked him back to the safety of the cabin. The bear climbed the three steps and standing, on her hind legs, began violently pounding on the door. They knew the sliding bolt would not withstand the battering the door was taking, so Hank snatched a kitchen chair and forced its backrest under the door handle, giving it enough rigidity to outlast the attack. Next, Hank located a first aid kit neatly tucked away in a kitchen cabinet. With Joe's help, Hank's wounds were dressed and treated with an antibiotic.

The sun had set, and darkness engulfed the cabin. Exhausted, they used their flashlights to illuminate their way to the bedrooms. They rehashed the day's events and were almost asleep when thundering vibrations arose from the floorboards. They both sat up, flipped on their torches, and realized that the bear had entered the elevated crawl space beneath them and was trying again to gain entry.

Joe pointed at a ten-inch fillet knife he had taken from the tackle box. It sat pitifully on the nightstand next to his bed, and they both knew it would be woefully ineffective against this beast. Then as quickly as the pummeling started, it ceased, producing a sinister silence that kept both of them awake through most of the night.

When dawn finally broke, both men walked to the sunroom and vigilantly surveyed the visible grounds around the cabin. No bears were spotted, and Joe made his way to the Suburban and brought back a package of ground coffee and several water bottles. Bear or no bear, they would make a pot of coffee and start the day off right.

They turned on the LP gas tank and, using a crumbling farmer's match, ignited the first burner on the rusted stove.

They used a dented aluminum saucepan to bring the water to a near boil, poured it through a makeshift paper filter holder, filled coffee grounds, and watched as it dripped slowly into the waiting pot. The system didn't look like anything you would find at Starbucks, but it still produced a fine cup of wilderness coffee.

As they finished their second cup of coffee, Joe glanced out the window and quietly said, "We've got company."

Once again, the three bears appeared at the far end of the field. Hank glassed them and said, "There's something unusual going on out there. The sow is standing on her hind legs and is skillfully scenting the air."

A moment later, the sow forced her yearlings out of the field and into the thick timber. They disappeared, but within a few seconds, a giant male black bear weighing at least five hundred pounds appeared at the opposite edge of the field. He probably was hungry and extremely horny. Male bears often kill cubs to bring the female back into heat; in this case, he may have been looking for a leisurely breakfast. Whatever the case, the female and her family were long gone, and that was precisely what Hank and Joe intended to do within the next few minutes. They locked the heavily scarred cabin door and rushed to the waiting vehicle, slowly meandering their way off the property. They expected to see bears on the trail back to Armstrong but they were still waiting to be sighted.

Victor was driving into his garage as they pulled up to the house. He had just returned from meeting Charlie and had the cabin keys in his hand. They both told him about the bear encounter, and Victor said he would go out to the cabin in the afternoon and assess and repair any damage to the property. Then, he stated, "I'll personally deal with this aggressive bear in no uncertain terms."

They thanked Victor for the hospitality but wanted to avoid staying around for a detailed explanation of what he intended to do.

CHAPTER 50

Driving northeast of Armstrong, they witnessed the damage from five days of severe thunderstorms. The blue skies and sunshine certainly masked much of the catastrophe, but water standing in the ditches and deep washouts around every bend, made for slow-going on the logging road. It was mid-afternoon when they found the overgrown trail that eventually led to an improvised boat landing on the east side of Keezheekoni. They shifted the Suburban into low-range, four-wheel drive and guardedly crept along the rain-soaked pathway. Small, flooded creeks crisscrossed the jack pine forest, and the beaver population had been busily trying to dam up some of these vessels. Water backed up over the trail, sometimes bumper deep where they had been successful. The Suburban slipped off the barely visible track several times, causing sudden anguish and fear in both men, as evidenced by their cadaverous complexions. Hank had made this journey several times, but he had never encountered conditions like they were now experiencing. It was almost dark when they reached a familiar rock-embedded clearing. Hank knew the small downhill cutoff to the lake was just ahead on the right. They were less than five hundred yards from the lake. He also knew it would require work with a chainsaw to clear brush and fallen trees blocking the final push.

He said, "Joe, there is no way that we will tackle this project tonight. It's too damn dangerous to be working in the dark! Let's rearrange a few items from the back of the Suburban and see if we can make room for two sleeping bags. We'll spend the night right here."

In the morning, they woke to another beautiful day. Joe found some dry cedar limbs, and after making a circular rock enclosure, he started a fire. Hank found an old piece of grated steel that someone had thrown in a nearby thicket, and he carefully placed it over the fire, forcing it down on the rock ring.

He unpacked a box of cooking utensils and located a seasoned, cast-iron frying pan and his favorite enameled coffee pot. Next, Joe opened one of their coolers and removed a half-dozen eggs, a large slab of bacon, and some butter.

Having had nothing to eat for almost twenty-four hours, they sat on a fallen log next to the fire, gorging themselves on a breakfast for a king.

The decision not to tackle the final descent in the dark proved to be the right one. It took most of the morning to clear a pathway to the landing. Hank used the chainsaw on well over a dozen fallen trees. He cut each one into a workable length for maneuvering off the trail. With all the fallen moisture, a fresh crop of biting Canadian black flies and Aedes Vexan mosquitoes found their carbon dioxide trail and punished them for intruding into their world. Then, finally, they could move the wagon train down the path to the gravel landing. They unloaded the boat in the shallow bay and positioned the Suburban, off the trail, in a dry, sandy clearing.

The cabin, located on the north side of the lake, meant at least two boat trips to carry all their gear to the site.

The wind had increased from the west and produced white caps and two-foot swells. The fully loaded boat rode low in the water. The gunwales were only about six inches above the lake's surface, and during the first trip, waves forced their way over the right side of the boat several times. Hank had forgotten to include a dipping can when he made his checklist, so they were sitting in ankle-deep, frigid water as they neared the cabin. They quickly unloaded the gear and began carrying it up the steep bank. The dwelling had a covered front porch with rotting pine boards for a base. They stacked everything against the cabin wall and hustled back to the boat. Joe took a short jaunt down the trail to a dilapidated, foul-smelling outhouse. He used the facility while holding his breath. As he was about to depart, he noticed a one-quart plastic vinegar jug with an affixed handle near the door.

He carried the bottle to the boat and cut off the tapered top with his Swiss Army Knife. It became a perfect bailing device. The return trip was quick and dry, with the boat empty and their backs to the wind. Again, they loaded the remainder of their gear into the boat. This time they packed everything with weight on the right side of the boat, thereby keeping the left gunwale much higher, stopping any wave intrusion. It worked perfectly.

With all the gear portaged to the porch, they walked around the cabin and noticed the heavy metal bedsprings that were securely screwed and fitted over each window.

Hank said, "They bearproofed this whole cabin with the bedsprings and by reinforcing the front door with a sheet of quarter-inch steel. I can see old claw scrapings at the windows and around the front door, but none of the marks are recent. This cabin has become a real fortress, and I know we'll sleep soundly tonight."

Next, they checked out the two storage barns erected at the property's rear. They opened the padlocked doors using the owner's set of keys. Each building contained basic supplies for the cabin, two ancient birch-bark canoes, and three small outboard motors. They also found a large, opened bag of quicklime. In the bag was an empty Campbell soup can, and Joe took a full scoop of lime and hurried to the outhouse. He opened the door and sprinkled the powder into the one-holer. They would repeat this treatment for several days until the flies and odors were eliminated or deemed tolerable.

As they unlocked and entered the front door of the lodging, they were amazed at the cleanliness and organization of its interior. A small wooden table in the main room revealed carvings and initials made by visitors from the past. At each end of the table were two nicely padded chairs. A kerosene lantern with a smoke-smudged glass chimney sat in the middle of the table. The cabin had no electricity, but they noticed a small, portable generator in one of the storage units, probably used to power electric tools. A four-burner La Cornue LP stove was sitting under a north wall window. Joe had located the LP tank and turned on the gas supply valve. For cabin heat, a Drolet wood stove was anchored to a metal floor covering hammered to the floorboards in the middle of the room. Next to the cook stove was a small sink mounted in a plywood cabinet. The drainpipe was plumbed directly through the wall and emptied into a buried pile of river rock about ten feet from the cabin. They would put only gray water down the drain. The sink had no faucet, so they used a wall-hung five-gallon plastic jug with a spigot for their water supply. A cupboard in the kitchen contained a full array of pots, pans, dishes, glasses, and cooking utensils, but they decided to use the items they had brought.

They unloaded their supplies and brought in the two food coolers lined with dry ice. Everything made the trip without incurring any damage. They reloaded most of the fishing gear back into the boat and carried their dry sleeping bags upstairs to the bedroom. Two comfortable-looking double beds filled most of this floor. Windows, located on each of the gable walls, produced adequate ventilation across the whole room. They each picked a bed and unfolded their sleeping bags. Hank went downstairs and retrieved their backpacks. He opened a zippered panel and pulled out two small, battery-powered lamps that could stand on a flat surface or be hung by attached chains. One would stay in the bedroom and the other in the kitchen.

Canned stew was on the menu for their evening meal. They sopped up the juices with several slices of bread, washed their dishes, and retired to the lawn chairs they had borrowed from one of the storage sheds. Joe pulled out two of several Cuban cigars he had purchased in Thunder Bay while Hank broke the seal on a bottle of eighteen-year-old Aberlour Scotch. They toasted to good health and success as darkness fell.

CHAPTER 51

The distant howl of a lone gray wolf and a well-fed raven's more immediate throaty caw welcomed them to the waters of Keezheekoni. They sipped coffee as they removed the tarp cover from the boat. Today, breakfast would consist of a couple of energy bars and a hastily prepared Thermos of hot coffee. Then, as they used a pair of oars to separate themselves from the shoreline, a frightening, massive swirl on the water's surface meant only one thing; hungry pike were on the prowl.

Hank did not start the outboard motor but elected to slowly paddle the boat through the sunken cabbage weeds to avoid disturbing any monsters in the area. Joe checked the depth finder to locate the sudden drop-off outside the weed bed. Unfortunately, northern pike were opportunists and often lay motionless and camouflaged in the weeds, awaiting an easy meal. Finally, Joe said softly, "We just cleared the weed bed, sitting in twenty feet of water. So, I'll lower the anchor, and we can start fishing."

They both were using Shimano pike rods and reels. Hank snapped on a yellow and red, five-of-diamond, Daredevil with a silverback while Joe started with one of the artificial pike minnows that Hot Lures had supplied. The trick was to cast the lure over the weed bed and create a rapid retrieval as soon as the attraction touched water. It kept the lure away from the pesky cabbage, and hopefully, it would entice a pike to strike. The only problem with working the weed beds is that it gave the fish a tremendous advantage. They would often ingest the lure and dive deep into the thick foliage, twisting and turning to dislodge the lure or snap the line. Even with a 40 lb. braided line and 60 lb. steel leaders, they only managed to land about thirty percent of the hookups. Joe fought a thirty-minute battle with a twenty-nine-pound beauty that taped out at just under fifty inches and was the day's biggest catch.

Around noon, they decided to switch gears and try to jig in a few walleyes for lunch. They rigged up two ultralight rods with quarter-ounce jigs and began casting into deep water on the other side of the boat. Within minutes they caught several keepers that would make a perfect meal. They pulled anchor, and because they had remained within a few hundred feet of the cabin for the entire morning, it was a leisurely paddle back to shore.

They cleaned the walleyes, coated the fillets with Shore Lunch Beer Batter, and fried them with sliced potatoes and onions. After the feast, Hank said, "I think eating our big meal mid-day is a great idea. Fishing tends to slack off at this time of day, and most biting insects have taken a siesta in the dark timber. We can also catch a few rays of sunshine, nap a little and maybe enjoy a beer or two." Joe nodded and grinned as he twisted the cap off another Labatts Blue.

During the next few days, good fishing and excellent weather prevailed. Again, the lures they tested passed with flying colors, but they could not locate any world-class pike.

Within a few days, the cabin felt like home, and even the obnoxious outhouse became tolerable after a few treatments of lime. Except for a few field mice that scampered across the kitchen floor and two inquisitive moose walking in knee-deep water along the shoreline to avoid bothersome insects, no other forms of wildlife appeared.

At the beginning of week two, on a dead-calm day, Hank asked, "What do you think about putting the Fold-a-Boat through a series of maneuvers to test its buoyancy, stability, and handling capabilities? We'll use the eight-horsepower outboard and stay in shallow waters for the maiden voyage."

Joe responded, "Let's do it now! If it proves seaworthy, we can throw in some rods and tackle and see how it holds up to some real pike action!"

The twelve-foot vessel was nothing short of amazing. The small outboard effortlessly pushed the boat through the water at almost water-skiing speed. It handled tight turns and sudden stops with ease. The gunwales were exceptionally stable, and the boat was unsinkable with its foam composite construction. However, getting used to the sponginess of the floorboards was disconcerting, and the hard plank seats provided little comfort for much more than short excursions.

After the initial test, they returned to the cabin and loaded their fishing gear.

Hank muttered, "Don't take anything that isn't necessary. A few choice lures, a landing net, a small anchor, and one tackle box is about all we can afford to take. Don't forget the life jackets."

They had one helluva evening of fishing from the little craft, and the pain in their cramped and stiff bodies seemed to disappear as they thought about the numerous, good-sized pike they had hooked and released. They agreed the boat passed all their tests and filled a unique niche.

Then, as darkness crept over the lake, they turned the little boat toward home.

CHAPTER 52

Toward the end of their second week on the lake, they decided to take a break from fishing and do some exploring.

Hank had been studying a topographical map and discovered three other small lakes located northwest of their camp. They put on their hiking boots and loaded a daypack with bottled water, snacks, a first aid kit, and a compact 35mm camera. They followed a well-trodden moose trail that skirted a narrow whitewater river with ever-increasing elevation. The brush was exceptionally thick, and the bugs were insatiable as they pushed and stumbled up the first two miles. The roar of the rapids was deafening at times, but they could never see the flowage because of the impenetrable foliage. Finally, they emerged from a beaver clearing and came out on the first lake.

Hank became deliriously happy with what he saw. The lake was more extensive than he expected, and he could see the shoreline waters dotted with cabbage weeds and several secluded bays.

He looked at Joe and said, "I'll bet this water has never been fished, at least not recently. I know monster pike are lurking in each of the bays. Let's remember this when we make another trip."

They continued their journey up to the subsequent two lakes on the map, but they turned out to be little more than a swollen section of the river, stretching the imagination to be even called lakes. The return trip was downhill, except for a short photo session on the first lake. They were back at the cabin before they knew it. They were famished after the arduous hike and fried up another walleye meal as they planned the final seven days. Joe wanted to try what looked like a good bay on the west side of the lake. He said he felt goosebumps over his body as he examined the map. This spot could be pike nirvana. They would take the big boat and venture up there in the morning.

The morning sky was overcast, and there was a light chop on the water from a low-pressure front that was moving in. Hank knew the terrific weather would not last. They stopped the boat several hundred feet from the bay. Unfortunately, an active beaver family had constructed a vast, stick-laden house right on the edge of a forty-foot drop-off.

Hank lowered the electric trolling motor into position, and they silently trolled right up to the beaver dwelling. They methodically started preparing their gear after carefully dropping a front and rear anchor. Hank threw out the first cast, using a standard Daredevil with a copper back. The lure no sooner hit the water than a torrent of water exploded on the surface. He immediately set the hook with a violent upward swing of the rod. The fish lunged for deep water, and Hank knew he had a trophy on the other end. The drag was set perfectly on the Shimano as the line spiraled off the reel.

Finally, the beast stopped moving, and the line went slack. Hank glanced at the reel, knowing he had at most ten feet of braided Dacron on the spool. He started turning the handle slowly with a guarded retrieve. When Hank had drawn up the slack in the line, the fish reversed its direction and was heading directly back to the boat. Reeling like there was no tomorrow, he kept pace with the monster while Joe grabbed the pike landing net and placed it in the water beside the boat. The pike began to tire and could only muster two half-hearted runs under the surface. They had a full glimpse of the fish in the dark water when Hank guided it directly into the awaiting net. Joe tried to lift the monster into the boat, but with the weight of the fish, he thought the aluminum frame would collapse, and all hell would break loose.

He roared at Hank, "Put your rod down and grab the front edge of the net. We'll hoist her in together. I can't do it on my own!"

Hank quickly reacted, and within seconds the enormous pike lay exhausted on the carpeted, flat bottom of the boat. Hank had to sit down as his knees failed him. He started to unravel the fish from the netting, but his hands were shaking so badly he couldn't complete the simple task. Finally, he could straddle the fish with both legs and with Joe's help, the Daredevil came free from the shark-like jaws. Joe took out a tape line and determined the length to be fifty-six inches. Hank fumbled in the tackle box for his Manley Brass Fishing Scale and warily placed the sharpened S-hook through the skin of the lower jaw. Just as she felt the penetration of the hook, her jaws slammed shut like a steel bear trap, puncturing Hank's misplaced pointer finger with a two-inch, razor-sharp tooth. Bleeding profusely, he raised the fish to the vertical and gasped in disbelief as the scale registered a whopping forty-five pounds! It was a world-class pike, and they needed return it to the water immediately. Joe moved to the front of the boat and pulled out his Nikon camera from the front storage compartment. He rapidly snapped a dozen pictures, put the camera down, and helped Hank remove the prize from the scale. They lowered the fish into the water while Hank maintained a firm grip on her tail.

He gently moved her forward and backward, forcing oxygen-rich water over her gills. It took several minutes to revive the pike completely, but without warning, she slapped her tail against the aluminum hull and swiftly disappeared.

Hank reached for two Blues in the cooler, and they clinked the bottles without saying a word. This fish probably weighed slightly less than Peter Dubuc's American record pike caught in New York's Sacandago Lake in 1940, but Hank didn't care. He was happy to have released the trophy unharmed, and it would live to fight another day.

He looked thoughtfully at Joe and said, "Who knows? That pike just might put on another pound or two before our next trip and could become a new North American record." This Keezheekoni treasure would remain a best-kept secret, avoiding undue attention to this fragile pike domain.

Rain was starting to fall as they returned to camp. Joe said, "Hank, you're still dripping blood from that wound. I'll bring the first aid kit to the cabin and patch you up. Puncture wounds can be dangerous, and God only knows what germs lay on those ancient teeth."

Joe pulled out a tube of antibiotic cream and carefully dressed the damaged finger in gauze and tape. It throbbed like hell as he stared at the bandage. Finally, Joe chuntered, "That scar will be with you forever, triggering memories anytime you want to bring them up."

He fished out two Cuban cigars from the cooler and a fresh bottle of Drambuie. They smoked and drank the afternoon away, sheltered under the corrugated front porch of the cabin.

Heavy rains came and went for the next four days, accompanied by savage winds. Fishing was out of the question. They packed up and left at the first sign of a break in the weather. Then, on Friday morning, it happened. They awoke to calm water and bright sunshine. Their spirits rose as they made two round trips across the lake, hauling their gear to the staging area. Three weeks was a long time to be in the bush, and they looked forward to the drive home.

CHAPTER 53

Saturday afternoon, they exited 35W and drove directly to Hank's house. Lydia was outside pruning some English roses she had planted in the spring. She dropped her tools and clippings and ran to the Suburban, exclaiming, "Gosh, I had no idea how long three weeks could be. I've been so lonely! I was worried about you guys, and the more I worried, the more helpless I felt. So, get out of the truck and give me a big homecoming hug!"

They backed the boat into the second bay and started the unloading process. Within an hour, Joe was on the road again, and Hank was sprawling out and dozing in his favorite leather recliner. Lydia started preparing dinner and would get the trip's details over a glass of wine later, but she just let him dream for now.

He awoke to smell homemade lasagna and freshly baked garlic bread.

At that moment, he didn't fully comprehend how much he missed a home-cooked meal. Yes, the walleyes were exceptional, and even the canned stew tasted great after a day on the lake, but those camp-side delicacies couldn't compare to proper home cooking. So, he devoured the first helping and asked Lydia for another and then another.

"You've outdone yourself with this meal," he exclaimed as he munched on another crunchy bread stick.

She couldn't believe how much he had consumed and was hesitant to mention the dozen cannoli she had prepared for dessert.

She poured two glasses of creamy, white chardonnay, put on a new *Bill Evans* piano collection, and settled into their overstuffed loveseat. He told adventure stories until midnight, and she never once lost interest. Then, finally, they retired to the bedroom. He showered first, and when she showered and climbed into bed, he peacefully snored away into his goose-down pillow.

She woke up first on Sunday morning, reached over, and started to caress and stroke his lifeless body. Within seconds he was wide awake, and before they knew it, the sun was beginning to set.

It was like their first few days in Italy but with all the comforts of home. First, they shuffled into the kitchen in the early evening and ate some leftovers. Then collapsing back in the bed, neither one moved another muscle throughout the night.

Almost a month had floated by since Hank returned from Canada. He recapped his successful trip to all the department heads at work but has yet to mention the world-class pike he had encountered. However, Hank pulled up his pant leg several times and pointed out the scabby scars from the terrifying bear attack. Hank enjoyed telling this tale as his audience hung on to his every word. His team treated him as a battle-proven warrior and hinted about the possibility of joining him on a future expedition. All the product trials he had conducted were compiled and graded. He informed all manufacturers of the results. Unfortunately, several products did not meet the grade, including one tackle box with poorly engineered hinges. As a result, it fell apart in pieces on the first day of fishing.

On the other hand, Fold-a-Boat came through with flying colors and six impressive lures from various tackle companies.

Finally, Hank invited Eldon Vatsaas from Marketing to join him for lunch to discuss the items earmarked for the Fall marketing and sales campaign. It was quite a shock when Eldon, who had consumed two glasses of wine, said, "What's this I hear about an invention you've patented? I attended a Lion's Club meeting in Minneapolis. The President of Anderson Fish Finders mentioned your name and said you were sitting on a breakthrough that could revolutionize the whole industry."

Stunned, Hank regained his composure and evasively replied, "Oh, come on, it's just an idea I had while attending grad school. No big deal. It's just a simple way of identifying fish in the water. Maybe someday, I'll work out all the kinks, and some cash-heavy investment firm will bite on my idea. In the meantime, let's get back to the task and determine what we can add to our inventory."

This deflective response subdued Eldon's curiosity.

However, Hank knew it was just a matter of time before he would be confronted again with this issue, and he needed to start preparing an action plan. First, he would explain his predicament to Lydia that evening and ask for her advice. Then Hank would contact Winnie and Arnie and schedule a meeting to fill them in on the latest events. *When God closes a door, he opens a window. It may be the push he needed to step out on his own.*

Lydia arrived home at almost eight o'clock. She had left a voice mail, explaining she would be late and that he was on his own for dinner. The moment she walked in the door, she sensed something was amiss. Hank was sitting in his office with a neat glass of Scotch in one hand. She startled him as she placed her hand on his shoulder. He swiveled his chair, stood up, and embraced her, saying, "You can't believe how much I need your advice and support right now!" He relayed what had happened at lunch with Eldon.

He felt a decision would have to be made soon regarding his plans for VisualFish.

"Should I prepare an immediate resignation letter or continue to work at FishNautics for another two years, as planned? I know there is no conflict of interest with the Company, but how would Mark Branigan and the Board of Directors react? Maybe they already know about my patent, and could they also be aware of my plans to resign?"

Guilt clouded his thinking, so he needed good advice and some astute perspective from Lydia and his two partners. In typical lawyer fashion, Lydia dismembered every possible conclusion to this predicament. By the end of the evening, the answer became abundantly clear. Hank would tender his resignation to FishNautics, giving them at least a thirty-day notice. It would be the professional, and prudent course of action, not burning bridges. Now he could focus most of his time on building the new business stratagem. He would honor the remaining eighteen months of the warehouse lease agreement, but it would not be renewed or extended. Because the lease did not include the front office space, Hank would immediately begin using it as their company headquarters. He telephoned Winnie and Arnie, briefed them on his plan, and set up a Wednesday evening meeting to discuss the minutiae. Hank was excited and relieved.

The next day, he arrived at the office before six a.m. He knew Mark Branigan was an early riser and hoped to catch him in his office before the workday started. So, he poured two cups of Kona and carried them directly to Mark's office. Deep in thought, Mark was seated behind his desk while staring at his computer screen. Hank knocked gently on the door and said, "I think even workaholics deserve a coffee break now and then."

Surprised, he replied, "Hank, give me a moment, but please have a seat."

After a few minutes and several taps on his keyboard, he said, "Besides bringing coffee, what's on your mind this fine morning?"

Hank did not attempt any small talk and carefully explained his intentions. Mark closely listened to everything he had to say, making no comments.

"Although we tried to challenge you in your position with the company, I knew this day would eventually come. You have a great head for business and a wonderful knack for developing people. Starting your own business is a feat to be envied. I heard through the grapevine that you received a patent for some fish identification software. The idea is intriguing, and if I can help in the future, please call on me. The team you've built here demonstrates your dedication and loyalty. I wish you all the best," Mark concluded.

Then he continued, "Would you be interested in buying the Suburban you've been driving for the past couple of years? I'll give you a helluva deal on it. The Board has decided to purchase a fleet of new vehicles, trick-out with our company logo. If you don't buy it, I'll send it to a local car auction."

Hank accepted the Suburban offer, rose from his chair, shook Mark's hand, and placed the official resignation letter on his desk.

Hank said, "You can see I have given a thirty-day notice, but if you need more time from me, I'll make it happen. I'll meet with my team this morning and make the announcement. Mark, I hope you will consider offering my position to Dylan Sanders.

He has proven to be an outstanding leader in every sense of the word, and I know he will have the support and backing of our entire team."

Hank knew he had done the right thing when he left Mark's office. He returned to his office and found Rose working on several new product additions to their Fall lineup. He asked her to step into his office. She had an apprehensive look on her face as she heedfully took a seat. He started the conversation by saying, "Rose, you have always been an outstanding assistant."

She swallowed hard and speculated: *What have I done? I can't afford to lose my job!*

He continued, "We've always appreciated your loyalty to the Company. But beyond all of that, you have been a true friend. I have always been able to share my innermost thoughts with you, and now I have something important to say before the team arrives. Effective in thirty days, I will be leaving FishNautics to pursue a new venture. I met with Mark Branigan early this morning and officially handed him my resignation. You're the second person to know of my intentions, and I'd appreciate it if you would organize a team meeting for eleven o'clock in the conference room."

Rose sighed profoundly and nodded in the affirmative while tears rolled down each cheek. Then, all she could muster was, "I'm going to miss you!"

As she left the office, Hank became emotional and hastily pulled a tissue from his desk drawer to dry his watery eyes.

He put on his happy face as he entered the conference room, but sensing something was wrong, everybody sat silently with their heads slightly bowed. He looked around the room at each employee and then commented, "My God, it looks like we just had a death in the family!"

He picked some carefully chosen words, and smilingly, explained that he would be leaving the company. They all had questions and wanted to know what prompted this decision. It took the better part of an hour, but everyone seemed to accept his explanation, and they were about to return to work when Mark Branigan appeared in the doorway. He asked, "Could you delay the adjournment of the meeting and let me say a few words? Hank has been a valuable part of this Company's spectacular growth, and we will all miss him. He has built a solid foundation and assured me that this team could take the Company to heights we could never imagine. However, it will take continued leadership, and I am so pleased to announce that this morning, Dylan Sanders has accepted the challenge and with it, the new role of Vice-President. Hank's recommendation and Dylan's exemplary service record since joining FishNautics made him a shoo-in. Dylan, please stand and accept our congratulations and best wishes." Hank was thrilled to know his recommendation of Dylan was now a reality.

CHAPTER 54

Hank spent most of his working hours with Dylan at his side for thirty straight days. Because he had been grooming him for this challenge, passing the baton was a relatively painless event within the company. However, Dylan was disadvantaged, needing more personal contact and field experience with the suppliers and manufacturers of the products they sold. As a result, Hank set up formal meetings with key players.

I knew most people feared the change process, not the actual change itself, thought Hank.

He drew on his well-honed communication skills to individually announce his departure and to establish a seamless pathway for Dylan's success. Seeing how well all parties accepted and applauded the changeover was beautiful.

Rose was working behind the scenes to plan a farewell luncheon for Hank on his final day.

With all the company employees attending and special guests, she realized the best option would be a catered meal in the company's main auditorium. Close and personal friends, including Winnie and Lydia, would be seated centerstage and conduct a good, old-fashioned roast. Rose asked Mark Branigan to be the master of ceremonies to ensure everything proceeded as planned. Next, Eldon Vatsaas and his marketing team produced a short movie highlighting Hank's accomplishments and adventures at FishNautics. Immediately following the film, Hank made a few opening remarks, followed by the highly anticipated roasting. Lunch would follow, with a modified, open bar that purposely limited any overindulgence.

The special day went off without a hitch. Hank laughed continuously through most of the roast and couldn't believe how many humorous and often embarrassing moments had occurred during his tenure. However, he took it all in stride and made a point to shake hands personally and thank everyone who attended and contributed to this memorable farewell. He and Lydia held hands as they walked down to his office for the last time. Everyone had departed the premises except Rose and Dylan, who were laughing and joking about the afternoon highlights. Lydia had never visited FishNautic's corporate office and wanted to see where Hank had spent so much time during the past few years. She was impressed with the whole facility and understood Hank's important role in its development. While standing in his office, she added, "I am so proud of you and for what you have accomplished. I couldn't completely appreciate your dedication to this organization until today. So, let's go home and continue the celebration if you know what I mean?"

Hank was up before sunrise and was pacing the kitchen floor. He knew it was the weekend, but the future of VisualFish seemed to have taken control of his thought processes. Even after a night of passionate lovemaking, he was unexpectedly invigorated and full of boundless energy. He wanted to go to the warehouse to start putting plans into action. Then Lydia seductively appeared in the hallway, saying, "Come back to bed. I'm lonely and freezing without you." In a heartbeat, all of Hank's business plans came to a sudden halt.

Winnie knocked forcefully on a milky warehouse window to get his attention. It was the beginning of the week, and Hank was sitting in his new office chair, formulating and prioritizing a thing's to-do list. The intense rapping finally drew Hank out of his trance, and he glanced over to see Winnie's smiling face framed in the window. He rushed to the front door, latched onto his elbow, and pulled Winnie into the room. Hank then made an athletic leap to his new Bunn coffee maker, poured two freshly brewed cups, and slid the first down the counter to Winnie's waiting hand.

Winnie spoke, "Excited is not even close to describing you this morning. Being in business for yourself certainly seems to agree with you!"

Next, Hank exclaimed, "It's not even eight o'clock, and I already have two confirmed local appointments for tomorrow, and I've left messages with at least six more companies requesting a callback. So, I'm telling you, Winnie, right here and now, VisualFish is about to take off!"

Winnie coasted over to a leather-padded Scully & Scully director's chair and thoughtfully nursed his brew. He was not prone to showing his emotions, but he began to connect with his partner's enthusiasm and shouted, "You damn right, this company is going places, and you're the man who's going to make it happen!"

Hank had a grin on his face that rippled from ear to ear. Winnie got to his feet and said, "I came down to see if you needed some encouragement or help on your first day, but obviously, you don't need any assistance from me. I'll check in with you tomorrow to see how many more fires you've lit." Hank didn't hear or see him leave the office as he was busy on the phone with another potential buyer.

Many improvements and refinements materialized from the initial patent during the next few months. With Arnie's ingenuity and Lydia's legal help, Hank was delighted to receive patent approval or pending status on five additional applications that would meticulously protect his invention. Nevertheless, he spent most of his days meeting with skeptical clients who demanded proof that his brainchild could be married to their unique products without compromise. Hank maintained a ninety-five percent success rate with his applications, and the five percent failure rate was due to old technology used by companies that might soon be out of business. At the end of their lease, the snack food company vacated the warehouse overnight. It was eerie to walk into the warehouse and sense the enormity of the facility when it was empty. Hank planned to lower the ceiling, intensify the lighting and add an air filtration and conditioning system to meet ISO standards for clean room certification. After all, computers and their peripherals would occupy most of the newly designed space, producing software and microchips for company applications. He would rely on Arnie's technical expertise to help recruit employees to fill these specialized positions. Hank would build the front office team and a marketing and sales department. Winnie said he would assume the role of Chief Financial Officer, and within six months, he would formally request a buyout for the shares he owned in the law firm where he had made partner. This move made it apparent that Winnie had become an adherent believer.

CHAPTER 55

The years passed in somewhat blurred vision. Sales skyrocketed well into seven figures. With their success, VisualFish acquired several fish finder companies. These acquisitions provided a secure gateway to test new ideas and developments with controlled consequences. It also allowed them to market their product line. Hank witnessed how stagnation and resting on one's laurels had been the demise of untold business ventures. As long as he was at the helm, he would not let this happen to VisualFish. The company buzzwords were loyalty, teamwork, and innovation, and Hank would generously reward employees who personified those traits.

In 1984, after the birth of their first child, Lydia joined the Company as Chief Legal Officer on a part-time basis. She resigned from Strighton and Williams in Edina, wanting to spend the critical, formative years, at home, with Anthony. Hank never imagined how much enjoyment came from being a father. Little Tony touched and reformed their lives. Lydia was a natural when it came to raising a child. Her boundless energy was something to behold. Even on days when she was feeling under the weather, her enthusiasm never faltered. Hank often said, "I don't know how you kept up the pace, but I now nominate you for *Mother of the Year*."

He repeated this phrase when his daughter Melissa was born two years later. Parenthood seemed to agree with them, blessed with two healthy babies so late in their lives. Finally, however, they decided their limit was two children, and they were assured of that number when Hank willingly went under the knife.

Little Tony followed him everywhere he went. He was like a shadow. By the time Tony entered kindergarten, Hank was amazed at how many of his mannerisms and traits were evident in the little guy. He loved to be outdoors and never missed an opportunity to go fishing with him. He called Hank, Pa. Not Papa, Dad, or Daddy, just plain Pa. It was his first word, and Hank was proud to be called Pa.

Melissa, on the other hand, was Mommy's little girl. She had a smile that made you feel warm all over. The two distinct dimples on her rosy cheeks, with wispy blonde hair and a pair of sparkling blue eyes, completed this precious bundle of joy. She perfectly exemplified her Norwegian and Swedish heritage. She loved going on long hikes, picking colorful flowers, and helping Lydia with chores around the house. She also loved reading; unlike girls who became attached to dolls, she became attached to books. Even when she agreed to partake in an afternoon of fishing with the family, she preferred holding a book instead of a fishing rod. She would snuggle down on the front seat of the boat, block the sun with an embossed Little Pony pink umbrella, and then read until her eyes became heavy and gently closed. Hank could not imagine a daughter who was closer to perfection.

Hank was now in his mid-forties. The business ran on all cylinders, and he wanted to spend more time with his family.

Sixty to seventy hours a week had taken its toll on him, and he needed some relief before it was too late. So, he approached the Board, now consisting of Winnie, Arnie, Lydia, and himself, with a proposal to hire an Executive Vice President to oversee company operations.

Lydia had set the groundwork for this change. She witnessed

firsthand the negative impact of the brutal schedule he had maintained for years. She could see it in the trenchlike, dark crevices that appeared overnight across his forehead, the furrowed crow's feet that nested on both sides of his face, and bloodshot eyes from little or no sleep. His ever-increasing short temper with employees and friends was so uncharacteristic of Hank. She had prepared Winnie and Arnie for what was to take place. She wanted the proposal to seem as though it was utterly Hank's idea.

The recruitment of a new VP started immediately. Lydia would do all the prescreening of applicants and conduct initial interviews. Their small Human Resource Department would do reference checking and resume verification of selected finalists. However, the Board members would make the final selection and appointment. Lydia was overwhelmed by the number of viable candidates who applied for the position.

The entire industry knew of VisualFish and its *Cinderella* rise to the top. Many applicants came from companies and were acquainted with Hank in the past. One candidate, in particular, caught everyone off-guard; Rose Climber, Hank's assistant at FishNautics, had thrown her hat in the ring. When Lydia passed the news to Hank, he was surprised and intrigued. He asked himself: *Why would she consider a move after all these years?*

Lydia said, "I know what a dedicated employee she was at FishNautics. I think she deserves an interview, and I'll see if I can arrange it sometime this week. However, I feel you should not be present at this first meeting. I'll analyze her background, education, abilities, and her reasons for making an application. Then, if she can sell herself to me, we'll move her forward. You can rest assured I'll be completely fair, and I'll always consider what's best for the company."

Hank agreed and skittishly walked out of his office. He concealed his jubilation until he had passed through the warehouse door, skirted down the long hallway, and entered the men's room. Once inside, with the outer door securely closed, Hank released a scream of exuberance as his face turned bright red, and his jugular vein looked like it was about to erupt. He took several deep breaths and stared at the stranger in the mirror.

He tried to convince himself that he didn't feel as bad as he looked. *Could Rose be the answer to my unanswered prayers?*

Rose did impress everyone she met in the interview stages. As a result, she was one of the final three candidates invited to meet with the board. Once again, Hank put on his best poker face, never outwardly revealing his pent-up feelings or emotions.

The first of the finalists was a Vice-President of Operations with a major sporting goods company. They had been a direct competitor of Hank's while working at FishNautics. He was aware of the top-down corporate management structure that still existed at this company. After the Board members questioned him, it became evident that his management style would not fit at VisualFish.

Number two was a fascinating individual. He had worked his way up, through the ranks, in the competitive computer industry. He currently holds the position of Chief Information Officer with a sizeable upper-Midwest tech firm. He had earned a Ph.D. in computer science but was bored in his current role and wanted to make changes. The years of working in a controlled lab environment certainly had not helped him develop his communication skills. Although his resume was superb, his interpersonal skills could have improved more. When questioned by the board, his answers could have been more precise and easier to understand. He was unable to make eye contact with anyone in the room. After the grilling, Arnie, in particular, was very vocal about not needing another nerd to join the team. Lydia said she was shocked by what she had just witnessed. One-on-one, he had been amiable, relaxed, and self-assured. However, in front of the Board, it was as though he had taken a Dr. Jekyll potion that transformed him into an unwanted guest. In this case, they all agreed that judging a book by its cover was the proper thing to do.

That left only Rose. Hank remained silent as the other Board members posed their questions. They specifically wanted to know why she had not pursued a career in international business after completing her MBA. Rose explained how her father had been diagnosed with early-stage Alzheimer's Disease. In addition, her mother had passed away several years earlier, and Rose felt it was her responsibility to provide initial care for him as an only child. Then turning in her chair, she looked at Hank and said, "Mr. Wahlberg knew of my circumstances and still offered me a position at FishNautics. Moreover, he approved a flexible work schedule that met all my immediate needs, for which I will always be grateful."

Hank merely nodded as she confidently repositioned herself for more questions. Rose had evolved into a highly skilled professional. Every answer she gave to an array of thought-provoking questions was superb. Finally, after almost two hours, the session ended with a standard response: "Thank you for coming in, and we'll get back to you with our decision in the next few days."

Hank stood and walked over to the large whiteboard on the conference room wall.

He took a dry-erase marker and wrote the names of the three finalists across the top of the Board. Below each name, he added two columns; one titled PROS and one titled CONS. They checked their notes and verbally presented their observations while Hank carefully rendered every word to the appropriate column. Even before he finished the exercise, the board knew the answer. They discussed and agreed on a final salary and benefits package. Lydia would contact Rose to give her the good news, while Hank merely reveled in unaccustomed leisure, visualizing her return.

CHAPTER 56

Hank was hoarsely rattling out another rhythmic note when he suddenly opened his eyes and turned his head toward the silent alarm clock perched within arm's reach. He rubbed his eyes in disbelief. But then, he reflected: *Was it ten o'clock on Monday morning?*

Stark naked, he sprang from the bed and ran down the hallway to the kitchen. Caught by surprise, Lydia expounded, "Hank, you scared the living crap out of me! What's wrong with you?"

He stood motionless for a few seconds and replied, "I've overslept! Why didn't you wake me?"

Calmly, she lowered the book she had been reading and answered, "This is part of your new lifestyle, Hank. You can sleep in when you want to, and the business will not suffer or crumble in your absence. You have a fantastic team, and now you must learn to rely on them."

He breathed a sigh of relief and walked to her side, kissing her gently on the cheek, and murmured, "It was my type A, dark-side rearing up to, once again, meet the day. But I think I can get the hound under control with practice."

She gave him a solid pinch on his firm butt and laughed as he painfully hobbled back to the bedroom.

It was almost noon as he entered the parking lot. He missed his Suburban, but the 930 provided an exhilarating ride that his old

Chevrolet could never replicate. Rose was seated in her new office, and Hank went by the beverage center and poured two cups of brew. Carrying them to the office door, he couldn't knock, so he managed a mild throat-clearing cough. Seeing who was standing in the doorway, Rose rushed around the massive desk and threw her arms around him. Then, realizing what she had just done, she sheepishly released her grip, backed up, and profusely apologized.

Hank laughed and then spouted, "I've never experienced a greeting like this in my entire life! So, don't apologize, but maybe a handshake will suffice in the future?"

He took a seat as she returned to the far side of the desk. She explained how much she missed his management style and felt her talents needed to be more utilized by Mr. Sanders and FishNautics. She methodically analyzed the role of women in FishNautic's corporate structure and knew she was facing an uphill battle for any meaningful recognition or advancement. Whenever she had an opportunity to voice her specific concerns, they seemed to fall on deaf ears.

She then reported, "One of the sales reps from Hot Lures mentioned you were searching for a VP of Operations. Hearing those words was like an answer to my prayers. I had already prepared my resume, knowing I would soon leave FishNautics. So, I thought, what the hell, and I threw my hat in the ring! Rumors were flying about the number of qualified applicants interested in this position, but I was not intimidated."

He finally said, "You know I removed myself from the recruitment process. I was not even aware you had applied for the position until my wife broke the news to me. I could barely restrain myself, but I knew I couldn't interfere or impose any influence. When they announced the finalists, and I had time to review the resumes, I knew, barring some catastrophe, you had an excellent chance of getting the nod."

He closed by saying, "I want to welcome you to the company personally, and in the coming days, I want to explain my expectations and review your job description in detail." Hank left her office as a warm feeling came over him.

Winnie was standing in the conference room, talking with the Production Manager, Paul Nordstrom. They were discussing the influx of new orders, and in particular, an enormous order that had come from a German company named FischSucher.

Paul argued they would have to purchase additional equipment to handle this order, and Winnie suggested leasing may be a better alternative. Hank stood quietly in the hallway while this intense conversation took place. Hank would have stepped into the room in the old days, postured himself, and made decisions without further discussion. Instead, taking a lesson from Lydia's playbook, he did not enter the room but remained as quiet and observant as a fly on the wall. Paul presented his thoughts and reasons for purchasing the needed equipment. Winnie continued and waited until he had finished his argument.

Then, using his courtroom experience, he presented his case for leasing that negated the purchasing option. Once Paul heard the rationale, he reached out, shook Winnie's hand, and left the room, taking ownership of the new plan.

Paul had not noticed him standing against the wall, and Winnie was enjoying the thralls of victory as he settled comfortably into one of the conference room chairs.

Hank discretely returned to his office. He couldn't wait to get home to tell Lydia of his newfound success. He was like an alcoholic taking the first of twelve steps.

CHAPTER 57

It was early June 1989 when Winnie created a stir by arriving at the office before noon. Even Hank was surprised to see his Ferrari parked out front as he nosed his 930 into the lot.

Hank didn't even stop for his needed caffeine fix but hustled down to Winnie's office. He had his legs stretched out on the corner section of the desk and an uncharacteristic smile on his face.

Hank declared, "You're living proof that the dead do rise! So, what in the world are you doing here this early?"

Winnie dropped his feet to the floor, looked Hank directly in the eyes, and exclaimed, "I'm getting married! When I was down in Mexico last week, I proposed to Camila, and she accepted. The wedding will take place in six weeks, so bone up on your Spanish and get your passport in order." Hank reached out and gave Winnie a firm embrace. He stood back, smiled, and said, "Congratulations, you rascal! I never thought I'd live to see this day."

Within minutes, the word had spread throughout the facility like wildfire. Winnie repeated his story to everyone he met, always energized and energized. Hank thought about the world of Camila, and he couldn't have been happier for the couple as he reflected on the impact of marriage in his life. Finally, he phoned Lydia with the news, and she squealed, "I'm jumping in my car right now. Don't let Winnie leave until I get there!"

As he hung up the phone, he turned to see Winnie and

Camila rushing into his office.

Winnie sputtered, "She flew in early this morning, took a taxi from the airport, sneaked into my office, and scared the living daylights out of me!"

Hank jumped to his feet, dashed over, and hugged her, lifting her completely off her feet. Then, he exclaimed, "Camila, you've certainly cast a spell on this dyed-in-the-wool bachelor. He hasn't been this emotional since he purchased the Testarossa. I am so happy for both of you!"

Camila, in perfect English, explained their wedding plans in great detail. Because of the size of her family, they would be married in her church in Santa Maria. Winnie agreed wholeheartedly. There was no remaining family members after losing his only cousin in a tragic car accident.

Hank asked, "Where do you intend to call home after you're married?" Suddenly the room went silent. Neither Winnie nor Camila said a word in response to his question.

Finally, Hank broke the silence with, "Did I say something wrong?"

The skin on Winnie's face turned ghostly pale and was as tight as a snare drum when he muttered, "We'll be residing in my downtown Minneapolis condo for a while."

Hank dropped the subject and was grateful to see Lydia coming down the hallway like a jubilant jogger at the finish line. She offered her congratulations but was surprised to see Camila in the room. Once again, Hank listened politely to their orchestrated plans but needed clarification and clarification about the response to his previous question.

Camila suggested they go to lunch. After spending a night in Dallas and catching an early morning flight to Minneapolis, she was offered disgusting, highly preserved pastries and lukewarm coffee as the day's meal. She respectfully rejected the fare. She was now famished.

Lydia suggested Nicklow's Greek Restaurant in Robbinsdale. They all agreed, loaded themselves into Lydia's Lexus, and headed south on Highway 100. Hank and Lydia found themselves treated to some excellent homemade Greek specialties. They each ordered Moussaka layered with tomato sauce, sweet eggplant, and cooked minced beef.

Winnie and Camila settled for Pastitsio, a baked pasta dish with ground beef and béchamel sauce. They all shared a liberal serving of flaky Baklava for dessert. At the end of the meal, several Greek belly dancers entertained them. Dance students from the University of Minnesota were hired as on-the-job trainees to engage the less demanding afternoon crowd at meager wages. Winnie and Hank appreciated their efforts by clapping and cheering while they consumed several shots of Ouzo. The ladies nursed a single glass of Roditis Rose as they pretended to ignore the exotic display of beads and flesh. Together, they made several impromptu toasts to marital bliss and happiness before the merriment ended. Then they gleefully, arm in arm, promenaded across the parking lot to the waiting car.

Lydia was the designated driver and transported the revelers back to Spring Lake Park. Camila immediately got into the driver's seat of the Testarossa, and reluctantly, Hank agreed to leave the 930 parked in his designated spot until the next day. They said their goodbyes, and as they drove down Central Avenue, Hank told her about the awkward situation that had arisen when he asked a question about where they would reside after the wedding. Lydia pooh-poohed the silence and the delayed response as pre-wedding jitters, but it did not convince Hank.

CHAPTER 58

With the wedding only a week away, Hank and Lydia realized that no one else from Minnesota would be attending the event. Arnie was busy with an out-state work assignment, and nobody from Winnie's old law firm even responded to the invitations. Rose would not attend because someone had to stay home and manage the business. None of this seemed to bother Winnie. He was at the office daily, working with Rose and other team leaders to ensure his plans and responsibilities would be strictly adhered to in his absence. But Hank could not shake his uneasiness as he watched Winnie go through the motions. He appeared to have developed a severe case of PYA. Something was not right. However, Hank would not discuss his concerns and suspicions with anyone, including his wife. Maybe Winnie's reluctance to share his plans was a figment of Hank's imagination, as Lydia had suggested. But for now, he'd put a cap on this *stinkin' thinkin'* and celebrate this special occasion.

Hank and Lydia arrived at Xoxocotlán International Airport in Oaxaca after fourteen hours, with one stop in Dallas. Then, they rented a car and drove the forty-six miles up to Santa Maria, Jaltianguis.

Hank knew the area well and was ready for treacherous Highway 175. Going through the mountains is a scenic drive, but not for the faint of heart. So, he told Lydia to take a couple of Dramamine tablets before they started the journey.

The drive took almost four hours, with the last hour in total darkness. As they drove up to the villa's security gates, they were greeted by two intimidating security guards dressed in full military apparel and armed with AR-15s.

One of the men spoke fluent English and asked for their IDs. He found their names on a clipboard list and signaled his partner to open the heavy, wrought iron gates. He said, "*Senor*, please drive up to the courtyard, and someone will assist you with your luggage, park your car and show you to your room. *Gracias y buenas noches.*"

As they drove slowly up the pathway, Lydia remarked, "That was quite a welcome! Do you think we should be concerned?"

Hank glanced at her and said, "This kind of security was never in place on my previous visits. So maybe they've had some trouble. I'm sure Winnie will have some explanation!"

Lights erupted from everywhere as they stopped in front of the villa. Two men dressed in formal, black Mariachi outfits appeared out of nowhere. First, they formally welcomed them to the estate. Then, transferring their luggage to a magnificent gold trolley, they were directed through a pair of twelve-foot, lacquered entrance doors into a spacious foyer. A beautiful senorita, dressed in a traditional white, Oaxacan maxi dress, escorted them to their suite. Their accommodations resembled a five-star hotel, with a gigantic four-poster bed on an elevated mahogany platform. The bathroom featured a sunken jacuzzi tub and a walk-in shower, large enough to accommodate a small army. After they had time to freshen up and unpack their cases, they went to the main dining hall for a late dinner.

Winnie did not make an appearance, and when they had finished their meal, they went directly back to their quarters.

A maid tapped on their door in the morning and asked if they would like breakfast in bed or enjoy eating in the courtyard with several other guests. They dressed and were seated in a fabulous, enclosed atrium at the very heart of the villa within an hour. They ordered coffee and tried deciphering a Mexican menu when Winnie and Camila strolled up to their table. They exchanged hugs, and Winnie apologized for not meeting them when they arrived. Camila said they would join them for breakfast, but they had to make the rounds to seven other tables to introduce Winnie to her side of the family. The formalities took over an hour, and they consumed several cups of Café De Olla coffee before Winnie and Camila returned. Lydia said, "Thank goodness you're back. We're starving, and we need your help with the menu."

Camila laughed and said, "I'll translate, and you stop me when it tickles your fancy, and together we'll place an order."

Hank couldn't remember having a more delicious breakfast, with huevos rancheros cooked to perfection. Lydia decided on a hot pan of Mexican scrambled eggs served with various red and green chili peppers. Camila and Winnie had eaten an early breakfast, so they settled on two cups of Lucas dark roast and several Coyota cookies laced with cinnamon and brown sugar.

When they had finished eating, Winnie asked if they would like to tour the entire hacienda. Hank commented as they walked around the grounds, "You've certainly made some major additions and changes since I last visited. I don't recall a security force like this one. What gives?"

Winnie explained that the sleepy little village of Santa Maria was suffering from growing pains. He said, "Tourists, in particular, have brought attention to this slice of paradise, and with more people, there is more crime. I've suffered three burglaries in the past year and vandalism to some of my buildings and equipment. When I purchased an additional two hundred acres that adjoined the north side of my property, jealousy seemed to erupt from some of the impoverished locals and outsiders. My in-house staff can't effectively patrol the premises, but I have some friends in the local cartel who, for a price, have agreed to provide security. So far, it's worked, and crime has become a non-issue."

Hank replied, "I guess fighting fire with fire is an answer. But it sure as hell can rattle your nerves when you face a semiautomatic assault weapon in a quasi-military setting."

CHAPTER 59

It was a picture-perfect day for a wedding. Temperatures were in the 80s, and humidity so low that it could rival Death Valley, California, in mid-July.

The stately towers of Iglesia De Santa Maria Jaltianguis Catholic Church had received a thorough power wash and were gleaming in the late afternoon sunlight. The long, whitewashed church sanctuary had seating for about two hundred people, but on this day, it was packed with wedding guests, leaving standing-room-only for latecomers.

Winnie had asked Hank to be his best man, and Lydia was to be one of Camila's bridesmaids. The wedding party was picked up at the Villa by four beautifully decorated, horse-drawn carriages that would have made Queen Elizabeth II envious. They escorted the bride and groom-to-be into the first coach, and the rest of the wedding party scrambled for seats in the next three.

As they made their way to the center of town, the streets were lined with well-wishers, each pitching a variety of flower petals at the lead coach as it passed. Members of the wedding party entered the church first, positioning themselves at their assigned posts. Hank and Lydia stood on alternate sides in front of the church altar. Winnie, unescorted, made his way to the front of the church. He waited patiently for his bride to be ushered down the aisle by her father. The priest placed a cross above the groom's face and asked him to kiss it, signifying faithfulness and trust in a marriage. Camila repeated the ritual. She wore a simple white silk dress with elaborate floral embroidery that engulfed the upper half of the gown. Winnie wore a traditional black suit with an embroidered white-collar shirt called a Guayabera. Camila's youngest sister had her six-year-old son become the ring bearer, and her five-year-old daughter was the flower girl. Like many weddings, it became highly emotional as the ceremony progressed. Everyone seemed to be vicariously living out their past or future. Finally, cheering erupted as the priest gave his final blessing and presented the new couple to the congregation.

The wedding reception was held at their Villa because there needed to be a facility in Santa Maria to accommodate the large gathering. Festivities went on well into the wee hours of the morning, but Winnie and his bride left early to catch a honeymoon flight to Rome, Italy. Hank and Lydia volunteered to drive them to the airport in Oaxaca but would stay the evening at an airport hotel, not risking a return trip up the treacherous 175 in the middle of the night. Winnie invited them to stay at the Villa for as long as they wanted. Getting to any major tourist traps or beaches from Santa Maria was challenging, but the price was right, and they would persevere.

After two more weeks of enjoying Mexican food, sundrenched beaches, and complementary villa accommodations, they scheduled a return flight to reality. They both appreciated this part of Mexico and decided a return trip was definitely in the cards. As they lifted from the airport in Oaxaca, Hank was troubled about Winnie. But not wanting to upset Lydia, he kept his uneasy feelings in check during the flight home.

Their kids were staying with Lydia's cousin in Hudson, Wisconsin, so when they left the airport, they went east on Interstate 94 directly to her cousin's home. Tony heard the car in the driveway and ran across the front porch, yelling at Hank, "I'm so happy you made it home; did you bring me a gift?" But when Lydia stepped out of the car, Melissa bolted over to her with tears in her eyes, hugged her mom, and cooed, "I missed you so much when you were gone. Please don't ever go away again!"

They thanked Lydia's cousin for watching the children, and ten minutes later, they were on their way home.

As they entered their driveway off Lexington Avenue, Hank experienced a senior moment when he could not remember the combination of the entrance gate. He looked at Lydia, gulped, and quietly mouthed, "Help!"

She slowly lifted her hand and digitally fingered the gate combination so he could see it without alerting the children. Hank grinned while punching the numbers into the keyboard and felt relief as they swung open.

When they finally climbed into bed just before midnight, she lovingly said, "What happened to you at the gate this evening?"

Hank stammered, "I don't know. I just drew a complete blank. It honestly scared the shit out of me. I've never felt so completely helpless, and thank God you were there to rescue me."

She whispered, "We've all experienced moments like that, Hank. You didn't get any sleep on the plane, so let's see what a good night's sleep will do for you."

Hank sighed, turned over, and was lightly snoring within seconds. However, she lay awake for half an hour, unable to nullify her vivid concerns for him.

Hank woke up feeling refreshed. After all, it was mid-afternoon the following day, and he had been asleep for fifteen hours. His overactive bladder hadn't even awakened him. He could hear Lydia singing a familiar children's song in the kitchen. Melissa must be helping her because he could hear her squeaky little voice trying to add some harmony to the tune. Then the mouthwatering smell of chocolate chip cookies baking in the oven wafted into the bedroom, and Hank jumped to his feet. He silently sneaked down the hallway and peered into the kitchen as she placed the heavenly morsels on a cooling rack.

Melissa saw him first and ran to him, saying, "Pa, guess what I did? I helped Mommy bake cookies! Do you wanna try one?"

Then, picking her up and giving her a kiss and hug, he said, "I'll pour myself a coffee, and you and Mommy surprise me with the biggest cookie on the tray."

Lydia smiled and said, "You look like your old self. Sleep sure has a way of healing the body and the mind. Your head no sooner hit the pillow, and you were dead to the world."

He answered, "I didn't know how much the trip to Mexico took out of me. I'm calling Rose right now, and I'll tell her we made it home safely, but we won't be coming to the office until tomorrow morning. I've got more important things to do, like eating chippers with my two favorite girls."

CHAPTER 60

Early September was his favorite time of the year. Fall was in the air, and fishing was on Hank's mind. Winnie and Camila returned from their honeymoon and settled nicely into his Minneapolis condo. Finally, married life seemed to agree with him as he paraded around the office daily with an unshakeable smile. Everyone in the office noticed the difference. They could approach him with problems and concerns without the old fear of having their heads chopped off for bringing issues to his attention. Yes, Winnie was a new man, and Hank felt immense guilt for losing faith in his friend.

Hank received a phone call from his brother Arvid. He explained that he and his buddies Normie Spicer and Ken Newstrom were planning another trip to Keezheekoni and wanted to know if he had the time or interest in going with them. Arvid said, "I'll take my new Ford F250, 4x4, and piggyback two boats on my trailer. Four of us can fit comfortably into the extended cab, but having a second vehicle in the wilderness is always peace of mind.

Hank replied, "I told my wife last night I was getting antsy for another trip to Canada before freeze-up. So I'll call Joe Watkins and see if he would be interested in making the excursion. Joe purchased a Toyota Land Cruiser and is dying to put the behemoth through its paces. My boat and trailer are ready to go, but I'll check with Joe to be sure he has a two-inch ball on the drawbar, and the wiring works with an American four-prong plug. Those foreign vehicles can sometimes be a real pain in the ass!"

Arvid sputtered, "Give him a call! We leave on Saturday morning and plan to be gone for three weeks. We can meet you guys at the Cenex gas station in Knife River, just north of Duluth on 61. By the way, the Indian cabin is unavailable on this trip, so bring your tent, sleeping bags, and any other needed creature comforts you can pack. Normie is bringing a Coleman camp stove, a foldable picnic table, and a screened canopy."

He added, "Ken wants to bring his porta-potty as he can't stand crapping in the woods while devoured by black flies and mosquitos. Call me this evening to confirm the plans."

Joe was ecstatic when he received the invitation. He juggled a few family commitments but would be at Hank's home on Saturday morning at six o'clock sharp. He had checked the drawbar, coupled to a two-inch ball, but he had to go to the Toyota dealer in Bloomington and get financially ripped off for a seven-pin to four-pin adapter plug.

It was late afternoon on Sunday when they finally reached the shores of Keezheekoni. Their trip through northern Minnesota and into the wilds of Ontario proved to be one of the easiest they had ever made. Their only problem was getting down the last five hundred meters to the lake. Summer storms had blown over several trees, which required chainsaws to clear the trail. Two deep washouts at the first curve caused both vehicles to bottom out. They had to use a ratcheting come-along and farm jack to break free. Then, finally, they maneuvered their trailers into the rock-filled water and carefully unloaded the boats. The water level was shallow, and a green fall bloom, thick as glue, had settled on the surface. It smelled of decaying matter resembling a skunk gland's sulfuric spray.

They made several quick trips to their campsite on the lake's east side, hauling equipment and gear.

Luckily, the sandy beach spread along that part of the lake had no algae bloom, and the water was crystal clear. So, the tents were set up and dry, and cedar driftwood was set ablaze within a hastily constructed ring of rocks just as the sunset. Then, as they unfolded their lawn chairs and were about to settle in around the fire, Ken opened a cooler of Labatt Blue and yelled, "Come n' get it! There will be no fishing tonight. Just good beer, fresh air, exaggerated bullshit, and some of my smoked, homemade, venison-jerky."

Hank remembered bringing a Sony boombox, and Arvid had a box full of country music on cassette tapes. George Jones, Hank Thompson, Johnny Paycheck, and several other artists sent musical, sing-along shockwaves across the water until midnight.

Hank reflected that Ryman Auditorium couldn't have been better on a Saturday night in Nashville.

A full moon appeared and cast its softened, golden shimmer across the camp as each of the revelers zipped into their sleeping bags. There was no wind, and the only sounds heard were the distant din of turbulent whitewater as it entered the far side of the lake and an occasional grunting snore from one of the three tents. Hank lay awake thinking about the day and was already planning an assault on his favorite pike haunts when he noticed a shadow forming on his side of the tent. It grew larger and larger, soon encompassing the whole wall. Finally, he could hear the muffled crunch of an animal's paws in the soft sand. The tent was next to a ridge of brush that channeled along the entire edge where Hank slept. Suddenly, the visitor was on a narrow path between the vegetation on one side and the tent wall on the other. Shifting, it took one step onto the canvas covering, lost its balance, and fell directly on top of him. Hank drew his left arm from the sleeping bag, and with all his strength, he slammed his fist into the intruder's side. A loud, painful roar spilled out from the animal's mouth.

Then somehow, it managed to get to its feet, bounded over the nearby brush, and disappear into the darkness. Hank managed to shout only one word, "Bear!"

Awakened from a beer-induced sleep, Joe looked at him and mumbled, "You must've been dreaming. Now go back to sleep!" Members of the other two tents repeated this sentiment, and silence again filled the air.

Hank was out of the tent at the crack of dawn. He examined the evidence. Two sets of claw marks had viciously penetrated the canvas and several deep tracks that started at the water's edge and ended up too close for comfort. Hank let everyone sleep as he relived the nightmare, over and over, while sipping on a soothing cup of fresh brew. Then, blurry-eyed and zombielike, each member saw the evidence, and candid details of the whole event. Nobody said a word, but everyone thought: *better him than me!*

The flotilla of three Lund boats set out just after breakfast.

They sent each boat to a known pike hot spot, and they would meet back at camp around noon to review their efforts and have a bite to eat.

Hank and his brother were teammates for the day, but their attempts at catching a big pike were unsuccessful. After hundreds of casts that produced occasional cabbage weed, they decided to hang it up for the morning. Arvid had a terrible time getting the old Johnson outboard to fire up. He pulled on the recoiled starter rope at least twenty times. With curse words becoming more frequent, Arvid's face flushed crimson red. The engine finally started but was only running on one of two cylinders. They nursed the craft back to camp, and Arvid began rummaging through his tackle box, looking for a new set of Champion spark plugs. They still had over an hour before meeting for lunch, so Hank pulled out a two-liter bottle of Canadian Club and said, "It's five o'clock somewhere, so let's enjoy three fingers to see if it'll change our luck!"

As they sat at the picnic table under the bright blue canopy, Arvid observed, "The wind is picking up from the west. High pressure is moving in, and fishing should pick up this afternoon. So, let's finish our drinks, and I'll put the new plugs into the motor, and we'll test it."

Hank pushed the boat off the shoreline and waded into the incoming waves. Then, finally, he shouted, "Arvid, grab an oar and help me turn the boat around so we're facing into the wind."

Then he rolled and hoisted himself into the boat just as the engine came to life. Arvid hit the throttle, and the front end of the Lund rose to forty-five degrees and then settled down into a level plane. They cruised confidently, back and forth across the wind-swept waters, while the engine never missed a beat. Now convinced that it was a plug problem, they turned the boat toward camp. As the bow scooted onto the sandy beach, Hank noticed the canopy had partially collapsed over the picnic table and groaned, "The wind sure raised hell with our dining room. We'll have to put down some more stakes to secure it."

As he was about to leave of the boat, he froze, took a deep breath, and said, "I think we have company. There's a steaming bear scat on the beach right here, and pieces of paper towel are spread around the site."

Hank carefully exited the boat and slowly made his way to the downed canopy while Arvid remained seated in the rear with the Johnson still idling at the ready. He examined several rolls of paper towels that had massive bites taken out of them. The paper towels stuffed in grocery bags had several loaves of bread squeezed next to them. The towels had absorbed the bread odor, and the bear couldn't tell the difference. When it bit a mouthful of paper and discovered it wasn't edible, it simply spits out the shreds, leaving a huge mess. Hank managed to get the canopy back on its legs and retied several nylon anchor ropes when he glanced at the whiskey bottle in the middle of the table. Its plastic cap was gone, and bear drool completely coated the outside of the container. The bear had drunk the entire contents of the bottle. He turned and walked back to the boat and told Arvid to turn off the motor.

He grumbled, "Not only do we have a hungry bear in the area, but we have one who is highly intoxicated. It had probably been fattening up on fermenting fall blueberries, and it couldn't resist the enticing smell coming from the opened bottle of Club. He sucked down the entire contents like a baby getting its first milk feeding. When the boys return, we'll build a raised cache to safely store our staples out of harm's way."

They could hear the two boats coming across the lake as they finished a meal of franks and beans.

Fishing had been lousy for them too, and they welcomed a mid-day meal break. Hank told the second bear story of the day, and although they had cleaned up most of the chaos, they kept a couple of half-eaten rolls of paper and the slimy whiskey bottle as visual proof. After eating, Ken and Normie took a boat, returned to the parked vehicles, and loaded hand tools, a chainsaw, and a box of screws and nails.

They completed the cache in less than two hours and built a sturdy, removable ladder that allowed easy access to the elevated platform. With about two hours of daylight left, all three boats departed for a weed bed in front of the Indian cabin. Using the latest VisualFish locator, Hank identified several large pike sounding in about twenty feet of water. They appeared to be waiting for a school of walleyes, who generally start feeding in the shallows as the sun settles. They baited up with deep-diving HookSet lures painted to resemble a small walleye or perch. Within seconds, each boat was battling a monster pike. The furious action continued until sunset, subsiding as fast as it had begun. They all thought they should get back to camp before dark. The boats slowly approached the campsite, and each angler was highly apprehensive.

They remained in their boats, visually looking for any signs of an unwanted trespasser. However, everything appeared normal as they cautiously approached the tents. Ken and Joe collected some kindling branches and started a small fire. Arvid placed several large pieces of dried cedar on the fledgling flames, and they instantly exploded into a welcomed bonfire. Normie announced, "Dinner will be ready in about ten minutes. Tonight's main course will be Dinty Moore Beef Stew, hot chili peppers, and the remains of a partially eaten white bread. Hopefully, fresh walleye will be on tomorrow's menu."

Another evening of tall tales, laughter, good country music, and several bottles of ice-cold Blue continued until the hot flames in the pit had cooled to mashed orange and black embers. Finally, they gathered in the distant brush for a final beer piss before heading to their respective tents. No one wanted to venture out alone, considering what had happened in the past twenty-four hours.

CHAPTER 61

The air temperature had dropped significantly overnight.

Daylight disclosed some gnarly dark clouds sputtering a few light snowflakes. Nevertheless, the lake water felt warm as Hank brushed his teeth and washed his whiskered face. Ken was also up early and joined him on the beach, saying, "Thank goodness; we packed warm clothing for this trip. Who would've thunk we could go from the low eighties to freezing in a matter of hours!"

Hank nodded and replied, "Finish your morning ritual, and let's go up the north shoreline and catch a few lingering walleyes before they retreat to deep water."

The rest of the camp was dormant as they forced the boat free from the gripping sand and paddled silently away from the dock. They started the outboard when they were far from hearing and motored directly to the significant drop-off, just off the Indian cabin. Hank knew most of the walleyes survived last night's pike ambush, so they dropped anchor in that spot and began casting small, yellow, plastic jigs. The walleyes were still present, and they had almost caught their limit within twenty minutes. Hank made his final cast and set the hook into what he thought was a good-sized walleye. The fish made two prolonged, lengthy runs toward the weeded bay but never surfaced and was pulling the boat as it swam forward. Hank had the drag set perfectly on the lightweight Shimano reel but made no progress in trying to control the fish. Finally, she moved into a shallow cove where the water was less than three feet deep. Ken managed to use an oar to turn the boat around as the fish suddenly stopped moving along the boat's port side.

The water was dark, but they could see a reflected outline of the fish. Finally, Hank yelled, "Ken, she's a monster pike! Get the landing net, and I'll try to lead the fish into it."

Then Ken screamed, "There's no net in the boat. So, what're we going to do now?

Hank replied, "Take my felt pen and mark a spot on the gunwale where you see the end of her tail. Then hand me the pen, and I'll mark the front of her mouth on the bow. I'll never land this giant, but at least we'll know its length."

The pike had enough of this nonsense and began moving toward deeper water. It abruptly rose to the surface, snapped her head in one vicious, circular motion, and the pike was free as it tossed into the air. The fish seemed to look back at the boat for a moment as it rested on the surface, and then with a ferocious slap of her tail, she vanished.

Hank grew weak in the knees, lost his balance, and began to topple overboard. Ken grasped his feet and held on for dear life, preventing a near catastrophe. Then, lying in a prone position, he yelled, "Hank! Are you okay? I'm trying to pull you back into the boat, but I need your help! Answer me!"

Hank raised his face from the water and fumbled to grip the oar lock on the gunwale. Once he got ahold of it, he could twist and jerk himself sideways, and with Ken's help, plunked himself safely back onto the metal hull. Hank, totally spent, grunted, "What the hell happened? I felt myself falling, and the next thing I knew, I was gasping for air, and you were yelling something at me while pulling on my legs. I must've gone into shock! Thank the Lord you were there!"

Hank rested for several minutes and then pulled himself up

on the front seat.

He reached for his tackle box, pulled out a tape line, and said, "By Jesus, we're going to measure the length of that fish right now! So, hold the end of the tape on your mark, and I'll stretch it out to mine."

He looked at Ken in disbelief. The pike measured a full sixty-seven inches, and according to the *weight-to-length chart* he had glued inside his tackle box, her weight was almost seventy-two pounds.

The words came slowly, but Hank finally managed to say, "Do you realize that pike was a new world record, and I have no way of proving it! Let's take our walleye catch and go back to camp. I need a powerful shot of something to help settle my nerves!"

Everyone listened intently to their story, and although they were disappointed, he and Ken posed for pictures beside the two blackened marks that epitomized nothing but a memory. Then, as Hank downed another tin cup full of Normie's Cutty Sark, he roared, "Here's a toast to the one that got away, left to fight another day!" They all raised beverages and yelled in unison, "Hear, hear!"

They decided a freshly caught meal of walleye would lift their spirits, and Chef Normie, a role he coveted, was heating two black cast-iron pans on the Coleman stove. Arvid took a piece of weathered plywood and his seven-inch Wusthof knife and produced twenty-four boneless filets in minutes. Joe cut up some sweet Vidalia onions while Hank and Ken peeled and sliced a bowl of russets. They were like ravenous rats as they sat at the table and gorged themselves on the beer-battered fillets and all the fixings.

The air was still cool, but the sun had come out as they

reposed around another open fire, sipping a beer and trying desperately to digest the delicious grub they had just inhaled. Normie was giving a dissertation on the current plight of the Indian population. His opening remark was, "The only good injun is a dead injun," and from there, it went downhill. Next, he explained how being raised near three Indian tribes made him aware of their tendencies for drunkenness, theft, domestic violence, disregard for personal property, and hatred for white people, to name a few. He was about to go into another tirade against native people when he was interrupted by footsteps and conversation coming along the beach. It was a family of five native Cree, two adults, and three children, heading to their cabin on the north side of the lake.

The leader waved his hand and uttered a soft hello while the other members continued in single file past the camp, making no eye contact with anyone. Normie, a retired teacher with an imposing six foot seven inches of height and over three hundred pounds of well-nourished fat, got up from his lawn chair and was about to make more unwanted, despotic remarks when he suddenly clammed up. One of the children, a boy about ten years old, had turned around and was walking back to the camp. He was holding an object in his hand. Hank walked over to meet him, and they exchanged a few words. Hank took the thing from the young man and firmly shook his hand. Then, saying nothing more, he turned and ran to catch up with his family. Hank strolled back to the gathering and took a seat.

Normie looked at him and snarled, "What was going on down there? I hope he wasn't begging for something! If you give them something of value, they'll keep coming back for more. It's their nature!"

Hank turned to him and hollered, "Normie, why don't you

just shut the fuck up! I am so sick and tired of your rants and raves that I could puke! That young boy found a wallet in the water and returned it to its owner, who just happened to be me. When we returned from fishing this morning, it must've fallen out of my back pocket. So, I'm telling you, here and now, keep your god-damned indigenous opinions to yourself for the rest of this trip, or you'll never go on another one! I think I speak for everyone here!"

Heads nodded, and Normie didn't utter a word for the rest of the day.

CHAPTER 62

The lost wallet incident was but a memory as they entered the third week of the outing. Normie had remained in check since the confrontation and tried to engage in everyday conversation. However, with the unprecedented, day-to-day changes in the weather, fishing had been very hit-or-miss.

Additionally, another problem arose. A forest fire was burning in the area, and thick smoke engulfed the lake. Burning eyes and irritating coughs made life miserable for everyone.

Two days before leaving Keezheekoni, Hank decided to take a walk back to their parked rigs and invited Arvid to come along. Following an old moose trail, they would travel three miles through rough terrain. Once back with the vehicles, they would walk up the cleared entrance trail to the high ground. As they came out at the top of the trailhead, flames, and raining embers greeted them—from jack and white pine trees burning less than a mile away. The east wind was pushing the fire directly toward them, and they bolted down the hill and high-tailed it back to camp.

Reaching the base just before sundown, Hank howled, "Pack up your gear, break down the tents, and load everything into the boats as quickly as possible. We have a massive fire heading our way. We must get back to the vehicles and try to protect them the best way we can. Keep your sleeping bags handy because we'll probably spend the night floating on the water."

They worked like a team of trained Navy Seals, *and* in less than twenty minutes, they were motoring south to the boat landing. When they arrived, Arvid and Joe ran to their trucks and removed several plastic containers of gas and two small tanks of LP. They placed them neatly in a nearby creek and used anchor rope to secure them to exposed tree roots so they wouldn't drift away. Joe found several five-gallon buckets in the back of the Toyota and told everyone to fill them with water. They lined up like an old-fashioned English fire brigade and poured bucket after bucket on the defenseless vehicles, saturating the ground around them. They could see no blitzing flames through the trees, but the unmistakable roar of the fire could be heard in the distance, joined by an occasional ember that seemed to parachute from the sky leisurely. The boats were anchored just off the rocky shoreline in preparation for a hasty retreat. Night had fallen, and an ominous, orange glow hovered in the eastern sky as they looked to the heavens.

They took two-hour watches throughout the night, paying close attention to the trail that meandered up the hill. Floating in the boat's safety, Hank fully understood why the Native Tribes called this water Keezheekoni. The distant flames of color, reflecting in the rippling water, made it appear as if the water was on fire. The translation *Burning Fire* took on a new meaning as the flickering spectacle nearly hypnotized him.

When morning came, most of the smoke that had covered the lake was gone. Joe and Normie decided to hustle up the hill and assess the damage. When they emerged from the forest, they couldn't believe their eyes. Overnight, the wind had shifted to the west and had forced the flames to recede over burnt and smoldering ashes, miraculously extinguishing the fire.

Except for a few minor hot spots, the main trail leading out was free of obstructions. They rushed back to the gang with the good news. They took a vote and unanimously decided to load the boats and get out while the getting was good. Hank and Joe voted to stay another two days, but being outvoted, they reluctantly agreed to the immediate departure. Unfortunately, on the way out, they witnessed the widespread destruction that the fire had caused. The fire had consumed thousands of trees, and the carnage could be seen on both sides of the trail as they guardedly drove the twenty-five miles out to the connecting logger road. When they arrived in Armstrong, they stopped by Victor Lowbranch's home and reported the fire information to him. Victor worked part-time with the Ontario Department of Natural Resources and would pass this data to the fire crews battling blazes in two adjacent areas.

Victor explained, "We're short-staffed in this part of the province, and if a fire poses no immediate threat to people or structures, we often let it burn itself out. Fire is just a part of nature that you must accept when you reside in the trees. I hope to see you guys again next spring, eh? Call me in April, and I'll arrange for you to use the Indian cabin so you're not lugging your camping gear. Have a safe trip home, eh?"

CHAPTER 63

Hank declared that fall in Minnesota was the best time of the year, but he repeated the exact words about the other recurring seasons. This year, 1999, he was determined to drive up the North Shore of Lake Superior with his family to witness the leaves changing. Work had always taken precedence over family, but with a well-oiled team at VisualFish, he assured himself that he was about to start practicing the Roman metaphor, *carpe diem,* for real.

First, Hank established a monthly mystery date for an entire calendar year. He and Lydia would alternate months in creating and planning a special event or activity that would surprise the other partner. He wanted to add some spectacular excitement to his already perfect marriage.

Next, they asked the children to plan a monthly family event involving the whole family. Again, every member had to swear they would support and enjoy the choices, even if it weren't their favorite thing to do. Lydia and the children appreciated the tremendous changes in Pa, especially the absence of bad moods and a short temper. For once in his life, the role of husband and father took meaning. Although he always tried to mask his shortcomings at work, Rose, in particular, always knew when things weren't quite right. The employees first witnessed and applauded the changes in Winnie's behavior, but now they were treated to a double whammy with Hank getting on board. After that, life was pretty damn good in the *Walhberg world.*

Although Hank had already experienced an early taste of Winter on his last fishing trip to Canada, a major October snowstorm in the Twin Cities was unexpected. Twenty-two inches of wet, heart-attack snow had fallen overnight, still coming down, with no end in sight. WCCO Radio announced business and school closures and emphasized that no one should attempt to go out until the snow subsided. Plow trucks were out in force, but the white stuff accumulated more than three inches per hour and they could not keep up with the storm. In addition, the temperature was dropping, expecting gale force winds in the late afternoon. These conditions are how Minnesotans define the word blizzard.

Camila had never seen snow. As she stood on the balcony of their downtown condo, she was mesmerized by the white blanket that smothered everything in its path. She reached out and plucked several big flakes with a pair of strange hand covers called mittens.

She yelled, "Winnie, come over and look at these beautiful creations!" But they had melted and were gone when he reached her side.

He explained to her, "No two snowflakes are alike. Each crystal has a unique design, with duplication impossible."

She extended her hands over the balcony and let the magic happen. Winnie had purchased two insulated *North Face* winter jackets, Sorel boots, insulated long underwear, and several other pieces of winter gear. He would take her to Hank's ranch as soon as the weather improved and introduce her to cross-country skiing and maybe a ride on a snowmobile.

Hank had purchased a Polaris Ranger equipped with a seven-foot Myers plow. He had been working all night on his mile-long driveway, trying to keep up with the storm. Hank kept his driveway clear of snow, but like a bridge to nowhere, his efforts came to an abrupt halt as Hank faced an impenetrable, six-foot barrier of ice and snow on Lexington Avenue. With its front loader, he would need his John Deere tractor to remove the blockade, but only when the snow subsided. He returned to the garage and phoned Rose to see the conditions in Spring Lake Park. She had recently purchased a new home less than a mile from the office.

She answered on the first ring, "Hank, I've never experienced a snowfall like this. It just keeps coming and coming, with seemingly no end in sight. I put on my dad's Alaskan snowshoes this morning and walked to the office. It was probably not the smartest thing I've ever done, but I trudged on and made it in less than an hour. Our plow contractors had been busy clearing snow overnight. The lot appears to be in great shape. They'll need another sweep when the snow ends, but I couldn't be happier with the results. I contacted our team leaders and told them not to come to work until I notified them. They said they would get the word out to the entire team."

Hank thanked her for her efforts but instructed her to stay home. Next, he telephoned Winnie. Camila answered the phone and gave him a fascinating lecture about snowflakes. He could hear Winnie laughing in the background, and when he could finally commandeer the phone from her, he snickered, "Is there anything else I can add to help you understand the characteristics of snow?"

Winnie had never heard him break into such an uncontrolled belly laugh. He became concerned when Hank could not speak for more than a minute. Finally, gaining some composure, Hank told him what was happening at the office and that Rose had communicated with the team leaders. No one was expected at the office until the storm blew over. Winnie ended the conversation with, "I was wondering if you and Lydia would like some company when the roads open up? Camila is so excited about the snow, and I was wondering if you had some cross-country skis we could use to introduce her to the sport. Maybe we could even get you to fire up those Artic Cat snowmobiles you have in storage, and we can take a brisk ride around your property. What do you think?"

Hank thought it was a grand idea and replied, "With the weekend upon us, why don't you plan on staying for a couple of days so we can get into the winter spirit? I'll let Lydia know, and she'll get the guest bedroom ready while I work on snowmobiles and skis. Talk to you soon."

The storm ended as precipitously as it began. On a very cool Saturday morning, the sun reflected its rays over miles of shimmering white powder. Temperatures were hovering around twenty degrees. He could see distant traffic moving very slowly as he drove his tractor to the end of his driveway. It took him about an hour to move the compacted snow so he could gain entrance to Lexington Avenue. The county plows had cleared most of the snow and had deposited a heavy mixture of sand and salt on the roadway. It was doing its job because much of the black asphalt was now exposed, swabbed with a light coat of grimy water.

Winnie phoned while Hank was still on the tractor. The roads were in excellent shape downtown, and he and Camila were already on 35W, heading toward the ranch. Hank turned the Deere around, slammed it into road gear, and barreled back to the house. Lydia was shoveling the last few scoops of snow from around the front door when she saw the speeding tractor coming up the drive. Hank hit the brakes and slid to a complete stop. He stepped out of the cab and hollered, "We've got company coming, and they'll be here in less than forty-five minutes!"

Lydia nodded but kept shoveling as he nursed the tractor back into its stall. Next, they started looking for skis, boots, and poles, but their effort proved futile. Instead, they found the two snowmobiles, still covered and prepped for summer storage. Getting them running was going to be a chore.

Eventually, they found the ski equipment and laid it all on an eight-foot folding table. It was all in like-new condition. Then, several years ago, Hank stopped in Anoka at a local sporting goods store that was going out of business. On impulse, he looked at a complete collection of cross-country skiing equipment and made an offer for the whole lot. When he loaded it into the Suburban, he knew he had enough gear to outfit an entire high school ski team.

He rushed to the last garage and pulled off the tarps covering the snow machines. Next, he took a bottle of quick-detail spray and wiped down both vehicles with a microfiber towel. Unfortunately, their batteries needed charging, so he was stuck manually starting them with the recoiled rope. Surprisingly, both machines sprung to life with only a few pulls. Finally, he returned to the house and told Lydia what he had accomplished.

She handed him a honey-do list and said, "With all the piss and vinegar you've been exuding this morning, this should keep you busy until they arrive!"

Winnie and Camila encountered several horrible accident scenes on the interstate. With traffic backed up, they arrived at noon. Hank completed everything on her list and even took the snowmobiles out for a test ride, carving some new trails around the property's perimeter in the deep snow. Unfortunately, he couldn't find any of the four full-face safety helmets included in the price of the sleds. Hank searched every nook and cranny in the six garages but came up empty-handed. As Lydia came outdoors to check on his progress, he angrily barked, "The damn things have to be here somewhere! I won't let the kids do any riding without helmets. If Winnie and Camila insist on taking a tootle, I'll make a strong case for taking it slow and easy. Both machines can handle breakneck speed, but that's not happening without a freakin' helmet."

Snow was developing on the storm's backside, producing a distinct wrap-around effect. Winds had once again picked up, and the temperature was falling. Hank suggested they strap on the skis and follow the trail he had cut with the snowmobiles. Although there were a few problematic hills to traverse, the course could have been more active. Nevertheless, it was the perfect layout for the novice from South of the Border. However, Camila surprised everyone by taking to this unfamiliar sport as a duck takes to water. She experienced no spills or collisions around the entire route and begged Winnie to make a second run with her. Hank and Lydia, exhausted from making one agonizing, five-mile loop, happily volunteered to start dinner and had their skis and boots put away before anyone could create an argument.

After Sunday morning breakfast, everyone gathered in front of the snowmobile garage. Light flakes were still coming down, but the Chinook winds had subsided, and twenty-four degrees felt relatively balmy. Hank pointed out various features of the Arctic Cat El Tigre, including the sophisticated suspension system that provided the ultimate trail-cushioning ride. He then explained the emergency stop-kill switch, connected to the rider with a tethered cord and release key. Because this was one of the most important safety features found on modern snowmobiles, he drove one of the sleds down the driveway and purposely fell off.

As he fell, the key was pulled from the kill switch, instantly stopping the engine. Tony and Melissa gasped as they saw Pa tumble to the ground. He got to his feet and said, "Even experienced drivers can fall off their machines, and stopping the engine, prevents many accidents and injuries." He went on to talk about wearing an approved safety helmet and proper attire when taking to the trails. Finally, he announced, "I thoroughly searched the entire property again this morning and still can't find any of the helmets. I accidentally put them in storage at the office, but I won't know that until Monday. So, if you two want to take the sleds out for a ride, it's okay by me. But I want you to promise you'll go easy on the throttle and take no unnecessary chances."

They nodded, and he helped them power up the Cats. Hank was more concerned about Winnie's abilities, or lack thereof, to handle a snowmobile than he was about Camila's. She grew up with five brothers in Oaxaca and became a classic tomboy to survive her youth. They were all into motocross racing, and according to Winnie, Camila became proficient in the sport. Hank could tell she was comfortable behind the El Tigre controls, probably due to her motorcycle prowess. They waved and shouted, "We won't be back until late afternoon." Then, the crimson taillights slowly disappeared from view.

Hank looked at Lydia and said, "Why do I feel so uneasy about their little adventure? What could go wrong?"

She replied, "Don't be such a worrywart! Let's go in the house and warm up. I'll make a hot toddy, and the kids can sip some hot chocolate."

By late afternoon, Hank had become concerned. He walked outside and anxiously strained to hear any motorized sounds filtering through the air. Tilting his head and cupping his ears still produced nothing but muzzled silence. Finally, Lydia joined him as they were sharply alerted to a distant wailing ambulance. It was heading north on Lexington and suddenly turned east onto the section road bordering their property. Hank's heart sank as he heard the siren stop sounding. Then, without hesitation, he sprinted into the garage and jumped into his Polaris Ranger. He sped out the open doorway, turned on his lightbar, and located the partially covered trail. Lydia just stood shivering in the driveway as she watched him disappear.

It was slow going in the deep snow, but he finally caught a glimpse of flashing lights through a close-packed stand of white pine. It was dark as he shifted the Polaris into low range and headed off the trail, circling the snow-laden trees. He could see the outline of several more vehicles as he moved closer to his target. Finally, he stopped his Polaris and walked apprehensively toward a group of people standing beneath a gnarled, old oak tree, shining flashlights upward. He froze in his tracks when one of the beams illuminated an object positioned high on the tree trunk, about ten feet off the ground. A paramedic rushed toward him and screamed, "Sir! Stay back! Who are you, and what are you doing here?" Hank explained who he was and demanded to know what was going on.

The paramedic took him by the arm, escorted him back to the Polaris, and told him to take a seat. He quietly said, "There's been an accident. A female snowmobiler lost control of her vehicle and hit a forgotten farm implement, buried in a snowbank. She was probably traveling at high speed and was thrown from the sled and violently landed on the solitary tree. We're waiting for another ladder so she can be quickly released."

Hank murmured, "Is she alive?"

He replied, "We don't know her condition until we examine her, but I'll be honest, it doesn't look good."

Hank dropped his head to the steering wheel and began gasping and bawling while his tears froze solid as they dribbled on his frosted parka shell. Hank heaved himself up as the paramedic started to leave, and hoarsely cried, "Where's her partner? Was he also injured? Where is he?" Turning around, he returned to Hank, saying, "We found him lying beside her snowmobile, dazed and incoherent. They're transporting him to the hospital in Forest Lake."

Camila's body was lowered, placed on a yellow gurney, and loaded into a waiting ambulance. As the vehicle departed, he heard no siren and saw no flashing lights, and he knew her fate.

In total disbelief, he somehow piloted the Polaris back home. Lydia heard him drive into the garage, and she threw on a jacket and ran outside. She could see him slumped low in the vehicle, not moving. Lydia dashed to the driver's door and yanked it open with both hands. As he raised and turned his head, she recognized her worst fears.

She shrieked, "My God! What happened?"

CHAPTER 64

It was early Monday morning, and a deputy sheriff knocked on their door. Tony jumped out of bed, scampered down the hallway, and opened the door. He yelled, "Mom, there's a policeman here, and he wants to talk to you!"

She shouted back, "Tell him to come in. I'll be there in a minute."

The deputy explained that he had several questions for Hank and needed to verify a few points about last night's accident. She responded, "He's not here. He spent the night in the hospital with his friend, who lost his wife in that tragedy. He phoned just before you arrived and said he'd be home in about two hours."

The deputy made a note of it and said, "No problem. I'll come back later this afternoon. Thank you for your time."

Hank arrived home at just past eleven. His face was hauntingly pale, and his eyes were red and puffy. He plopped down on a kitchen chair and said, "This was one of the worst days of my life. Winnie was in pieces! He witnessed the entire event right before his eyes. He's still in shock, and the doctors are doing everything possible to make him comfortable. Unfortunately, there was nothing more I could do for him in the hospital, so I decided to come home. But unfortunately, I feel he'll not make a speedy recovery."

Hank was sleeping soundly when the deputy returned. Lydia woke him by gently rubbing his arm. He opened his eyes and muttered, "Has this been a bad dream?"

She lovingly looked at him and shook her head. Then she said, "The deputy is back. If you don't feel up to it, I'll tell him to come back later."

Hank grunted, "No, tell him I'll be out to visit with him in five minutes."

The deputy wanted to confirm ownership of the two snowmobiles and to establish permission had been given to use them. He explained that the accident had occurred on a section of the Carlos Avery Wildlife Area, which butted up to Hank's property. Removing the snowmobiles was a priority now that the initial investigation was complete. Hank said he and Lydia would drive the Polaris six-wheeler to the site and tow and drive the sleds back home this afternoon. The deputy gave him a copy of the official accident report, something he might need to make an insurance claim. The deputy thanked him for his cooperation, left him an official business card, and departed.

It was very late in the day when they arrived at the scene.

They both stood arm-in-arm and whispered a little prayer as they stared dumbfoundedly at the surroundings. Then, finally, Hank cleared his thick throat, rubbed his tear-filled eyes, and turned to grab the tow rope before she could see his fragility. The wrecked sled had sustained unbelievable damage. It was a total loss. Hank attached the tow rope and directed Lydia as she slowly inched the Polaris forward, removing the shattered Cat from the concealed snare. As they headed home, Lydia tried to stay on the hazardous pathway, but the recovery sled kept twisting and pulling her into deep, drifted snow. Hank was following on the operable snowmobile. Several times he had to move to the front and hook another tow rope onto the Polaris to help get it back on the trail. A journey that should have taken thirty minutes now approached two hours.

Tony and Melissa were face-first glued on the living room window as the convoy arrived in the courtyard. They were scared and worried and didn't want to go outside to see the damage. While Lydia went into the house, Hank managed to pull all three vehicles into the garage. He flipped the ceiling lights and found his Konica camera on the workbench. He took photographs of the destroyed sled, closed the overhead door, looked toward the heavens, and breathed a deep sigh of remorse. *Would a helmet have made a difference? Should I have stopped them from going for a ride? Would Winnie blame him for the accident?*

These thoughts and many more crossed his mind as he stood quivering in the bitter night air. Lydia peered out the porch window and saw him standing stoically in the middle of the driveway as light snow settled on his shoulders. She knew what he was doing and did not want to interfere. Lydia checked on him every five minutes but could not contain herself after an hour. Eventually, she opened the front door and gently beckoned him to come inside. Startled, he snapped out of his trance and began laggardly moving toward her. She held the door, and once inside, she wrapped her arms around him, hoping to provide some solace and relief. They talked well into the night, knocking the stuffings out of *shoulda-woulda-coulda,* and finally drifted into a deep sleep.

In the morning, Hank telephoned the hospital and discovered Winnie had discharged himself. Five minutes after talking to a nurse practitioner, the doorbell rang. Winnie was paying the taxi driver as he opened the door. When the taxi departed, he approached his friend, put his arm around his shoulder, and said, "Do you think it was a good idea to discharge yourself against the doctor's orders? I'm concerned about you."

Not making eye contact, he shouted, "Where are the keys to

Camila's car? I want to go home! No more bullshit from you! Just gimme the keys!"

Hank retreated into the house and found Camila's purse in the guest bedroom. He grabbed the keys and stepped outside.

As Hank approached and leaned on the car door, he said softly, "I still think this is a bad idea."

Winnie abruptly threw his hand out and barked, "The keys!"

Watching him drive away, Hank realized that things between them would never be the same again.

CHAPTER 65

Camila had been transported back to Mexico for burial. Winnie had not shared any of the funeral arrangements. He had not spoken to anyone at VisualFish, except for the few harsh words he had spoken with Hank the day after the accident. Hank had left numerous voicemails for him, but it was only an exercise in futility. Winnie would have to work it out on his terms, and he was not going to pry or interfere with the grieving process.

Christmas was approaching, and business was booming.

Lydia had stepped up to the plate and was stellar in handling her CLO responsibilities and Winnie's financial duties. Hank had heard, through the grapevine, that he was still in Mexico and had no plans to return home. However, the entire team at VisualFish had pulled together, and the whole operation was running like clockwork. Hank spent much of his day in the field with clients but maintained a personal time commitment to his family. Tony grew into a fine young man, and Melissa would melt many hearts with her enchanting smile. Words were impossible to describe the pride they had in their children. Hank was lying on the living room floor, admiring the lights and decorations on the Christmas tree, when Tony lunged in next to him.

"Pa, do you think I could run the business someday?" I love the way the company makes you happy. I can't think of a better job!"

Hank breathed profoundly and replied, "You make me proud, son. Of course, you could take over the business someday.

I'd be delighted to teach and mentor you along the way, but first, you'll need a formal education."

He sat silently for more than a minute, his little mind churning. Then looked at him and said, "What about the University of Minnesota? It worked for you. Do you think it could work for me?"

Hank answered, "You bet it could, but it'll take hard work, good grades, and dedication to get into the U."

He laughed and replied, "Pa, I know I still have a ways to go, but believe me, I'm up for the challenge."

Hank fought back the tears, reached over, and gave him a smothering hug with both arms while thinking: *He's growing up much too quickly*.

No one worked at the Company between Christmas and New Year's Eve, so they purposely held their annual holiday party at the Marriot City Center the week before Christmas. At the party, Hank announced that VisualFish would close on the Friday before Christmas and remain closed until January second. He wanted everyone to spend this time with their families, and as a Christmas gift, they would receive a regular paycheck for that period.

The day after Christmas, Hank and Lydia decided to go into the office to catch up on a few items that would need their attention in the new year. The kids wanted to visit friends in Coon Lake and do some tobogganing and skating at their lakeside property. They could drop them off on their way to the office and pick them up on the return trip. The company parking lot was empty, with both cars and snow. Hank put on a pot of coffee and asked Lydia, who was already seated in her office, to join him for a few minutes. She slid down on the couch next to him and inquisitively asked, "What's up?"

He began, "I'm concerned about the Winnie situation. It's been over two months since we've heard from him. I've left messages on his voicemail and talked to his property manager in Mexico twice, asking her to have him call me. Let's take some formal action to see if we can get him to respond. He is a partner in the company, and I still consider him a friend, but he is not fulfilling his obligations, and I want answers!"

Lydia was about to respond when they both looked up and saw Arnie Morgan standing in the doorway. Hank stood up, shook his hand, and invited him to sit. Arnie was a minor partner in the company and had played a vital role in developing the software that put VisualFish on the map. Arnie said, "I just stopped by to pick up some paperwork and was surprised to see your car in the lot. I didn't mean to eavesdrop, but I overheard part of your conversation about Winnie. So, what the heck are we going to do with him?"

Hank explained that Lydia would prepare legal documents that hopefully would force him to communicate. Hank said again, "We want answers. Once we know Winnie's plans, we'll deal with them. I think we've shown tremendous restraint. I know the grieving process can take some time, but life goes on. I'll keep you posted with any results."

They watched Arnie get into his car before they continued their discussion.

Hank spoke first. "Have you had an opportunity to check Winnie's financial projections for the company and the tactics and strategies he'll use to achieve those goals? Before the accident, I reviewed his FY plans for next year. I found them to be somewhat aggressive and extremely vague. He also wanted to change some financial checks and balances in our original partnership agreement. He proposed these changes for expediency and practicality because I was out of the office much of the time. He said he often found himself in a precarious position when important checks needed to be issued, contracts needed approval, and he could do nothing until I returned. As a senior partner, he argued that this was not good for business and that an either/or signature amendment should be approved and put into the company's SOP. Furthermore, VisualFish must immediately inform all financial institutions, business partners, and clients of this policy change." Hank muttered with his head in his hands, "I agreed."

Lydia was angry and grumbled, "Hank, he must have cast an evil spell on you. You should never have agreed to that change in policy. Checks and balances are there for a reason. It is a definite red flag. I've been using the two-signature requirement, yours and mine, since taking on the added responsibility of CFO. No one in this company, including you, ever informed me of the change. I certainly won't be part of it. I want it rescinded and the old policy reinstated as soon as possible."

Hank hung his head as the error of his ways completely sunk in. But because he and Winnie had agreed to the amendment and collectively put it into effect, any reversal would require approval from both of them. He released a deflated sigh and murmured, "I appreciate your advice, and I was wrong not to discuss it with you before I signed off on it. When Winnie returns to work, I'll deal with it."

CHAPTER 66

Another snowstorm had made life miserable in the upper Midwest. It had arrived on Valentine's Day, and Hank had to cancel a planned, romantic dinner at the Vineyard with his wife. It was almost ten o'clock before he departed for the office. Plowing had taken place, but a hidden layer of frozen rain made driving treacherous. He went into an uncontrolled skid as he tried to enter the icy parking lot. The Suburban hit a buried curb and brutally bounced him through the entrance. He slammed on the brakes and tried to grasp what had just happened. He exited the vehicle and checked for damage on the left front end. Except for a scab of wheel rash, he could see no other problems. As he lifted himself back into the driver's seat, he noticed a car parked in Winnie's reserved space. Because he didn't recognize the car, he thought it must belong to a visitor who apparently couldn't read English.

He stopped for his usual java fix and started down the hallway to his office. Rose met him about halfway and ushered him into the conference room. She softly gushed, "You'll never believe who just walked in the door before you!" She paused a second and yelled, "Winnie is back!"

Hank forced his way through the doorway and ran down the hallway. He burst into Winnie's office and startled the crap out of him when he shouted, "You're back!"

As he rose from his chair, Hank barely recognized him. He had lost weight, which he couldn't afford to lose, and his face was pale gray, and he had sunken, jaundiced eyes. Winnie extended his hand, and Hank did likewise.

His grip was weak, and it felt like he was clutching the bones of a skeleton. They both sat down and stared at each other for several agonizing seconds. Finally, Winnie broke the silence by saying, "I've had a rough go of it. Depression got the better part of me, and the weeks and months evaporated. Then, one day, Camila's father came over to check on me and found me collapsed on my bedroom floor, barely conveying a pulse. They took me to a hospital and treated me for severe dehydration. The good news is, I'm on the mend and anxious to get back to work."

Hank smiled and replied, "It's good to see you, my friend. I can't imagine the hell you've been through, but I want you to know I'm here to help in any way whatsoever."

Winnie closed his eyes and said, "I'm putting the downtown condo up for sale and selling all the furnishings. I don't like the idea of living there without her. I've rented an apartment in Brooklyn Center and will take occupancy this afternoon. My Ferrari is in storage, and I purchased a winter beater that you probably saw in the parking lot. Living on the north side of town makes a lot of sense, and I know I'll appreciate the short commute to the office."

Hank got to his feet and said, "Welcome home! You take as much time as you need to get settled. We have an exciting year unfolding, and I'm really in need of your help and commitment. Remember, if you need anything, my door is always open."

Winnie left the office that afternoon and didn't return for several days. The condo in Minneapolis had sold in less than a day. Winnie had rented a *U-Haul* van and was busy furnishing his new apartment. Rose told Hank that she thought he sounded more like the old Winnie.

Winnie seemed to be operating on all eight cylinders, and when inquiries had come in from several large companies *across the pond,* Hank asked him if he felt strong enough to do some overseas travel. With Winnie's extensive international law background and proficiency in several languages, Hank hoped he would accept the assignment. Without hesitation, he jumped at the challenge and spent the next two months in Europe and the UK, finalizing contracts with three major manufacturers. Winnie's performance put a big smile on Hank's face.

VisualFish had surprised the entire financial community, generating annual sales above thirty million. Hank had purchased two additional facilities to meet the increased demand. One is in Eden Prairie, and one is out-of-state in Fargo, North Dakota. He had also teamed up with a Chinese manufacturer who provided a springboard for new growth by removing the acute limitations of in-house silicon chip production. As a result, his company was focused on an intensified assembly-line approach to business, installing technology and turning products in a much more timely and profitable fashion.

With Winnie's return to full-time participation, Lydia had removed herself from much of the corporate environment and was donating more time to her favorite charities and hobbies. However, she realized that raising two kids, even with the help of a willing husband, was nothing short of a full-time job.

The endless ball games and extracurricular activities were often overwhelming, but seeing Mom and Pa in the stands or the audience brought immeasurable happiness to both children. It certainly brought everything into perspective.

Hank had yet to pursue the signature policy with Winnie. With so much new business coming from distant places, implementing and enforcing a policy change like this could be interpreted as a sign of weakness. Lydia had either forgotten her concerns or grown weary of fighting this battle. Hank agreed with Winnie on the one hand, but Lydia's warning words stuck in the back of his mind. Hank digressed: *There may be a compromise to this mess that no one has considered. I'll bring it up for discussion when the time is right.*

As the warm days of summer made their presence known, Hank had severalND fishing trips planned. The first one would take him to the steep breaks of the Missouri River in central South Dakota. Several fishermen had taken large pike on the River just north of Pierre, but he wanted to try snagging for the prehistoric paddlefish in the Gavins Point Dam area. Tony had researched and written a paper on this creature, believed to be older than the dinosaurs, more than three hundred million years old. Tony could barely control his excitement as Hank promised to take him along.

Another excursion he wanted to make was to Lake Coeur d'Alene, Idaho. Locals took several pike weighing in at close to forty pounds, but there were stories about much bigger giants lurking in the back bays. Hank had spent a lot of time in Spokane and Coeur d'Alene when he opened new sites for FishNautics, but he needed more time to wet a line. Nevertheless, he thought this could be an excellent summer vacation for the whole family, and he would start looking for accommodations as soon as he broke the news to Lydia.

They made journeys to South Dakota and Idaho over the summer months. The family trip to Lake Coeur d'Alene involved detours to Glacier and Yellowstone National Parks. They were away for the whole month of July. It was the first of many extended family holidays they would enjoy together. It was Lydia and the children's first trip west of the Mississippi. He grew tired of stopping at every bend in the road so they could take photographs of mountain scenes and abundant wildlife, but he willingly complied when he saw the excitement it brought to their faces. The cabin they rented in Idaho was a large family home on an isolated point with an expansive, western view of the lake. Lydia and Melissa enjoyed spending mother-daughter time on the groomed and sandy beach, although the water was a little too cool for their liking. With disappointing results on the fishing trip to South Dakota, Coeur d'Alene held active and hungry pike. Tony and Hank went fishing every day, returning exhausted but willing to get back on the water every morning with a newly charged frame of mind. Hank shared his skills and knowledge with his son. At the end of the vacation, Tony had developed into quite the angler.

CHAPTER 67

It was mid-September of 2000. Y2K had come and gone without incident. George W. Bush was elected President, and Hank had just arrived at his office when he noticed an envelope shoved under his office door. He sat on the front corner of his desk and carefully opened it. It was from Paul Nordstrom, Plant Manager. It read,

Mr. Wahlberg,
I don't know if I should even be writing this letter. I feel guilty and ashamed, as if I had opened a can of worms with no merit. But here goes my story.
Yesterday, Mr. Farrell and I had a weekly meeting scheduled in the conference room at nine a.m. I arrived on time and waited almost thirty minutes, but he didn't show. I finally returned to the plant and noticed our supply room door was open. I stepped inside, flipped on the lights, and found Mr. Farrell seated at a small typewriter table, his back to me. Startled, he used his arm to brush off the table, and I saw what appeared to be some white powder settling on the floor.
He turned and demanded to know what I was doing there. He told me to get the fuck out there and for me to mind my own business. I turned and left the storeroom, closing the door behind me. I went back to the storeroom later in the day. Maybe it was curiosity, but I wanted to confirm what I had seen. I checked around the small table and could find no evidence of any white

substance.

 I told myself that maybe it was chalk or dust that he had accidentally swept away with his arm, but I was not convinced, and that's why I'm bringing it to your attention. Please don't confront him with this letter. I've not told anyone else about this incident. I get along very well with Mr. Farrell, and I don't want to jeopardize my relationship with him, especially if there is a legitimate answer to my concern.
 Sincerely,
 Paul Nordstrom

Hank lowered the letter to his knees and shook his head in disbelief. Winnie swore he was drug-free. When Hank had caught him using in the men's room, he promised it wouldn't happen again, but this letter seemed to confirm his worst nightmare.

 Winnie pulled a disappearing act for several days but returned and behaved like nothing had happened. He must have felt guilty because he went into Hank's office and complained vehemently about Paul's intrusion into the storage room. He exclaimed, "I needed a yellow pad to take to my meeting with Paul, and I couldn't locate the light switch in the room. I floundered down an aisle, bumped into a chair, and sat down to get my bearings. Suddenly, the lights came on, and it startled me! The chair started to tip over, and I reached out to catch my balance, and I must have knocked over a box of board chalk on one of the lower shelves. I asked Paul to leave the room while I cleaned up the mess. Paul is a good guy, but you should talk seriously with him. Going around scaring people is not acceptable behavior."

 Winnie turned and left the office without saying anything.

Circumstantial evidence was not what Hank wanted or needed. Trusting Winnie had become a problem, but he had to give him the benefit of the doubt. He took the letter and locked it up in his desk drawer. *First, I'll talk with Paul, thank him for his concern, and then reveal Winnie's side of the story.* Hank sincerely hoped this would end it, although he still had unresolved doubts about Winnie.

During the last few weeks of September, Hank solidified his plans for the final fishing excursion of the year. He had seriously thought about canceling the trip and needed time to think. So, Hank and his buddy Joe Watkins planned to depart on October second, returning on the twenty-first. He loved Canada and especially Keezheekoni at this time of the year. All the hungry mosquitoes and millions of biting black flies were gone. The abundant blueberries were ripe and sweet, changing the sandy soil into a sea of azure blue.

The day before their departure, Joe telephoned and informed him of the unexpected death of his father and would be unable to make the journey. Lydia pleaded with Hank to forget about going on this trip. With no partner, it could be a lonely and dangerous outing. He assured her that he had made the journey alone several times. He would take every precaution and not put himself in harm's way. He had his mind made up. She continued to argue as the taillights on the boat trailer disappeared from view.

As he drove north on Highway 61, along the shoreline of Lake Superior, Winnie was constantly flashing into his mind. He knew he had been following an ostrich routine by putting his head in the sand. The problems had not disappeared and appeared to be multiplying. He had trusted his partner, but his personal issues had severely slashed that bond. He thought: *I'll be home in a few weeks and resolve this issue once and for all.*

The inviting view of the lake lifted Hank's spirits as he unhooked the boat and trailer. The waters were calm, and so was his mental state as he once again set camp on the magnificent shoreline of Keezheekoni.